"One of the most origin... ...ort story collections to have a... ...recent years . . . Experienced together, the collection reads as a sophisticated orchestration. So tightly interwoven are its themes, characters, and grim events that it is hard to imagine any one apart from the others. . . . An absolutely dazzling triumph . . . Shankman's skill for description paints the setting in brilliant detail. . . . Many stories reward with ironic twists and indelible surprises. . . . [*They Were Like Family to Me*] is a singularly inventive collection of chilling stark realism enhanced by the hallucinatory ingredient of top-drawer magical realism, interrogating the value of art, storytelling, and dreams in a time of peril and presenting hard truths with wisdom, magic, and grace."

—Jewish Book Council

"Moving and unsettling . . . Like Joyce's *Dubliners*, this book circles the same streets and encounters the same people as it depicts the horrors of Germany's invasion of Poland through the microcosm of one village. . . . Shankman's prose is inventive and taut. . . . Her writing is simple and matter-of-fact, never maudlin or sentimental. . . . A deeply humane demonstration of wringing art from catastrophe."

—*Kirkus Reviews*

"Every story in this remarkable collection reveals Helen Maryles Shankman's talent for surprising, disturbing, and enlightening her readers. Blending the horrors of war with the supernatural, she creates a literary landscape that is strangely mythical and distinctively her own. These stories haunted me for days after I finished reading them."

—Sarai Walker, author of *Dietland*

"Following in the footsteps of Isaac Bashevis Singer and Sholem Aleichem, Helen Maryles Shankman is an exquisite storyteller of early twentieth-century Eastern European Jewish life. . . . Readers of [*They Were Like Family to Me*] will encounter vibrant tales of extraordinary people, good and evil, in a twisted, macabre life. Here, the old rules are no longer valid. Subjected to inhumane conditions, with brutality and death around every turn, Shankman's characters alternately perpetrate and combat hatred while sliding inexorably toward a dark and surreptitious future."

—*New York Journal of Books*

"This is a book lover's book, filled with beautiful language and textured scenes. . . . There's no forgiveness in these stories, but explorations of human nature. With bold originality, Shankman has created her own literary blend of history, folklore, fantasy, myth, spirituality, and truth."

—*The Jewish Week*

"With unflinching prose and flashes of poetry, Helen Maryles Shankman spirits her readers back through history to the Polish hamlet of Włodowa during the dark days of Nazi occupation. Horrific reality and soaring fantasy meld in serial stories that include an avenging golem, an anti-Semite who shelters a Jewish child, brutal SS officers who lay claim to their own Jews, and an unlikely messiah 'whose breath smelled of oranges and cinnamon.' That scent will linger in the memory of readers, as will the haunting stories in which barbaric hatred is mitigated by the reflection of a survivor that 'love is a kind of magic.' There is, in fact, literary magic in these well-told tales."

—Gloria Goldreich, author of *The Bridal Chair*

"A short-story collection that revolves around the Holocaust is a tough sell. Make it colorful, or optimistic, and it's pure fairytale. Dwell on the ugliness, the death and depravity, and it becomes perverse—or simply unbearable. Besides, what is there left to say? Then along comes [*They Were Like Family to Me*] by Helen Maryles Shankman. Shankman shows us a world in which German officers, Poles, and Jews regularly cross paths. It's a deadly coexistence, but relations are more complex than we've generally imagined. . . . A less able writer couldn't pull this off, but fortunately for us, Shankman is skilled and she pulls this off beautifully."

—*Tablet*

"[*They Were Like Family to Me*] is a moving collection of beautifully written short stories that readers of Jewish fiction will celebrate. Not to be missed."

—Naomi Ragen, author of *The Sisters Weiss*

"[*They Were Like Family to Me*], with its sense of detached irony, mixed with tragedy and fantasy, simply takes your breath away. . . . The collection ends on a positive note that succeeds in being hopeful without sentimentality. These are beautifully crafted, moving stories, haunting in the dark complexities they portray."

—*Chicago Jewish Star*

"Populated with monsters and heroes (human and perhaps not), but mostly with ordinary people caught up in horrific events they neither understood nor controlled, this series of intersecting stories drew me in completely, making me read them again to find all the connections I missed the first time. The writing is fantastic, and I marvel at Shankman's literary skills."

—Maggie Anton, author of the bestselling *Rashi's Daughters* trilogy

"Many of the stories are almost childlike in the simple but elegant beauty of their language. Ms. Shankman turns tales of murder, whether methodical or casual, into fables that are rich in turquoise and tangerine sunsets, populated with mythical warrior bears who fight with the partisans and albino deer who summon nature's wrath, releasing tidal river waves upon the demons who have conquered the land and its population . . . Each story leads inexorably back to Ms. Shankman's fundamental questions regarding blame, courage, and responsibility. In a better world, no one would have to ponder these issues. Unfortunately, that world does not exist. One cannot read Ms. Shankman's compelling, beautiful, gut-wrenching book and not think long and hard about what we are and what we are capable of becoming."

—*Pittsburgh Post-Gazette*

"Well-shaped and often word-perfect, boasting a clear narrative structure and a sure, signature voice . . . Richly rendered . . . As time advances, the tales grow more lovely and layered . . . Shankman's talent comes fully into view."

—*Chicago Tribune*

"Only rarely do books have the literary wallop to break through my protective psychic defenses. [*They Were Like Family to Me*] is one such work."

—*Washington Jewish Week*

"Shankman presents a typical German-occupied Jewish town in an atypical way: through the lens of several non-Jews and their individual transformations, or lack thereof. We come away with something new in literature—a full portrait of a war-torn Jewish town, where a nimble application of the magical gently veils the harsh realities."

—*The Rumpus*

"Helen Maryles Shankman's story collection, [*They Were Like Family to Me*], blends mythology and history into a single, unforgettable voice."

—*Barnes & Noble Review*

ALSO BY HELEN MARYLES SHANKMAN

*The Color of Light*

# They Were Like Family to Me

stories

## Helen Maryles Shankman

ORIGINALLY PUBLISHED AS *In the Land of Armadillos*

SCRIBNER

*New York   London   Toronto   Sydney   New Delhi*

SCRIBNER
An Imprint of Simon & Schuster, Inc.
1230 Avenue of the Americas
New York, NY 10020

Originally published as *In the Land of Armadillos*

First Scribner trade paperback edition October 2016

SCRIBNER and design are registered trademarks of The Gale Group, Inc.,
used under license by Simon & Schuster, Inc., the publisher of this work.

For information about special discounts for bulk purchases,
please contact Simon & Schuster Special Sales at 1-866-506-1949
or business@simonandschuster.com.

The Simon & Schuster Speakers Bureau can bring authors to
your live event. For more information or to book an event,
contact the Simon & Schuster Speakers Bureau at 1-866-248-3049
or visit our website at www.simonspeakers.com.

Interior design by Kyle Kabel

Manufactured in the United States of America

3   5   7   9   10   8   6   4

Library of Congress Cataloging-in-Publication Data

Shankman, Helen Maryles.
[Short stories. Selections]
[title] : stories / Helen Maryles Shankman. — First Scribner hardcover edition.
pages cm
I. Title.
PS3619.H35474A6 2016
813'.6—dc23
2015023521

ISBN 978-1-5011-1519-6
ISBN 978-1-5011-1521-9 (pbk)
ISBN 978-1-5011-1522-6 (ebook)

For Brenda and Barry Maryles,
with love and awe

Our eyes register the light of dead stars.

—André Schwarz-Bart, *The Last of the Just*

# CONTENTS

# IN THE LAND
## OF ARMADILLOS

The man took up his pen and wrote:

*My own darling,*

*From my new office, I can see the village square. The houses are very old, with slanted roofs, all painted cheerful colors. In the distance, I can see church spires, little cottages with thatched roofs, lovely rolling fields. Just outside my window, a cherry tree has burst into bloom. All day long, I have been going around like I'm sleepwalking, remembering the day I met you, when we went for that long walk under the cherry trees in the Stadtwald, and the blossoms filled the air like snow. I couldn't tell you then, but I was trembling with desire as I picked them one by one out of your shining hair.*

*You scold me for my lack of letters. Well, my darling, you can hardly blame me for that! They keep moving me around, putting me where I am most needed, but finally, I have a posting where I can receive mail. Now I am sitting at my own desk,*

*in my own office, looking out the window of our new home.*
*Your new home, my darling.*

*Dearest little bunny, I wake up, I go to work, I sign papers,*
*I direct people to go here, to go there, to do this and that, but all*
*day long, I am thinking of you. How can I describe how much*
*you mean to me, the touch of your hand, your trusting smile?*

*My secretary has just walked in with an armload of work*
*for me to do; so I must say goodbye now, but I dispatch this to*
*you with a hundred kisses. Save some for yourself, and give*
*the rest to Peter, my brave little soldier. I am enclosing some*
*new stamps for his collection. I can't wait until we are together*
*again. Nothing makes any sense without you by my side.*

*Your adoring husband,*
*Max*

With care, he folded the letter around the stamps, slid it
into an envelope, sealed it, laid it in his out-box. That done,
he took a leather-bound diary from his desk drawer and
smoothed it open to a new page. After noting the date in
the top left corner, he wrote:

*Seems that I am General of the Jews again. This time*
*they've put me in charge of the work details, assigning them*
*to the jobs they are best suited for. I can't complain, at least it's*
*indoors, better than my last position, where I always had to*
*be ready to march off into the forest to do a job, no matter how*
*foul the weather.*

*Shooting women and children is not what I signed up for;*
*I'm a soldier, I miss the smoke and strategy of the battlefield.*
*Still, a soldier must do what he is told, or all discipline disap-*
*pears, and the war is lost.*

*Anyway, that's all over now. For my calm demeanor in the disposition of difficult duties, I have been rewarded with a promotion and this beautiful villa overlooking the market square. My years of hard work are finally paying off.*

*Still, I am left with some disquieting images: the composure of the Jewish women as they dug their own graves; the courage of the men who offered no pleading, no tears; and I cannot forget the attractive figures of pretty young girls as they put down their shovels and turned to face me. At least I did what I could to ensure that they didn't suffer. Those who came up before my rifle fell without a sound.*

*Only in that moment, as I sighted down the barrel, pointed it at their hearts, did I feel a flutter of emotion. Otherwise, I ate well, I slept like a baby. I should feel something, shouldn't I? What does it mean?*

*I can see that having my own office is making me something of a philosopher! I still have so much to do before my little Hasenpfeffer gets here. All in all, I am confident that everything will be better when I am together with my family again. I am counting the days.*

It was the end of October, and still Gerda hadn't arrived. One thing after another conspired to keep Max Haas the solitary occupant of the magnificent villa. First Gerda had wanted Peter to finish the school year with his friends. Then she had wavered about leaving her parents behind in Köln. The most recent delay was due to her fears over an increase in deadly attacks by those murderous partizans.

And in the meantime, the villa wasn't ready. The walls needed plastering, the pipes were leaking. Max sighed. What he needed were skilled construction workers, plumbers, painters. Instead, he was issued a steady parade of dentists, tailors, furriers, and law clerks. Irritated, he assigned them to a crew digging drainage ditches and sent them on their way.

It was the end of the day. He told his secretary he was leaving and went to see if Gruber was in his office. Max knocked; there was a flurry of sounds from within, then something fell and rolled slowly across the floor. The door opened and Gruber's secretary emerged, flustered and a little breathless.

His boss from the Sicherheitspolizei was seating himself behind his desk. He was a cheerful, heavyset man with sparse black hair and a square, pleasant face, which was now flushed and damp.

"I'm going," Max said.

"Oh," Gruber said in surprise, looking at the fat gold watch on his wrist. "How did it get so late? Will we see you tonight?"

There was a party at the SS club later, a Beerfest, an opportunity to express fraternity with the enlisted men. Max always went, it was good for morale. "Of course. And you?"

Gruber waggled his eyebrows, gave him an enigmatic smile. "That all depends on Honi. Listen, how is it going with your villa? Are you finding workers?"

A sensitive subject. "I find lots of lawyers and university professors. No bricklayers or housepainters."

"I think I may have someone for you." Gruber leaned forward, pushed a buzzer. "Honi, those papers I told you to put aside," he cooed. While he waited, Max looked out the window. An officer and a few SS men were having fun with some Jews, making them do jumping jacks in the middle of the market square. One of them, a juicy one, collapsed. The officer drew his gun and walked over to where he lay gasping on the cobblestones.

Just then the secretary opened the door and sashayed across the room, her skirt drawn tight over her hips, the fabric clinging enthusiastically to every stride.

"I don't know anything about art," Gruber admitted as he slid the form across the desk. "But I know you're looking for a painter. Honi tells me he's very famous."

"Oh yes, Sturmbannführer," she exclaimed, her eyes wide with excitement. "He's been in many exhibitions, he's even had books published. Maybe you've seen some of them. There was *The Thief of Yesterday and Tomorrow*, also *The Town Inside the Hourglass*." She was very proud of this Tobias Rey, obviously a local boy made good. Honi was Volksdeutsche, Polish-born but of German descent.

Max looked down at the paper in his hands. The photograph showed a man perhaps in his early thirties, gaunt, with longish hair, dark pouchy eyes, a small sardonic smile. Nothing much for a Jew to smile about these days, he thought.

"He can't be worse than my last painter," he said.

Gruber was caressing his secretary's cheek with a stubby finger. "Good," he said, but he didn't take his eyes from the bland, pretty face. "I'll see that he reports to you tomorrow."


Years later, alone in his cell, he would remember that morning, how the air was fresh from the east, bringing with it a smell of cows and wood smoke that was not altogether disagreeable; the sight of the cherry tree outside his window, the branches cased in clear ice; the color of the light as it fell in bars across the ashen, angular man at the other end of the table.

Max was in the dining room, taking his morning coffee from the set of Meissen china his housekeeper had found in the china closet, left behind by the previous owner, when the painter presented himself. Instead of shuffling in with bowed head, exhibiting the proper mix of fear and submission due to his position and race, the famous Tobias Rey shambled in and plopped himself down on a chair, folding one sharp knee over the other. He wore a chalk-striped suit that was too large for his slender frame. Max was no expert on these things, but even he could tell that the suit showed vestiges of a good tailor and an elegant cut.

Later, Toby would say that he had hoped Max would shoot him right then and there for his insolence. In his cell, Max would wonder again why he hadn't.

"So," Max said. "Ever paint a house?"

Tobias Rey shrugged, a simple lifting and dropping of the shoulders.

"Standartenführer Gruber's secretary is very impressed with you. Are you fucking her?"

A smile threatened the corners of the artist's mouth. Max could almost hear his thoughts. *If I smile, he'll beat me. If I don't smile, he'll beat me.*

"No."

"Well, what have you painted?"

There were dark smudges under his eyes. "I used to paint watercolors," he said. "Oil paintings. In the surrealist manner. Your Führer would probably find my work degenerate."

"Do you have any examples?"

The gray lips lifted in a bleak smile, and now he resembled the black-and-white picture on his work papers.

"No. But you do." He gestured at a stack of boxes in the corner, arrived yesterday from Köln. Poking out of the top was a snow globe from Berchtesgaden, some plush animals, picture books. "That book, the one on top. It's mine."

Max's eyebrows arched up. He retrieved the book and ruffled through the pages, smiling at the depictions of cinnabar-colored armadillos perambulating over electric-blue hills. It had been so long since he'd seen his family, his son was little more than the memory of a dark head on a pillow. "*In the Land of Armadillos* . . . this is Peter's favorite book. You did this?"

The artist shrugged again. Max found himself moved to offer the man a cigarette, leaning forward to light it for him. Tobias Rey wound his skinny body around his seat and blew smoke into the air, barely looking grateful. Max tried to keep the enthusiasm from his voice. "You're very talented. What else have you done?"

"Theater sets," he said. "In Vienna. Opera sets, once, for a friend in Warsaw. Murals for Szyk's dining room. Szyk was my dealer."

"Sounds like fun. You must know a lot of interesting people."

For an instant, the look the artist returned was unmistakably ironic. Then he shifted his gaze to the trail of smoke dissipating into the air. Max realized his mistake. Of course. They were probably dead now.

The interview was depressing him. He clapped the book closed with more force than he had intended, making Tobias Rey jump. The noise was like a gunshot in the quiet room.

"Come on, Rey, cheer up," Max said in an affable voice. "You're going to be fine here. I want you to paint some murals for my son's room. He's arriving in a few weeks. You'll have to hurry."

The next morning, his new employee presented himself at ten A.M., two hours late. Any other day, Max might have shot him. But he was already behind on his other duties, so today he let it go.

Last night he'd been having a wonderful time in Reinhart's castle, a medieval hunting lodge belonging to some departed Polish earl. Reinhart himself was at his table, along with some of the brightest lights of local Party society. Chief Engineer Falkner, who rolled his eyes and complained about how long his damned drainage operation was taking; Rohlfe, Gestapo chief of the district, who said little, but drank heavily and was surprisingly jolly; Hackendahl, Rohlfe's protégé. Cold and efficient, he had studied law before taking to the streets as a Brownshirt. Gruber, who beamed at Max from across the table, his face shiny and red, while his eyes followed Honi as she flitted from table to table, wearing a gold gown that was tight across the breasts.

Reinhart had a marvelous chef. There was game from his forest, venison, boar, grouse, duck, rabbit, all prepared from good German recipes. With dinner, one could have French brandy, Scottish whisky, Polish vodka, Czech slivovitz, and with dessert, a fruity German Riesling. Max had just discovered, over an apple strudel that melted on the tongue, that he shared with Rohlfe a lively common interest—they were both in the process of training a new cook—when Gruber called him aside.

"Sorry, Haas," he began apologetically. "Something's come up. We caught a group of Jews in the forest outside of town, and I need you to take over."

"Why me?" Max protested unhappily. "I don't do that anymore. Ask some of the other officers. Or the men. They love shooting Jews."

"Ah, that's just the problem," confided Gruber morosely.

He glanced around the room at the men in their dress uniforms, the ribbons, medals, and braid on their chests refracting the light of the chandeliers like the flashbulbs of many miniature cameras. "Just between you and me, they love it a little *too* much. I know that what we are doing here is for the benefit of mankind, but when I think of what it is doing to their souls . . . Something happened today during a perfectly routine operation . . . some of our men behaved abominably. Babies . . . bayonets . . ." He took off his glasses, rubbed his red eyes with fat fingers. Max noted that his hands were shaking. "What are we doing to them, Max? How we can send them back to Germany, to their mothers, their wives, their children, after the things we've made them do?"

Max glanced around uneasily, worried that someone was listening in on their conversation. He had never heard Gruber talk this way. Was it a test? A trap? Or was he cracking?

With a quick motion, his superior gulped down what was left in his glass. An involuntary shudder, followed by a forced smile. "That's why I'm asking you. With you, there's no circus, no hysterics, no fuss, one-two-three and it's over. I don't know how you do it. You have a way with them."

*Seems that I am General of the Jews again.* A muscle at the base of his skull was throbbing. He flexed his neck right, then left, until he felt a click. "How many?"

"A small job. Twenty-three. They must have been hiding out somewhere."

After so many of these lousy operations, what was one more? "Send a driver to my villa. First thing in the morning. I want this over with before breakfast."

Gruber squeezed his arm, bent close enough so that Max

could smell the brandy on his breath. "I won't make a habit of this, Haas. You're a good man."

Max led his new employee up a narrow passage of stairs to the top floor. At this hour of the morning, beams of sunlight streamed in through the windows, heating the space with a voluptuous warmth.

The walls were newly plastered, as chaste as the feathers in an angel's wing. There was a bare bed, a desk, a chest of drawers, a pair of tailor's dummies left by a previous owner. As if he had been placed there for the purpose of contrast, Tobias Rey slouched over by the pristine white wall, the very picture of doom and gloom.

"What happened to you, Rey, stay up too late dancing?"

The circles under his artist's eyes had grown darker, if it was possible, the stubble on his long face, longer. Max offered him a cigarette from a gold case, then took one himself. Smoke waltzed in lazy spirals with the dust motes in the bare room.

"So, what are you going to paint for me?"

Tobias Rey spoke slowly and deliberately. "I'm sorry for your trouble, Sturmbannführer. Someone should have told you. I don't paint anymore."

Max considered this for a moment, then pulled out his pistol and jammed it into the hollow under the artist's cheekbone. With a satisfying click, he relaxed the safety catch. The bereaved eyes stammered shut.

Sturmbannführer Maximillian Haas was not an introspective man. He believed in neither God nor an afterlife. He was a man of medium height and build, with plain looks, of moderate intelligence. As a schoolboy, he'd never excelled at anything, his grades were nothing to brag about. Before he joined the Nazi Party, he'd been a machinist.

But as he stood there, his finger curled around the trigger of a gun pressed to another man's head, Max came to a startling conclusion: Tobias Rey wasn't being disrespectful. Tobias Rey wanted to die.

The arm holding the gun fell to his side. "What's the matter with you, Rey?" he asked, curious. "Why don't you want to paint anymore?"

The shadowy eyes opened, recognized that the risk of imminent death had passed. Max could tell that he didn't know whether to be relieved or disappointed. Wearily, he replied, "With death circling all around us, the practice of making these chicken scratches seems ridiculous to me. I feel like I am mocking the dead."

Max thought. "It's not ridiculous to want to live. Toby— may I call you Toby?—you know what your problem is? You think too much. For now, all you have to do is work. Okay?"

When he sucked on the cigarette, Max could see a cut shaped like a crescent moon where he had socked his gun into the starved cheek. "What do you want me to paint?"

Since yesterday, the box with Peter's possessions had moved upstairs. Max paged through *In the Land of Armadillos* until he found the picture he liked. "This one," he said, pointing to the parade of red armadillos trundling up and down blue hills.

Leaving the cigarette dangling from his lips, the artist took up a pencil and squinted at the wall behind the bed. In his black pants and black shirt, he was pitiably scrawny, reminding Max of a broken umbrella, ribs inverted by the wind.

With a pencil in his hand, Toby's entire affect changed.

His back straightened, realigned. His shoulders relaxed and, with that small adjustment to his posture, broadened. He seemed to grow several inches taller all at once. Simultaneously, the muscles in his face tautened to a kind of concentration Max usually associated with animals of prey. Inhabiting his element the way a lion inhabits the savannah, Toby radiated power and confidence.

He lunged forward and began to draw. With a single undulating line, he brought forth a series of rolling, round-topped mountains. Max watched, entranced, as he feinted back, frowned, then darted forth to add palm trees and tufts of grass. With an intense flurry of strokes, Toby outlined a chubby armadillo. Before Max's astonished eyes, the picture in the book came to life.

"My God," he said. The words burst out involuntarily.

Now Toby seemed to remember that Max was in the room. He glanced at his drawing, gave him a wry smile. "Well, boss, what do you think?"

Max was confused. In the white room, watching the thin, pale man in dark clothes summon forth images from the air, he felt an elation not unlike the awe he had experienced when he was a child in church.

He shook his head to clear it of the dreaminess that had settled over him. An office full of work awaited his attention. "You look like you're going to faint," he grunted. "I'll send up some breakfast."

In the following days, Max was preoccupied with a whole Pandora's box full of problems. Jews were pouring in from everywhere. There was a transport from Vienna, one from Kraków, another one from Skorodnica, all needing evaluation, labor assignments, housing. A crew of Jewish stone-cutters complained that they were being mistreated by their employer and refused to go back to his shop. They wanted assurances that the abuses would stop. Furthermore, the Jewish Council was screwing around, unwilling to come up with a list of people who were too old, too sick, or too worn out for employment, having finally figured out what it meant when a large group of Jews was assembled for a walk in the woods. Up until now, the Judenrat had done everything they were asked. The time was right for his first visit.

It wasn't that the ghetto was walled off, or fenced in with barbed wire. Still, it bore all the signs of involuntary incarceration. The trees were dead, the crumbling buildings displayed leprous facades, the paving stones were cracked and missing. The gutters were swollen with an oily black runoff fed by melting snow. A fading, outdated movie poster peeled from a kiosk, advertising *Gone with the Wind;* a flyer demanding that Jews turn in all furs was tacked over it. Here and there Max could see a house destroyed at the beginning of the war and never repaired. Color had fled the Jewish quarter; the houses were gray, the snow was gray, the shingles were gray, merchandise in shopwindows, faces, too.

On the sidewalk, Yids scattered at his approach, scurrying across the street to the other side. Children stopped playing as he strode by, observing with wide eyes the shiny death's-head badge on his officer's cap, the billowing skirts of his overcoat, his gleaming leather boots.

The offices of the Judenrat looked like offices anywhere else. A desk, a telephone, a receptionist, rows of ledgers, a potted plant, the clatter of women typing in another room. There was a flutter of activity at his arrival. The members of the Jewish Council emerged from their offices, looking prosperous and harried. When enough of them had gathered around, peppering him with explanations and concerns, he handed his coat to the receptionist, pulled out his pistol, and shot them.

### From Max Haas's diary, November 1, 1942

*. . . fifteen men, well dressed, cultured, with beautiful manners. I didn't enjoy shooting them, but it was the quickest way to get their cooperation. The list of names I requested will be in my hands by morning.*

*This is wartime. There are the victorious and the vanquished, and unfortunately for them, they belong to the side of the vanquished. I didn't write the rules, that's just how it goes. From now on, I expect the Jewish Council will be more compliant.*

### From his letter to Gerda Haas, November 1, 1942

*The most exciting news! You're never going to guess who I found to paint murals in Peter's room. Tobias Rey, what do you think of that! He's painting some scenes from* In the Land of Armadillos. *Please don't tell Peter. I want it to be a surprise.*

*How are my little soldier's riding lessons coming along? Tell him that Lilo is a little lame from a fall she took during a hunt, so she is getting a good rest in the barn right now, but when he gets here, we'll go riding all the time.*

*My dearest darling sweetheart, how I miss you! Today I am thinking in particular of your little bunny nose, and your little bunny chin, and the softness of your hair when I put my fingers through it. How I long to be alone with you in our little den! All this romantic talk doesn't sound much like your old Max, does it? The closer the day of your arrival comes, the faster my heart beats for you.*

The tall clock in the stairway chimed ten times as Max climbed up the steps. At the threshold of the nursery, he pushed open the door. He caught his breath, speechless with delight.

Using the word *red* to describe the armadillos would have been laughably inadequate. The color was scarlet, or carmine, or madder lake, boiling crazily into a neon sunset orange, overflowing into an ecstasy of bronze, cinnabar, rust, before finally bleeding back into crimson. A wide swash of blue was brushed exuberantly around the outline of each armadillo, a pure, burning hue he had seen only once before, in a painting of the Virgin.

Max was just returning home from the cinema, a gala premiere for a new German film. A young, handsome scientist was developing a top-secret weapon that would win the war for Germany. Disaster struck when a foolish secretary let the secret slip to her new boyfriend, who, surprise surprise, turned out to be spying for the enemy. Order was restored in the end—the handsome scientist shot the traitorous spy and married his virtuous blond fiancée—and the foolish secretary learned a tough but valuable lesson. Max loved movies, especially movies like this one, thrillers that delivered a timely political message.

Toby was standing in the middle of the room, his thin arms crossed over his chest, lost in contemplation. There was something glamorous about him, Max thought, a certain inborn elegance, as if he belonged to a lost branch of a forgotten monarchy. He had already begun sketching out the next mural, which showed the armadillo Aramis and his lady love, Bianca, at the café they opened together in Paris. Men in homburg hats soared through the air, while fantastic animals of every shape and color populated the little round marble-topped tables. Bianca, the blue cockatoo, was in her white apron, Aramis, his vest and bow tie. Max barely stopped himself from clapping his hands with childish joy.

Under his protection, and with a steady diet, Max had expected Toby to fill out a bit or, at the very least, to cheer up. But if anything, he looked worse, the lines in his elongated face etched too sharply for his thirty years, the angles of his body growing more extreme by the day.

"You've got to stop fucking Gruber's secretary," Max growled, plopping heavily onto the bed.

Startled from his trance, Toby nearly lost his balance. "I'll try, boss," he began to say before breaking into a harsh cough.

Max removed his officer's cap and flipped it onto the desk. "That doesn't sound good," he said. "How long have you been coughing like that?"

Toby was bent over double; it took him a moment to catch his breath. "Since yesterday," he rasped.

Max frowned at the artist's shirt and trousers, too thin to be of any use against the eastern cold. "You should dress warmer. It's cold as a witch's chuff out there tonight."

It was the end of a long day. There had been an action at the hospital, all the patients shot in their beds, concurrent with a raid on the orphanage. His presence had been required at both operations. A cloud of fatigue was descending over him, assisted along its journey by the champagne served at the premiere. With a sigh of relief, he unbuttoned his dress-uniform jacket. He kicked off a boot, pushed the other one off with his toes. As he made himself comfortable, something nosed its way into Max's perception.

"You do have a warm coat, don't you, Toby?"

The artist shook his head, coughed lightly into his fist.

"Well, why not?"

He shrugged, his shoulders rising and falling with indifference.

Max sat up straight, indignant. "This is outrageous. We have warehouses full of clothing. I'll see to it that you get another one right away."

"Don't trouble yourself. When I die of pneumonia, you'll be commended for saving the Reich the cost of the bullet."

"You're not allowed to die just yet. Not before you finish Peter's room, anyway. I'm joking, I'm joking. Don't go anywhere. I know just the thing."

Max padded down the stairs in his socks. This late at night, there was only an oil lamp burning in the kitchen, the corners of the room sunk in murky shadow. He could have woken the housekeeper, but making the preparations himself gave him a certain proprietary pleasure. When the copper kettle began to sing, a voice from behind him murmured, "Can I be of service, Sturmbannführer?"

With all the extra duties of the last month, he had nearly forgotten about his new cook. On the petite side, with a pleasing round rump and a small, nipped-in waist, she had that dusky skin tone some of the Jews had, wan but pretty. Her eyes were large and hooded; to him, it seemed that they swam with myriad unfathomable secrets.

"I've forgotten your name," he said.

"Saltzman, Adela, Sturmbannführer."

"And how long have you been working here?"

"A month, Sturmbannführer."

Slowly, deliberately, he poured hot water over the tea leaves. "Was it you who made that saddle of rabbit for dinner last night?"

The shoulders were bowed, the eyes cast submissively downward. "Yes, sir." A husky voice for such a slight figure.

"Relax, relax," he said in a tone that was meant to be congenial. "That was the best rabbit I've ever eaten. Where did you learn how to cook like that?"

"From my mother, sir."

"Well, Saltzman. The next time you see your mother, you can tell her that Sturmbannführer Maximillian Haas says her daughter is the best cook in the entire country."

"Thank you, Sturmbannführer," she answered, her gaze still trained on the floor.

"Call me Haas. You can go back to bed."

"Yes, Sturmbannführer," she said, and evanesced into the shadows beyond the door.

When the tea was ready, he slowly climbed the stairs. On a tray, he balanced a tall glass set on a china saucer, filled with a transparent ruby-red liquid. For himself, there was a bottle of vodka. "Here," he said brusquely, setting it carefully down on the desk. "Oma's recipe. Tea with wine and honey. Drink up."

Toby took the glass in his slender, aristocratic fingers. "Honey," he murmured. "I haven't had honey since . . ." He didn't finish the sentence. Closing his eyes, he brought the tea near to his nose, abandoning himself to the sweet fragrance. The lines in his face eased, faded. Without them, he looked ten years younger.

It was late. Max should have gone downstairs to sleep, but after the unusual pressures of the day, he found he was hungry for company. He sat back down on the bed. "Tell me something about yourself, Toby," he said, stifling a yawn. "Do you have a wife? Sweetheart?"

The artist cupped the glass with both hands. "No wife, no sweetheart. Before the war, there was someone."

Max loosened his belt a couple of notches, slid down farther on the mattress. "So what happened? Why didn't you marry her?"

It was some time before Toby answered. "She isn't the marrying type."

"Oh, come on. All women want to marry, to become mothers, care for a home . . . It's in their nature. You're not making sense."

"All right, then, it was me. *I'm* not the marrying type." Toby's smile was too quick, the hand that ran through his lank hair, too unsteady.

Max turned this preposterous statement over in his mind. He couldn't conceive of a man who didn't yearn for the comforts of hearth and home. An idea formed in the depths of his consciousness, swirled slowly into focus.

"You're hiding something. Come on, Toby. The truth."

Toby went rigid, his graceful slouch frozen into corners and edges. "The truth is . . . I was seeing my translator. She isn't Jewish. It wasn't illegal then, you can't arrest her for that."

"I'm not looking to arrest anyone. It was just a friendly question."

Toby brushed the tips of his fingers across his forehead, as if he had walked into a cobweb. "The war started. She left me. But that was a long time ago. What about you?"

"Me? What's there to know? I'm married to the prettiest, cleverest, most wonderful woman in the world. I have a son, Peter, my brave little soldier." He felt around in his jacket for his wallet. "Here they are, take a look."

In the small black-and-white image, Gerda was propping Peter up on a carousel horse. Toby accepted the photo in his pale fingers, regarded it for a moment before handing it back. "It's a nice picture," he said.

There was a soft knock at the door. Guiltily, as if he had been sharing a confidence, Max leaped to his feet, buttoning his jacket.

But it was only the housekeeper. "Yes?" he said impatiently. "It's very late."

Even this hour of the night, not a single hair escaped the tight blond bun. These Poles. Such a tidy people. "Telegram, Herr Haas," she said. "It came while you were out." He took the envelope from her hand, and she left as silently as she had arrived, closing the door softly behind her.

Max tore it open and scanned it, his heart beating wildly. It was from Gerda. Peter had come down with bronchitis. Their move was being postponed until after Christmas. The doctor thought he should remain where he was for now.

Panic filled his throat the way wind fills a sail. Rattled by the unexpected emotion, he fumbled for a cigarette and tried to light it; when his hands shook, Toby held the match. Max took a few puffs, then angrily stubbed it out on the tray.

"She's put it off again," he said, trying to sound matter-of-fact. "Now you don't have to rush." But his voice betrayed his agitation, and he reached up to rake his fingers through his short hair, parted with martial precision. "They should have been here months ago, but always something holds them up. First it was his allergies. Then she was concerned about school. Last time it was those fucking partizans. I'd shoot them all myself if it would get her here any sooner." His next words were so forthright, so baldly honest, that he startled even himself. "What's the matter with her, anyway?"

he burst out bitterly. "I haven't seen them in so long, I hope I recognize them when they get here."

God, it was good to say those words out loud. He loosened his tie and poured himself another two fingers of vodka. "Forget I said anything. Let's change the subject. Tell me the truth, Toby. Do artists really draw naked women?"

With the hand holding the glass of tea, Toby waved indifferently at a flat case leaning against the wall, bound in marbleized paper. "I was going to ask you if I could leave my portfolio here for safekeeping. See for yourself."

He lifted the portfolio onto the bed and untied the strings. It fell open to an ink sketch of a woman lying back on a bed, her knees apart. One hand rested behind her head, the other lay lightly on the dark isthmus between her thighs. Max felt himself grow warm all over, felt the shock of adrenaline to his brain, his throat, his balls. In the drawing, she wore black stockings and a camisole that rode up over her breasts. At the bottom, he could read the inscription. *Paris, 1938*, it said.

"Who is this?" he demanded. "A model?"

The corners of the gray lips curled up in a slight smile. "A friend."

Max studied the girl in the drawing. From her dreamy expression, it seemed to him that she was enjoying herself. "What was Paris like?"

"Exactly what you want Paris to be like. Girls willing to sleep with you for the price of a meal and a good time. Interesting people, from a hundred different places, with a hundred different opinions. Food of the gods. Streets overflowing with books and art and beautiful women. And the nightlife!" The burnt-out eyes sparked at the memory. "Frankly, in Vienna, it's the same thing, only with better pastries. And the girls are kinkier. But for sheer quantity and variety, nothing beats New York."

"New York," he exclaimed. "What were you doing in New York?"

"I was invited to teach in an art school there."

Max was intrigued. All he knew about New York was what he saw in the movies. "Are the buildings really as tall as they say? Did you see a baseball game? Al Capone? Did you go to Coney Island?"

"There's nothing like it. It's a city of immigrants, everyone is from somewhere else. But that's its strength. There's an energy in New York, an attitude, that you don't find anywhere else in the world . . . like they can do anything, with a little luck, if they try hard enough."

"They're like children, living in Cloud Cuckoo Land," said Max, dismissing the Americans with the wave of a hand. "So, tell me, Toby. Why did you come back?"

A shadow crept across the gray, exhausted face. "It seemed like the right thing to do at the time. My life was here. My dealer . . . my publisher . . . my family . . . a woman . . ."

"Do you still think it was the right thing to do?"

"No, I think I was an idiot. What do *you* think, Herr Sturmbannführer?"

They both laughed.

Max turned the page, hoping for another sexy pose. But the drawing that followed was a portrait of a woman, handsome, with a long, thin nose, dark eyes, and the traces of a knowledgeable smile playing about sensuous lips. "Who's this?"

There was an uncharacteristic halt in Toby's voice when he answered. "My mother."

Max surveyed the drawing for a time before he spoke.

"She looks very intelligent," he said. "And yet like she is a woman who enjoys life."

Toby's face took on a healthy color when he smiled. "That's her, exactly. She was a dress designer up until the war. I must have inherited her artistic sensibilities. My father was an academic, a physicist. He was obsessed with the study of time. Can we go back in time. Forward in time. Are there universes parallel to our own. Is it possible to exist in a time other than the present. It could get very abstract."

"Where are your parents now? Are they in the ghetto with you?"

"They were taken away in April," said Toby. The afflicted look that lifted when he talked about the past returned, drew a curtain over the conversation. "I should go," he said, unmolding himself from the chair. "It's late."

"Are you kidding?" Max objected. "It's past curfew. You'll be shot."

Toby shrugged his thin shoulders and smiled his cynical smile, as if to say, *At least it will be quick.* "It hasn't happened yet."

So this was his regular routine. "Yes, well, they're trigger-happy tonight. There was an *Aktzia* at the hospital, another one at the orphanage. You're not going anywhere."

He sank slowly into the chair. "Is that what all the shooting was about?"

"Yes."

Toby looked like he might faint. Max leaned forward, gripped his arm. "Come on, Toby. Have some courage. Better them than you," he said.

When the artist opened his eyes again, he looked ill. "Lie down," Max instructed him gruffly, getting off the bed.

"You look terrible. I'll bring you a blanket. You're sleeping here tonight."

"She's here," said his secretary.

"Oh, good," said Max. He hurried to his office, careful to close the door behind him. "So glad that you could come, Fräulein Rozycki," he said enthusiastically, turning to the woman seated in the chair. "Did my secretary offer you something to drink? Tea? Coffee?"

"No, thank you," she said. She was struggling with her composure, as any woman would when called upon to visit the offices of the Gestapo on Staromiejska Street. "And it's Lipowa now. I'm married. What have I done? I have a right to know why I'm here."

He was relieved to hear that she spoke a good German. So few Poles did. Without the need for a translator, their conversation could be kept private. "It's nothing like that. This is a social visit. It turns out we have a mutual friend." Her expression showed that she found that difficult to believe. Max was struck by the feeling that he had seen her somewhere before. "The artist, Tobias Rey."

Few words could have had a greater impact, he was sure. Her face blanched as white as her pearls. Spots of color burned high on her cheeks, contrasting attractively with her milky skin.

"So he's alive," she said with a rush of emotion. "Thank God." Then, reacting with despair, "I had hoped he might have escaped by now." She put a gloved hand to her forehead, an eloquent gesture of grief.

He hastened to reassure her. "Don't worry, he's safe. You could say I am his protector."

She needed a moment to take in the information. Clearly, hearing his name had been an enormous shock. Emotions collided across the even surface of her flawless face. "How is he?" she said, feigning something like normalcy.

"Oh, he's fine now that I'm looking after him. He's painting for me, some scenes from *In the Land of Armadillos*."

A light came into her eyes. "I worked with him on that one."

"You were his translator."

"Yes, on that one and two others, *The Thief of Yesterday and Tomorrow*, also *The Town Inside the Hourglass*. How did you know?"

Max was very proud of his detective work. "Bianca Rozycki. He wouldn't tell me your name. I had to call the publisher to find you. Were those also for children?"

"None of them were for children." She turned her lovely head toward him, surprised. "Have you ever read any of his books, Sturmbannführer?"

He was insulted. "Of course. *In the Land of Armadillos* is my son's favorite storybook. I've read it many times."

"You'll know this, then. In the story, the armadillos live alongside the cockatoos for years, peacefully sharing the savannah, until an armadillo named Lazarus comes along and tells the others that cockatoos are bad, greedy creatures. The armadillos trample the blue cockatoos' favorite food, the indigo plant, and then they drink up all the water. In town, they don't let them rest in the trees, and they close down all the birdseed stores. The cockatoos fly away, never to return. On his way home after the celebration, an armadillo named Aramis comes across a cockatoo hiding in the roots of a baobab tree. Because of a broken wing, she is unable to leave with the others."

"Bianca," he said helpfully. He was listening with rapt attention. It was thrilling to hear the story told by someone involved in its creation.

She continued. "He takes pity on her, brings her home and fixes up her wing, tells her she can stay until she heals. Though she is a bird and he is an armadillo, they fall in love. In the meantime, things aren't going well in town. No one knows how to make the armadillos' favorite poppy-seed cookies. The cafés close down because the cockatoos were the only waiters. And finally, no one can purchase new shoes when their old ones wear out, because the cockatoos were the cobblers, too.

"Aramis realizes that if he and Bianca want to be together, they must leave. They move to Paris, where they open a café, the Blue Cockatoo. It's a smashing success, welcoming all kinds of animals, two-legged, four-legged, and flying. They live happily ever after." She cocked her eyebrows at him. "What does that sound like to you, Herr Sturmbannführer?"

"It's about an armadillo and a cockatoo," he replied, thinking of himself and Gerda. "They are very different from each other in many ways. Maybe their families don't approve of the match. But they love each other above all. So they move away."

She regarded him as if he were an interesting exhibit at a museum.

"The cockatoo," he said suddenly. "Her name is Bianca." The meaning of the coincidence dawned on him. "He named her after you." She bowed her head graciously, permitted him a small smile. "You left him when the war started," he went on, trying to work it all out. "Because of the anti-Jewish laws, I presume."

"*I* left *him*?" she repeated in disbelief, her eyes narrowing. "Is that what he said? Let me enlighten you, Sturmbann-führer. After he came back from the United States, he was afraid. Things had deteriorated. He thought I'd be harassed, beaten, maybe worse. So he told me he didn't want to see me anymore."

Max was astounded. He tried to imagine having the strength to leave Gerda, faced with a similar situation, and he realized he would never do it. He couldn't survive without her. "That was very noble of him."

"Oh, yes. Very noble. My hero. Of course, he didn't ask me what *I* wanted. He made the decision for both of us. I would have been happy to face those pigs together with him."

Max was surprised at her vehemence, at the hurt Toby's betrayal still inspired. "But how can that be? He came back from New York, where he would have been safe, to be with his family, his girlfriend . . . I don't understand."

She stared past him, out the window at the market square, giving him the opportunity to observe her in profile. The almond-shaped eyes—blue? gray? hazel?—were spaced widely apart and set into high, chiseled cheekbones. There was a straight, regal nose and a domed forehead that gave way to hair the color of a wheat field in autumn. She was like a poster advertising Aryan perfection.

"He didn't come back for me," she said, biting off the words. "He broke it off with me a week after he returned. I don't think it was for his family, either—they begged him to stay. No, I have another theory about why he came back to Poland. I think that, for him, it was too easy over there in America. Too easy to be a Jew, too easy to be an artist, too easy to be alive. Celebrated not for his work, but for his status as a refugee. 'Look, there goes Tobias Rey, he escaped from the Nazis' clutches.' And then they patted him on the head and invited him to dinner, and they gave him a job in one of their nice, safe schools, where there were a hundred wealthy girls who all wanted to be titillated by his terrible stories before they fell into his bed. He could say anything he pleased, do anything he liked. It cost him nothing, and it gave him nothing. It was too easy to forget the real world out there beyond Coney Island, where knowing the wrong people or being born to the wrong parents could mark the difference between life and death. Here, each tiny gesture matters. Every breath of a condemned man is an act of defiance. That's why he came back."

Max tried to get the visit back on track. "Excuse me, Frau Lipowa. I apologize if I am bringing up sad memories. But the reason I brought you here, what I would really like to know, is if he has always been this way." He laced his fingers together, leaned across the desk. "I know something about Jews, Fräulein," he said. "Generally, they are cooperative, they are helpful, they beg to be given a chance to be useful. They want to live, you see. Toby doesn't do any of those things. In fact, he does exactly the opposite. If I had to describe him, I would say he is a man who is waiting to die."

"Look around," she said bitterly. "Can you blame him?"

"The war will not last forever," he reminded her, ignoring the provocation. "He's an essential worker to the Reich. He's safe. He has plenty to eat. You would think he'd cheer up a bit."

She looked closely at the man behind the desk. In his thirties, not thin but not heavy, either, just now an earnest expression on his blunt bully's face. She noticed, too, the black uniform trimmed with silver braid; the SS eagle on the cuff, the twin lightning slashes on the collar; the red swastika armband, the gun in the smooth leather holster on his belt.

"Why is this so important to you, Sturmbannführer?" she asked curiously.

Years later, at the trial, she would recount this part of the conversation, and his response would save him from the gallows. "I don't know," Max admitted, his voice dropping a notch lower as he probed himself for an answer. "It's not like me at all. I've seen many people die, Frau Lipowa. I won't get into the specifics. And usually, what I feel is nothing. The way I see it is, today it's them, tomorrow it's me, it's a throw of the dice who gets the bullet. But with Toby . . . there's something about him, I can't explain it. I don't care whether he is a Jew, a Catholic, or a Buddhist. I want to help him if I can."

She regarded him with an expression he could not read; and then there was a little sigh, a drop of the shoulders, and she gave in.

"He was always very sensitive," she offered reluctantly. "He tried not to show it. A man beating an animal, a mother screaming at her child in the street, these things would bring tears to his eyes. He pretended it was all very funny, the world, a great big cosmic joke, but it would find its way into his drawings or another one of his stories. But waiting to die? No . . . you wouldn't use that phrase to describe Tobias Rey. He loved clubs, the theater, restaurants, women. All of it. He had a tremendous appetite for living."

Interesting, though ultimately not very useful. Still, she had given him some ideas. "Thank you, Frau Lipowa," he said. "You may go now."

Slowly, she rose to her feet, took a few steps, not yet

believing that she was being allowed to leave Gestapo headquarters. At the door, she turned. "Where's Aliza?" she asked.

"Aliza?" he repeated, puzzled.

"His sister," she said, fastening a stole made from some ferrety animal around her neck. "He adores her. He was always sending her little gifts from wherever he was, postcards with funny drawings. She must be fourteen or fifteen by now. Try her first."

"Thank you, Frau Lipowa," he said, pleased. "You've been a great help. I'll send Toby your good wishes."

"No," she said after a moment's hesitation. "Don't say anything at all."

He watched her walk out the door, tall and long-limbed and desirable, and suddenly he knew why she looked so familiar. She was the naked woman in the drawing titled *Paris, 1938*.

Circumstances conspired to keep Max from putting his plan into action for the next few days. First there was the matter of the stonecutting crew who refused to show up for work. As a solution, he had the striking workers lined up in the market square, where he whipped them, then shot them himself.

But that was a tea party compared to the next item of business that landed on his plate. Now his superiors wanted him to deliver twenty-five hundred Jews for resettlement. Max was at the end of his rope. It would take an enormous amount of time to select and train new laborers to replace them, to the extent that it might actually harm the war effort. What was Berlin thinking?

He was in this frame of mind when he clomped upstairs to Peter's room. Toby was there, of course, working. Max unbuckled his jacket and undid the first buttons, throwing himself onto the bed.

"What a day," he grumbled. "You can't imagine the stupidity I have to deal with."

Toby didn't answer right away; he was just finishing the last stroke on one of the patrons in the café. Max was seething from the way Reinhart had gone behind his back. A week ago, he had informed the commandant of the work camp at Adampol that he required a list of his nonessential workers. Today he had received a heated tongue-lashing, by telephone, from an unknown brigadier general calling all the way from the General Government in Kraków, telling him to keep his fat fucking hooks off of Reinhart's precious Jews. His ears were still ringing.

But here in Peter's room, time stopped, all such cares drained completely away. Red armadillos tramped up and down blue hills and paraded past cotton-candy-colored shops in the village, while blue cockatoos nested in the lofty branches of baobab trees. At the café, all kinds of creatures sat together in fantastic, whimsical combinations. A dog shared a table with a cat; a fish buttered a baguette for a canary. A bull wearing bifocals read a *Journal* while his friend the sea serpent stirred an espresso; a pink pig in a striped shirt and a beret-wearing poodle posed before tiny glasses of a clear cordial; a crocodile shared a kiss with a hare. Stranger yet were the humans: a blue man with a striped face; a beautiful girl with scales and a tail. "I know this one!" he exclaimed, pointing at a walrus who looked uncannily like Soroka the saddlemaker.

Max noticed a man in a blue mackintosh and a blue

bowler hat who bore a striking resemblance to himself, accompanied by a svelte red fox who looked very much like
Gerda. Despite the overall shittiness of the day, he smiled.
"It looks just like her," he said, planting himself in front of
the painting, his hands clasped behind his back. "Though I
would have made her a rabbit."

"You know, I tried that," Toby said. Without warning,
the frail body convulsed in coughing; his palette clattered
to the floor as he doubled up, resting his hands on his knees.

"Are you wearing the coat I sent you?" Max demanded,
concerned. Toby managed to bob his head yes. "You should
see a doctor. It sounds like it's getting worse. Maybe he'll
prescribe something for that cough."

Toby groped for a chair, sat down. "The only thing the
doctors prescribe around here is a bullet in the back of the
head."

"What's the matter with you, Toby?" Max said plaintively. "One of these days you're going to say something like
that to the wrong person, and *bang*." There was a soft knock
at the door. "I asked the kitchen to send up some dinner,"
he said to Toby, feigning casualness. "Come in and leave it
on the desk, Adela."

The cook glided into the room in carpet slippers, set the
plate on the desk. There was an apron tied around her small
waist, making her look even more fetching, Max thought.
"So. Have you two been introduced?" he asked slyly, taking
half a sandwich.

"No, Sturmbannführer," she replied in her provocative
alto.

"I told you, call me Haas. Adela, this is Tobias Rey. He's
doing some paintings for us."

It was an old house. Just then a gust of wind whistled

up the stairway, blasting the door wide open. Too late, Max saw it coming: the door slamming squarely into the painted couple at the café table, obliterating the delicate brushwork, possibly cracking the plaster as well. In the blink of an eye, Adela's small hand shot out and caught the doorknob.

Max let out his breath. "Quick reflexes," he said admiringly. "We could use someone with your instincts on the eastern front, Adela."

"I've read your books," she said to Toby.

Max thought he saw a glimmer of interest touch the gray, wasted face. "Really," Toby said. "Which ones?"

"My favorite was *The Thief of Yesterday and Tomorrow*. The use of the dolls to tell the story was hallucinatory. Like the dreams you have when you are running a high fever."

"I hope you didn't find them too pretentious," said Toby.

"Oh, no," she murmured, and there was a trace of amused irony in the sultry voice. "That is not a word I would use to describe them."

The smile was thin and fleeting, but it was there. So far, his scheme was working, Max thought gleefully. "Adela, our artist is wasting away," he announced. "From now on, I'm holding you responsible for making sure he eats."

When she left the room, Max saw that Toby's gaze followed her until the door closed behind her.

"Not bad, hey?" said Max.

"Not bad at all."

"The best cook I've ever had," he added as further incentive. "What was that book she was talking about? The one with the dolls?"

"*The Thief of Yesterday and Tomorrow*," Toby said, dropping his brushes in a can of turpentine.

"Is it also for children?" Max asked hopefully.

"No. A short story."

"What's it about?"

Toby looked reluctant. "I don't think you'll like it."

"Try me." Max took out his cigarette case, lit one for himself and one for Toby. Between them, the smoke revolved lazily into the air.

"The setting is the interior of a large old-fashioned house. Oversize furniture, Oriental rugs, heavy drapes, urns with artificial flowers. The family is all at home. Mother says she heard in the marketplace that a tremendous rainstorm was coming their way. Someone should check that the windows are shut, the laundry taken off the line, and the chickens locked safely in the henhouse. Father is in his study, lost in his research on a particular species of beetles in the Amazonian rain forest. Brother can't be bothered, he's too busy flirting with the sexy servant girl. Sister doesn't believe it, she only wants to talk about the party last night and how she needs a new dress for the big dance. Mother goes off to check on something cooking on the stove, then lies down on the couch with a headache. Just then there is a threatening roll of thunder in the distance. A giant hand descends through the roof and snatches them up, one by one. They scream and scream, but it's as if no one can hear them.

"Suddenly, the point of view changes: A small boy is taking dolls out of a large, elaborately decorated toy house. When he is called to dinner, he leaves the dolls naked in a heap on the playroom floor."

Toby took a deep drag on the cigarette. Max waited for more, but it became apparent that there was none forthcoming. "That's it?" he said, puzzled. "Then what happens?"

"Nothing. The End."

Max was disappointed. He couldn't put his finger on it,

but the story was too vague and disquieting to be enjoyable. "Not your best work," he advised him. "Don't feel bad. The next one will be better."

He unbuttoned his jacket the rest of the way, settled back on the bed with a satisfied sigh. He liked to watch Toby work, the movements of his hands as they drew looping lines and angles that became animals, or trees, or buildings, or people. This was how he ended his days now; there was something comforting in the regularity of the nighttime ritual. Had anybody asked him, he would have denied it, but the truth was, he could let down his guard with Toby in a way that wasn't possible among other Germans.

"Where do you get your ideas from?"

Toby, hunched on the chair, peered at him through the haze of smoke. "Everywhere," he said. "It's like a game. It starts like this. You see the paintbrushes, right? Look at them, all clustered together in that vase. What if the brushes were alive? What sound would they make, rubbing up against each other? What if they could talk? What would they say to one another? Would they have an ongoing feud with the paint about who is the most important? What would they think of the current political situation? You get the idea."

Max shook his head in wonder. No, he did not get the idea. His mind didn't work that way. In his brain, every word, every thought, every action, had a slot, like a well-organized toolbox, where he stored them until they were needed.

"But *how* do you do it? I can't draw anything, not even a straight line."

"I don't know. A picture appears in my head, and my fingers do the rest." Wearily, Toby rubbed at a place under his eye. Max could tell he was tired. The pouches were more bruised-looking than usual. "Sorry, it's late," he said. "Anything else?"

"Listen," Max said, coming to the second part of his plan. "I met an old friend of yours." A more observant man would have seen Toby turn pale, but rapt with enthusiasm, he plunged on. "Bianca Rozycki," he said, wagging a naughty-naughty finger at him. "You didn't tell me how pretty she is!"

"She's not in any trouble, is she?" There was a queasy tremor of fear in Toby's voice.

"Oh, no, not at all. She looks very well. She didn't want me to tell you I'd seen her. Probably didn't want you to worry. Now, Toby," he went on earnestly, "she did tell me one thing that was useful. You have a sister."

Toby bleached a deathly white. The hand holding the cigarette began to shake.

Max leaned forward. "It's all right, Toby. Trust me. I want to be your friend. Just tell me where she is. Maybe I can help her, too."

On his chair in the middle of the room, Toby hunched his shoulders closer together, as if in defense from imminent attack. Max thought he understood. "I know. When you look at me, maybe all you see is this uniform. I am an officer of the German Reich, yes, I do my job very well, yes, but inside the uniform, I am also a man. I know what it is to worry about someone you love. Come on, Toby. Let me help you. At least give me an idea."

"I can't. I mean, I don't know where she is." The long sensitive fingers had a life of their own, creeping across his forehead. "She was in a hiding place on the other side of town. For a while, I was getting regular messages from her. She was hungry, she was bored, could I bring her some movie magazines . . . a few weeks ago, they stopped. I went to the house, but it was empty. It looked like it had been ransacked. A neighbor told me there had been Jews hiding there, but someone gave them away. When they tried to escape into the forest, they were caught. I haven't heard from her since." His hands were trembling so much, he spilled ash over his pants. He brushed at it with fumbling fingers. Absently, like a worried mother. "Silly girl . . . the last time I saw her, she wasn't even dressed properly for winter . . . I had to give her my coat."

Max had a bad feeling about this. "When was this, exactly?"

"It would have been around the time I came to work for you."

*Something's come up. We caught a group of Jews in the forest outside of town, and I need you to take over. A small job. Twenty-three. They must have been hiding out somewhere.* Two dark-haired girls at the far end of the line, fourteen or fifteen, clasping each other for support. The celebrated artist and writer Tobias Rey, on a day so cold that the branches outside his window were jacketed in ice, showing up to his first interview without an overcoat. One of the girls, delicate, with legs like two spindles. Dark eyes in a sensitive face, wearing a coat many sizes too large for her. He saw it now. The girl looked just like her brother.

"Did you say she was wearing a man's coat?" he inquired cautiously, his eyebrows fanned upward.

At first Toby's eyes fixed on him with something like hope. But as the silence dragged grimly on and on, the import of the SS man's words dawned slowly across his face. Suddenly his features were changing shape, melting, breaking apart. A wordless cry forced its way out of his throat, his voice shattering into silvery pieces that fell to the floor and rolled away into the corners like balls of mercury from a broken thermometer.

"She didn't feel a thing, Toby," Max said urgently, sitting forward, putting his hand on his arm. "You hear me, Toby? She fell without a sound."

"Was it you?" he cried out. "Did you do it?"

"No. But I was there," Max said. Quietly, to calm him. "It was Krause, from my team. A good man. It was over in seconds. She didn't even hear the gunshot, I swear it."

There was another bleat of anguish, and the thin, pale fingers plowed into the unkempt hair, hiding his face from view.

Max knew what to do. Swiftly, he hurried down the stairs, came back up holding a bottle of vodka. He poured a tall glass for Toby and another one for himself. He pulled up a chair and sat down next to him. "Now, Toby, you listen to me," he said firmly. "It's over for her, okay? She's out of it. No more pain, no more suffering. Do you think she'd want you to give up, to go through all this drama, acting like it's the end of the world? No, of course not. She'd want you to be happy, to get on with your life. That is how you honor your sister's memory."

But the dark, shaggy head was rocking back and forth, *no, no, no, no.* Max sighed, rubbed his hand over his own stubby hair. Oh, he'd really put his foot in it. This was going to be harder than he thought.

"Listen, Toby," he started again, more gently this time. "The war won't last forever. One day all this business of killing will be over, and we will have to start again with the business of living. And on that happy day, we'll have a drink together in friendship. But for now we just have to get through this. Come on, drink up."

Toby stopped shaking, but behind his hands, he was

making small, unintelligible sounds, as if he were crying in the language of animals. Finally, his head lifted. His face was puffy, smudged with tears and paint. He wiped it off on his sleeve and downed half of the vodka in a single gulp. "You want to drink? Okay, then. Let's drink."

Toby's eyes were rimmed with red, but there was a menacing junkyard-dog quality to his movements that was setting off alarms in Max's head. "Hey, does the Gestapo ever play bar games? As a patron of the fine arts, I think you're really going to like this one."

In his time in the Einsatzgruppen, Max had seen a lot of drunks. Most of them slurred their words, became sloppy, or angry, silent, or sentimental. Toby, on the other hand, seemed to grow more awake, more aware, more precise. He roamed through his portfolio, pulling out a sheet of laid paper. Max caught his breath. It was an ink drawing of a man prostrating himself on the floor beneath a naked woman seated on a bed. The man was worshipfully kissing the underside of her foot. Toby said, "Here we go. You draw a line, and I have to make something out of it."

"I don't want to ruin your picture."

"Don't worry about that. I've got lots of dirty pictures. Come on, it'll be fun."

"No, Toby." He was uneasy. "You've just had a terrible shock. You need to sleep."

Toby's voice had changed, darkly colorful, slippery, and raw. "Not really. I don't sleep much these days. Drawing makes me feel better. Go on, Herr Sturmbannführer. Draw."

"I told you, I can't draw. And don't call me that. There's no 'Herr Sturmbannführer' between you and me, Toby."

"Okay, then, I'll go first."

Toby took a pencil, scribbled on the back of the paper,

then shoved it across the desk. Reluctantly, Max fingered the pencil, then looked at the line. It was just a meaningless squiggle. How could you do anything with that? He stared at it and stared at it, and then, in a flash, he had it. Squinting and tilting his head, he began to draw. A few minutes later, he slid it over to Toby, almost fearfully awaiting his judgment.

"I see. A rabbit. Clever, very clever," he mumbled. He tipped the glass upward, finishing the vodka. "Come on, Max. My turn."

"What do I have to do?"

"Just draw a line. After that masterpiece, it should be a piece of cake. I'll do the rest."

With the tip of the pencil touching the paper, Max hesitated. He had the distinct feeling that he was on the point of losing control of the situation. Best to just say no, turn Toby out into the night, with a guard, of course, to get him home safely. Better yet, he could just leave, locking the artist in the attic room. By morning he would surely be back to himself. But then he would miss the pleasure of seeing Toby draw. On the paper, Max made an irregular zigzag line, the lightning insignia of the SS, and pushed it across the desk.

Toby studied the scribble, tapping the end of the pencil against his teeth. "Perfect, just perfect," he said. With fierce joy, he bent over the paper and began to draw. Max wished he would just stick to drawing, but Toby wouldn't shut up. "It's bedtime, isn't it? How about a story?"

The pencil went *scritch scritch scritch*. The grandfather clock in the stairway bonged midnight. Outside, the wind wept and tore at the windowpanes. The hairs prickled up on the back of Max's neck.

"Once upon a time, there was a handsome and powerful prince. He owned a castle filled with servants, but still, he was lonely. The prince fell in love with a princess who lived in a faraway land. He wrote her many beautiful letters filled with poetry, inviting her to visit him. He decorated his castle with the finest flying carpets from Persia, drapes woven by enchanted spiders, furniture built by captive fairies, but still, the princess wouldn't come. It turns out the princess was actually fucking her son's riding instructor. The End."

Max lifted himself from his seat and punched Toby in the face. His chair teetered on two legs for a moment before falling over backward. Bunching his hand into a fist, he stood over the emaciated, angular figure and punched him again. Blood spurted from Toby's nose, ran from the split lips, the twisted, insolent mouth. Max yanked his gun from the holster and whipped it savagely across the unprotesting face.

Toby's eyes rolled up into the back of his head and he passed out. Breathing hard, the SS man stood over the prone, crooked body and pointed his pistol at Toby's heart.

Astonishingly, the hand with the gun faltered, dropped back to his side.

"No," he said forcefully to the ruined, unconscious face. "I won't do it, you Jew bastard. I won't kill you, no matter how much you want me to. You're going to live, you little shit, whether you like it or not."

He checked to make sure that Toby was breathing, threw a blanket over him, and walked to the door. The pen drawing of the naked girl and her foot-fetishist lover lay under the upturned chair. Max righted the chair, picked up the drawing, and turned it over.

Bars, walls made from stone, a sink, a bed, a toilet. On the bed sat a man in a prison uniform, reading a letter. Despite his fury, Max could still admire the attention paid to detail in the little portrait of himself.

He gave the artist a good swift kick, then headed down the stairs to get Adela.

From Max Haas's diary, November 12, 1942

> . . . *a dreadful night, up until dawn selecting Jews for transport, another thousand, and I'm expected to replace them and have the businesses up and running again by the next day. What are they thinking?*
>
> *There are rumors flying, something bizarre happened in the forest. Either no one knows, or no one wants to say. Many good men lost their lives, Krause and Hanfling from my team among them. It was brutal, barbaric. A man disemboweled and hung in a tree, another found without skin . . . of others, they are finding only body parts. There isn't even anything left to send home to their families. Some say it was the Communists. I'm sure it was the partizans. These people are animals.*

From a letter to his wife, posted on the same date.

> . . . *a firm date for when you are coming. No more excuses! You can't imagine how urgently I need you. The murals in Peter's room are almost finished. After our artist is done with the nursery, I think I'll put him to work in the dining room.*
>
> *P.S. Please discontinue Peter's riding instruction. I'm anxious for his health. He can resume his lessons when he gets here.*

A Siberian wind was blowing down from the steppes. Max's handsome overcoat was made of the finest fabrics, from the finest German mills, by the smartest designers, but it was small comfort against the eastern cold.

Earlier in the day, he had taken Lilo out for a ride. This time of year the landscape was flat and dead, frost lying between the furrows. Lilo snorted, dipping her head up and down, happy to be freed from her stall. Patting the side of her neck, Max urged her into the forest.

Leaves and small branches snapped beneath her hooves, and the pleasantly astringent smell of pine needles rose into the air. Unexpectedly, they came upon a big operation, hundreds of Jews patiently waiting to take their place in front of the pit. Rohlfe was there with Hackendahl, Reinhart, too, looking pinched and serious. Reinhart had visited Max's office a number of times in the past month, always congenial, always with gifts: a gold watch or a diamond bracelet in exchange for one Jewish craftsman or another whom he would whisk away to his labor camp. Max was rather sorry he'd let him have Soroka, he would have liked to keep the saddlemaker in town. He himself had recently ordered a new saddle from him; he was the best in the region.

Gruber called and waved. But Max couldn't stay and socialize, he had a full desk of work waiting for him, so he turned Lilo around and headed back for town.

Near the edge of the woods, he came upon a cadre of ragged, starved-looking Jews. When Max ordered them to put their hands in the air, they turned instead and fled, forcing him to give chase. He'd shot three of them, two men and a girl, when Lilo stumbled on the uneven ground and fell.

The long bone of her right front leg was fractured. He couldn't even coax her to her feet. It was obvious he would have to put her down. As if to break his heart, she put her velvety nose into his hand, snuffling around for the treat

that he always carried for her. Running his fingers across the
smooth hard hide, he looked for the last time into the liquid
brown eyes and almost cried. He was grateful for only one
thing—that she didn't know what was coming.

Capping off a perfect day, just as he returned to his villa,
Soroka arrived, bringing with him the new saddle. Max almost lost it right then and there. By the time he reached his
office, he was practically bawling. After signing a few papers,
he picked up his files and went home.

Before he was halfway through the door, his senses were
captivated by the smells of plums and cinnamon. Adela was
baking. From the upper floor, he could hear music playing—
Marlene Dietrich sighing throatily, *falling in love again,
never wanted to . . . what am I to do, I cahn't help it.* He went
straight to the kitchen.

Adela had turned out to be an able and trustworthy comrade in the struggle to keep Toby's feet planted on this earth.
After cleaning him up that long bad night, she had stayed
with him until morning. Since then, a bond seemed to have
been forged between his artist and his cook; she could often
be seen dashing upstairs with a plate of something delecta-
ble, and it could be some time before she was seen again in
the kitchen. Once he had come upstairs to find them close
together in the darkened room. They'd sprung guiltily apart
at his entrance. They had no idea how excited he was by the
proof that his little matchmaking scheme was working. As
she left, he'd intercepted a stealthy look of passion meant
only for Toby, her hooded eyes gleaming, her lips wet and
parted. Max had been so aroused that he'd had to excuse
himself to rush downstairs and write an ardent letter to
Gerda.

"How is our *luftmensch* today?" he asked. The Jewish

meaning of this word, a man whose existence was so airy that he might blow away in a strong wind, described the artist perfectly. Toby's spirit was so fragile, it seemed to be in danger of evaporating into the air altogether.

Adela made a seesaw motion with her hand. *So-so.* He handed her his coat and hurried up the stairs two at a time.

The day after his beating, Toby's eyes had displayed a sensational combination of hues, all the colors of a peacock's plumage. The sight of the purpled eyes and the gouge across the cheek gnawed at Max, made him feel bad. It wasn't like him to feel this way; he couldn't explain it.

In the days since he'd received the news of his sister's death, Toby had grown even thinner, his fragile connection to life more tenuous. Which was why Max was so glad Toby had hit it off with Adela. There was a strength to her, a solidity, that he found immensely reassuring; this was a woman with both feet firmly on the ground. Though he was not normally an imaginative man, he harbored a vision of Toby as a kite bobbing restlessly in the sky, Adela holding tightly to the end of the string.

It was from Adela that Max finally learned the source of Toby's despair. He had assumed the most obvious reasons: fear, uncertainty of the future, the loss of his family and friends, the dissolution of his nice, comfortable life. But the truth was more insidious. It was Toby who had found the hiding place outside the ghetto, Toby who had sold the last of their valuables to buy his sister's way in, Toby who had insisted that she go. Aliza had begged to stay with him, to share her brother's fate, but he alone had made the decision that she would be safer in the bunker. If he had relented, she might be alive right now. He felt completely and irredeemably responsible for the girl's death.

All of which was incomprehensible to Max. Fate had a way of playing havoc with the best-laid plans. It could just as easily have gone the other way, with Toby shot dead, the sister safe in the bunker. How could a man hold himself so overwhelmingly culpable?

The radio was tuned to a banned station. The music was very loud; Max was sure they would have heard it all the way over at the Gestapo headquarters if it weren't for all the shooting and shouting going on in the streets today. At the top of the stairs, he pushed open the door and switched off the radio.

Here, the smell of turpentine prevailed over the delicate trance of cinnamon that bewitched the rest of the house. Sunlight filtered through the apothecary jars of linseed oil, turpentine, and varnish that Toby lined up like soldiers on the windowsill, filling the room with an ambient amber light. In a corner, the heap of rags he used to wipe his brushes clean climbed ever higher, resembling a snowy mountain range. The surface of the desk had disappeared under disciplined rows of paint with evocative, Old World names, verdigris, malachite, aureolin, madder lake. It was like visiting an alchemist's laboratory.

Hunched on a tall stool in the center of the room, Toby sat with his legs crossed, surveying his work. "Well, boss," he said, taking a drag on a cigarette, "it's finished. You can kill me now."

"Why do you have to say things like that?" Max complained.

The indefatigable armadillos marched up and down the perimeter of the room. Blue cockatoos filled the artificial skies in their flight, evolving seamlessly on the next wall into businessmen with homburgs and suitcases, flying like miniature airplanes over Paris. Toby had a memory for faces, and his choices were quixotic. Among the customers at the café, Max recognized the miller; Reinhart's pretty girlfriend; Hammer, the tailor; and of course, the lovely Adela.

Elated, he turned around and around, drunk with the crazy sensation that if he sat down at one of the tables, Bianca would waddle over on yellow claws to take down his order in her little receipt book. He clasped the edge of the desk for support, overcome with the unaccustomed emotion of unalloyed joy. "Sorry to disappoint you, Toby, no one's going to kill you. You're just too good."

Toby got up and drifted toward the window. While the characters in the paintings grew more vital, their creator's strength seemed to ebb with each passing day. "I've been hearing a lot of shooting," he said.

"Yes. Big *Aktzia* today, most of the Jews. We're just keeping essential workers."

The artist paled. In a strangled voice, he uttered something in a language Max didn't understand.

"What did you say?"

He shoved his hands into his pockets and stared down at his town. It was some time before he answered. "I said I can see my house from here."

"Where?" Max got up, went to the window.

With a long, skeletal arm, Toby gestured at a pretty white eighteenth-century townhouse trimmed with elaborate carved architectural details. Wisteria vines climbed the walls, bare this time of year. A stork's nest sat on top of the chimney pot. A denuded apple tree stood sentry in the front garden among the ivy. The facade glistened with a fairy-tale charm. "That one, at the corner of the market square."

"You live there now?"

"Oh, no. We had to leave it to move into the ghetto. That's the house I grew up in. I don't know who lives there now."

"It's pretty," Max said. "Maybe you'll live there again someday."

Toby faced him with weary incredulity. "Don't you know, Max. They're going to kill us all."

"You're being melodramatic," he objected, but the words sounded weak even to him. Late at night, he had seen the flames shooting from far-off chimneys, he had smelled the greasy stink of burning fat. Max sighed, dropped heavily onto the bed. "Look, Toby. The important thing is, you are safe, Adela is safe. I can't save everybody." He opened his jacket, kicked off his boots. "Anyway, don't give me any grief today. I had a rotten morning."

"What happened?"

"Lilo. My horse." His voice cracked a little. "She fell and broke her leg. I had to put her down. I know, I know. It's not like she's a human being. But still . . ." He bent his fingers over his eyes, then looked at his hand in surprise. He was crying.

But Toby was distracted, looking out the window at the crowds of people being herded through the narrow streets by soldiers with guns. "Why do they shoot horses, anyway?"

"Oh . . . they're so big, their legs are so thin . . . you can't tell a horse to stay off her feet while she recovers. And the truth is, they're in so much pain . . ." He was wiping his eyes with the back of his hand. "Please. I don't want to talk about it anymore."

They sat a little while in silence. Outside, there were more gunshots. Far in the distance, a woman screamed.

"I had a letter from Gerda today," Max remembered,

breaking the mood of quiet contemplation. "She's coming in the spring. You'll like her," he said, cheering himself up as he went along. "She's not an artist, but she has very good taste. And Peter. You can give him art lessons." The stripe he had made across Toby's face with the muzzle of his gun was still visible. He averted his gaze. "You're getting to be very popular. Standartenführer Gruber wants you to paint some naked ladies for his girlfriend's boudoir. Very tasteful, I'm sure. Oberführer Rohlfe wants you to do something for the Gestapo headquarters. Kommandant Reinhart was asking about you, too, some frescoes for his castle at Adampol. But none of this happens until I'm finished with you. I'm thinking of frescoes in the dining room, too . . . maybe a border. Fruits, flowers, that sort of thing."

But Toby was frozen at the window, riveted by the madness convulsing the streets of his town. Max could see the points of his shoulder blades through his shirt, as sharp as knives. If Adela was bringing him all these treats, why was he still so skinny? "Listen, Toby," he said, sitting forward on the bed. "When is the last time you wrote anything?"

The artist turned to stare at him, honestly perplexed. "I don't even remember . . . before the Germans came, I think."

There was a knock on the door. Adela entered, bearing a tray. On it was a teapot and the plum cake that had smelled so heavenly. "I thought you might like some tea, Sturmbannführer," she demurred.

When Adela was in the room, Toby's bereaved eyes came to life, there was color in his cheeks, he even straightened up a little. Max was delighted.

"It's Haas," he rebuked her mildly, then took a bite of the cake. It had the texture of pudding, tasting of butter and plums, of childhood, reminiscent of a bracing walk through autumn leaves, sitting around a good fire. He cut a wedge and offered it to Toby, who refused it with a terse shake of the head. "You've got to live, Toby," he reminded him.

"Those are your rules, not mine."

Max grimaced at Adela, arching his eyebrows and tipping his head to one side, *See what I have to deal with?* She bent a fierce, tender look at Toby, then left the room. Together, they listened to the sound of her slippers scuffing down the stairs until it disappeared.

"You have feelings for her, don't you," he said jubilantly.

Toby glanced at him, fear stuttering to life in his eyes.

"Why are you looking at me like that? I couldn't be happier for you. You need a woman in your life, Toby. I don't know what I'd do without my Gerda. For me, my family is an island of peace in a crazy world."

"I have no peace," murmured Toby, leaning his forehead against the glass. "I will never have peace again."

"Toby," he said gently. He quelled the desire to put his arm around the drooping shoulders, to ruffle the unruly hair, to make shadow animals, anything to distract him, as if he were Peter, from whatever nightmare had sent him into tears. "You can't go on like this. The world is a harsh place for someone as sensitive as you. You need to be more like me. You have to learn to let some things go. Otherwise, how could anybody go on living?"

Toby closed his eyes, thrust his head away. A small, choked sound escaped his throat.

"I know it hurts you to talk about these things, but someone has to say it. A man like you needs a man like me. Believe me, Toby. You have to get back to work.

"I want you to write me a story," Max continued. "A children's book. A present for Peter."

Toby pressed the heels of his hands into his eyes. "I know you mean well, Max," he said dully. "But I can't. I just can't."

"I'll help you," he said, encouraging him. "You tell me the words. I'll write it down."

"I'm clean out of ideas, Max. There's nothing left."

His fingers drummed on his uniformed knee. "How about this. A good German story with a knight in it. Maybe he has to slay a dragon . . . rescue a princess . . . there's a treasure."

"Knights and princesses?" Toby was half dismayed, half amused. "I don't know. I'm not Walt Disney. It's not really my style."

"Well, you're the author. Do it in your own style."

Toby breathed on the windowpane. With his finger, he drew a forlorn little house in the fogged glass, a square with a triangle for a roof, a chimney with smoke coming out of it. "What do you have against dragons?"

"Don't be silly. Dragons steal sheep, ruin crops, burn down the town. They have to be destroyed. Even children know that."

The artist sighed and bowed his head. Max waited. Just when he was beginning to think that Toby was purposefully toying with him, the dark rumpled head snapped to attention, the pouchy eyes narrowed. The wisp of light in his pupils kindled into flame. "Once upon a time . . ."

"Now you're talking!" Max said enthusiastically, rubbing his hands together. "Is Peter going to be the knight?"

"Patience," Toby said. He closed his eyes, repeated the four words as reverently as if they were a prayer. "Once upon a time, there was a little boy."

"Wait a minute! I need to write this down."

"Here, use this." Toby pounced on his portfolio, slipped

out another drawing. A clown and a skeleton flanked the
wings of a dark stage, peering out of furled theater curtains.
Below them, a naked beauty sat astride a prancing white
steed with a flowing mane. A drawing for a theater poster
advertising a play whose curtain had rung down long ago.

"Toby, this is beautiful. I can't."

"Of course you can. This is important." He swept away
the tubes of paint with the side of his arm, slapped the
drawing facedown on the desk. Then he returned to his post
at the window, wrapped his bony arms tightly around his
scarecrow body. "As I was saying . . . there was a little boy
who loved birds more than anything in the world. When
the boy was little, he begged his mother to leave food outside their window for the pigeons, and colored strings for
the sparrows to build their nests. The year he turned ten,
his grandmother gave him an illustrated book of birds with
large, colorful plates. Instead of playing with the other boys
after school, he would go home, climb upstairs to the attic,
and study his picture book. In this way, he learned about
big birds and small birds, swimming birds, flightless birds,
drab birds, and birds that looked like they had been painted
by madmen. He studied the faraway lands they came from,
their individual calls, their diets, and their habitats.

"It was inevitable that one day the birds would commu-
nicate with him. The first bird to speak was the white stork,
of the kind you can see nesting in tall chimneys. 'Peter,' it
said in the voice of someone old and wise. 'You who admire
us and are loyal to us, you who have been a true friend to all
birds, upon you we have bestowed the gift of flight. Go to
the window. Flap your arms, and you will see you can fly.'"

There was a loud slap as Toby flung open the attic
window.

"Peter threw open the windows," he continued in a thrilling, powerful voice. "It was a warm evening in late spring; a cloudless sky beckoned him. He spread his arms, closed his eyes, and jumped.

"The birds were true to their word: The boy could fly. Flapping his arms, he swooped over the roofs of the town. In a delirium of joy, he soared over the school playing fields, he made loop-de-loops over the church's bell tower.

"Meanwhile, in the town square, a crowd was gathering. What was it? 'A bird,' someone ventured. No, it was judged to be too large. 'An eagle is large,' said someone else. 'That's no eagle' was the reply. Someone shouted that they saw horns. Another, sharp teeth. A third, a whiplike, pointed tail.

"One of the boy's classmates picked up a loose paving stone and let fly. The stone struck the creature's head and bounced off.

"It seemed to hang in the air for a moment, dazed by the blow. Now each villager reached for a missile. Under a barrage of pebbles, bricks, and stones, it plummeted to earth."

Toby's voice changed now, dark, fluid, impassioned, like a tune played on the Pied Piper's flute.

"When the citizens of the town gathered around the corpse of the demon they had stoned out of the sky, they saw only the broken body of the dreamy little boy who had lived in the house on the edge of the square. One of his classmates recalled that he had loved birds. Also that he had been good at playing marbles.

"Just then Peter's mother came out of her house, drawn by the crowd in the market square. The throngs of villagers parted guiltily before her. 'What happened?' she cried, cradling her son's lifeless body." Toby thrust out his arms as if reaching for the boy himself. "There was a long, drawn-out silence. And then the mayor spoke. 'He jumped out from there,' he said, pointing at the open attic window. 'He thought he could fly.'

"The boy's blood ran between the cracks of the paving stones. As it soaked into the earth, a sapling shot up out of the ground at the very center of the market square. While the people watched in awe, it grew into an enormous acacia tree, towering over every building in town. Stranger still, upon each branch sat a bird: strange, exotic birds, of every shape and color, birds that were not native to the town or even to the continent of Europe. The birds stared down at the townspeople; the people stared up at the birds. As if someone had given a sign, the birds all rose up with a deafening cacophony, their wings flapping, each bird cawing or clattering its bill. The birds flew around the town square once, then disappeared.

"All at once, nature went silent. No nightingales sang, no mockingbirds. No doves cooed, no hummingbirds flew, no starlings, no sparrows, no wrens, no owls. The storks abandoned their nests, the pigeons, the square. Even the crows deserted the town.

"After burying her son, Peter's mother hurriedly moved away. As if by agreement, no one spoke of the shameful incident.

"Years passed. In the summer, the tree gave shade. In the spring, racemes of tiny heart-shaped flowers. In the winter, its bark was a beautiful collage of silvers and grays. But in the fall, the leaves flamed a bloody red, and the people would remember the boy who had loved birds, and the atrocity they had committed together in the name of fear and superstition."

Here, Toby paused, aiming a sideways glance at Max.

Max grew impatient. What was he waiting for? "Go on," he urged. He wanted to know how it ended.

Toby shot him a look of incredulity before going on. "No one knows who left the first note," he said. "But one day there it was, lying in the tree's roots, pinned to a red poppy. It read, *I remember.*

"By the next day, there were twenty notes, by the third, hundreds.

"*I'm sorry,* they said. *I missed you at school. I missed you at aviation club. I think of you every day of my life. I never meant you any harm. My father made me. Everybody else was doing it. I am ashamed of my behavior on that day. Forgive me. Forgive us.* By the end of the week, an avalanche of notes and flowers spilled over the plaza, the flowers sanctifying the air like incense.

"Finally, a cry was raised. The townspeople mourned for the boy who dared to fly, and atoned for their terrible crime. At that very moment, a great swarm of birds blackened the sky, descending on the town in numbers never seen in recorded history. Flamingos and egrets, starlings and macaws, peacocks and sparrows, cranes and canaries, the rarest exotic birds of the world could be seen roosting side by side on the enormous tree in the middle of the marketplace; you couldn't see the leaves for the feathers."

Toby paused here, his index finger caressing his lower lip. Did he already know how the story would end? Or was he making it up as he went along?

"One by one, the people of the town came out of their houses to join their neighbors around the tree. When the last citizen had arrived, the birds began to caw and flap their wings. And then they took off, blinding the villagers with a whirling vortex of multi-hued feathers.

"When the thick cloud of grit had cleared, the tree was gone, crumbled into powder at the villagers' feet. Mourning doves with purple throats strutted through the sawdust, cooing, leaving delicate footprints. A snow-white stork settled onto a long-abandoned nest on top of a house. Sparrows picked up straws in their beaks and went straight to work. From that day forward, wherever the townspeople went, they were accompanied by the songs of birds. It filled their lives with beautiful music, but it also reminded them of what they were capable of. *Remember,* the songs warned them, *and do not forget.*"

Toby was finished. The delirium evoked by his voice evaporated, leaving a husk of a man standing before an open window, with the cold air blowing through his hair.

Max got to his feet. With an ominous thunk, he pulled the windows shut. "I don't like it," he grumbled. "Not at all appropriate for a child."

The fire in Toby's eyes died back to a flicker. "Everyone's a critic," he said.

The SS man caught Toby's arm above the elbow and squeezed hard. "I get it, Toby," he said softly. "I know what the story is about. The villagers throwing stones at the innocent boy are the Germans, aren't they. You're saying that after this period of senseless killing, there will be an era of remorse and reflection, and then we will all have to learn to live with what we've done. Do I have that right?"

Toby cringed under his touch. Max leaned over him, bringing his flat, smooth face even closer. "You're an artist, Toby. You have the luxury of being able to think in this way. As for me, I am a soldier. I deal with reality. And the reality is, Germany has enemies everywhere, enemies who wish to see her destroyed, enemies who must be put down with force. You know as well as I do, Stalin is the real villain in this war. Although it comes at a price, we must be vigilant." Affectionately, he patted Toby's shoulder. "Don't feel bad," he said. "We'll keep working on it. Maybe we should just go with my idea. The knight slays the dragon, finds the gold, and marries the princess. The important thing is, we made a start today." He shook his head, marveling at the randomness of life. "If you would have told me six months ago that my Peter would be a character in a book by Tobias Rey . . ."

"A book that will never be published," Toby murmured, looking down into the street.

"Uch, such a pessimist," said Max cheerfully, getting to his feet. He buttoned his uniform jacket, pulled on his jackboots. "I'd better get back to work. Lunchtime already, and just look at me, sitting around with my feet up, listening to fairy tales."

His good humor had been restored. At least Toby's story had taken his mind off of the loss of his horse. Feeling generous, he said, "Why don't you take the rest of the afternoon off? Adela, too."

Toby stood out in silhouette against the window, his gaunt body bent and black like a punctuation mark. Behind him, the outside world, slanted tile roofs, elegant townhouses, empty yards full of yellow weeds, soldiers pursuing Jews down dead ends and narrow alleyways.

"Thank you, Max," he said. A smile of surprising sweetness touched the ironic lips. Suddenly, he doubled over, his whole body wrenched by deep, hacking coughs.

Max slipped on his gloves. "That does it. I want you to see a doctor. I'll have my secretary arrange it."

"Why bother."

Max was learning to ignore it when Toby said things like that. At the doorway, he took a last delighted look around the room. "Beautiful, just beautiful," he said, and he closed the door behind him.

It was like the Wild West out there. Everywhere, Max had to fight his way through massive crowds being hustled toward the marketplace, the movie theater, the synagogue, the high school, the train station. In addition, he had to dodge Gestapo men running down Jews with phony papers, hidden Jews exposed by neighbors, the occasional and illegal settling of a score. It was loud: Soldiers shouted directions, children cried, women screamed, there was the regular crack of gunfire. The pavement rang with the echo of thousands of footsteps.

In the market square, near the Great Synagogue, he came across Gruber, Rohlfe, and Hackendahl at the head of a broad column of civilians that snaked back into the distance farther than he could see. Impatiently, Rohlfe corralled Max into helping with selection. That was how he happened to see Toby, waiting to cross the street at the corner of Solna and Mickiewicz streets, half a block away.

He was bundled in the new coat Max had procured for him—an imported, nicely tailored camel hair, the exact color of Lilo's tail—and he was accompanied by an attractive woman, Adela, Max realized after a moment. She was wearing a crimson wool coat and a stylish green hat with a feather in it. Had she not been standing next to Toby, he wouldn't have recognized her. He had never seen her without her apron.

She said something to Toby, who glanced down and responded with a smile. When she turned her face up to his, Max could see she had put on lipstick.

A strange feeling stole over him. In the street, outside of his villa, under the blue sky, Toby and Adela were not his workers, not his prisoners, not his playthings, they were just people. If they hadn't been wearing the white *schadenbands* with the blue stars, they might have been his neighbors in Köln. He had to overcome the temptation to raise his arm and wave hello; after all, to his fellow SS officers, they were the enemy.

He turned to find Hackendahl staring at him. Max viewed him with a certain amount of childish envy. Rohlfe's protégé always appeared so flawless, his conduct irreproachable, his performance invariably correct. His wife had moved to Włodawa with him, too, the lucky bastard, and she headed up a little culture group for the women. Though he and Max were about the same age, he was already an Obersturmbannführer.

Right now he was standing perfectly still, his breath coming out in little white gusts. Max saw the officer's eyes flick away from him and fasten on something in the middle distance. Then he took off, sprinting quickly across the square in the direction of Solna Street.

The next moments unspooled with a sense of unreality, as if they were happening in a movie. Max saw Toby looking carefully up and down Mickiewicz Street. Adela took his elbow, and they stepped down off the curb. Halfway across the intersection, Hackendahl caught up with them, coming up behind Toby and putting his arm around him, pulling him close to his chest. Toby looked frightened; Max saw his hands come up to pry at the SS man's grip, his long white fingers fluttering against the black uniform.

Even in the best of health, Toby would have been no

match for the strapping SS officer. The gun was already in Hackendahl's hand. He raised it to Toby's temple and pulled the trigger.

Did Max really scream the word *no*, or did he just think he did? As he lurched forward, his legs numbly pumping, Hackendahl fired again, then stepped away. Toby was a crumpled heap at his feet.

Time warped and stretched like a rubber band as Max elbowed his way through the crosscurrents of soldiers and civilians clogging the street. He squatted beside Toby, aghast. His hat had fallen upside down in the gutter; blood was leaking out of a ghastly hole in the side of his head. Gently, he took his arms and rolled him onto his back.

There was no mistaking it, Toby was dead. His eyes were wide open, the pupils dilating. On the gray, wasted face, the deep lines were fading, replaced by an expression of ceaseless wonder.

Max seized him by the shoulders. Toby's lips parted with a click, as if he were going to say something. But his mouth was full of blood.

"Are you happy now?" he shouted down at the dead face. "You finally got what you wanted, you dumb Jew bastard. Is this better?" Helpless with fury, he shook him, Toby's head rolling loosely from side to side.

Gruber was standing over him. "Stop it, Haas," he said quietly. "He's dead."

Max blinked. A gaggle of townspeople was gawking at him in horror. When he looked up, they scattered, continuing hurriedly on their way. Slowly, he let Toby sink back onto the cobblestones, then got to his feet. Hackendahl was posed like a recruiting poster for the SS, legs apart, smoke drifting from the muzzle of his pistol.

"Last month," he said, spitting out the words. "At the Judenrat. Remember? You killed fifteen Jews." Max stared at him with repelled amazement. "One of them was Liederman, my dentist." Incredibly, he was wiping his eyes. "He was not a bad little fellow," he blubbered. "Why did you have to kill him? Do you know how hard it is to find a good dentist?"

Hackendahl prodded Toby's flank with the toe of his boot. "There," he said shortly. "You killed my Jew. Now I killed yours." The skirts of his coat billowed in the wind as he turned on his heel and went back to join Rohlfe in the market square.

Max wanted to tear his fucking head off, beat him with his own gun until his brains came out of his ears, but that wasn't possible. There was nothing he could do. He squeezed his eyes closed, pressed his shaking hand over his mouth. He was afraid he would scream. At the same time, his throat was closing up; it was hard to breathe. *He didn't feel a thing,* he told himself savagely. *It was over in seconds. He fell without a sound.*

But none of that brought even the slightest glimmer of comfort. There was a tightness in his chest that was swelling rapidly into bottomless, insurmountable, desolating, terrifying grief. The world staggered beneath his feet.

That was when he remembered Adela. Max looked up, and found her standing a little distance away. When she noticed him seeking her, she vanished into the milling crowd.

Gruber was calling his name, and he heard himself automatically answer yes. After a last sorrowful glance, he turned away. The body lying in a halo of blood wasn't Toby anymore; whatever Toby had been was gone.

Slowly and deliberately, Max walked back to the market

square. With every step, he battled for control over his emotions, forcing the ugly and unfamiliar feelings down, down, down, as far away as possible, where they would stay safely locked up in a dark and unexamined vault at the back of his mind forever and ever. To his surprise, water was leaking freely from his eyes. *Gerda will be here in the spring,* he told himself, clenching and unclenching his fists. *Everything will be fine when I am with my family again. Nothing makes sense without my little bunny by my side.* But the tears wouldn't stop coming.

By the time he reached Rohlfe and Gruber, he was outwardly calm, able to assume his duties again. Lucky for him, it was freezing; he could blame his running eyes and constant sniffling on the cold.

At his trial, witnesses would remark on his demeanor that day, known forever after as Black Thursday. They would tell the judge how subdued he was, how often he wiped his eyes, how kindly he addressed them, a remarkable aberration in the career of Sturmbannführer Maximillian Haas, famed throughout the region for his reputation as a cold-blooded killing machine.

By the time the day was out, ten thousand Jews had been transported to nearby Sobibór. Two hundred more shared Toby's fate, shot dead on the streets, empty lots, stairways, and back alleys of Włodawa. Their bodies would lie upon the pavement until the following day, when they would be picked up in a wagon and burned in a field outside of town.

Late that evening, Max plodded through the market square back to his villa. As he handed his coat to the housekeeper, she reported that the cook was missing. Exhausted, barely listening, he took the bottle of vodka and climbed up the steps to the attic.

The light was out, it was dark. With all the activity of the day, he had almost forgotten that Toby was gone. He left it off. In the dark, Toby might still be there, sitting languorously on his stool in the middle of the room, watching the smoke from his cigarette make pictures in the air.

Max collapsed on the bed, unbuttoned his jacket, and upended the bottle of vodka into his mouth. The liquor burned his throat, sent a stinging glow through his body. It was the first time he had felt good all day, so he did it again, and again, and again, until the bottle was empty.

That was when he heard something scuttle across the floor.

In astonishment, he watched a small armored creature, red, oblong, with a head like a squirrel and a tail like a pointing finger, waddle under the bed. Looking up, he realized that the paintings were in motion. The creatures at the tables sipped their cappuccinos and bantered with their companions. The little men in homburg hats soared across the ceiling in tight formation. As for the armadillos, he could hear the sound of their marching feet, locked in step, tramping in perfect synchronicity up and down the undulating hills. It was so real, he could hear the clink of dishes being washed in the café's kitchen.

The tailor's dummies tilted toward each other, conspiring like spies. On the table, the brushes clacked their handles in an accusatory way; it was obvious that they blamed him for their master's demise. In the corner, the discarded painting rags seethed like a pile of snakes. With a silky, slithering motion, they knitted themselves together and stood erect. The pile swayed back and forth, trying to get its balance; then it lumbered toward him in the form of a man.

"Max," it hissed in Toby's voice. "*Maaaaax . . .*"

The SS officer stared at the entity made from rags, his eyes starting from his head. With a sibilant sound, it moved in his direction, sliding one ropy leg in front of the other like a baby learning to walk. Max was too frightened to scream.

He covered his head with his arms, waiting for the inevitable blow. The air moved around him as the thing approached, reeking of turpentine and pine resin. When he worked up the courage to peer between his fingers, he found it standing before him, close enough to touch.

"Where am I, Max?" it whispered. "Where am I?"

Slowly, understanding swept over him. The apparition wasn't violent, or angry, or vengeful; it was confused and disoriented and lost.

"I'm sorry for what happened to you, Toby," he said timidly. "I wanted to help. You know that."

The thing had no eyes, no mouth, no face, but he saw it turn its head to the side as if someone were calling its name. "I have to go now," it sighed in a voice like dry leaves scraping across a sidewalk. Unbelievably, it slogged its way to the door and turned the knob. He could hear it mourning all the way down the stairs. "Where am I, Max? Where am I? Where am I?"

He woke up the next morning to a clear blue day, sprawled on the bed in the attic, still dressed in his uniform. When he rolled over, an empty vodka bottle clattered to the floor. Outside the window, a net of high herringbone clouds streaked across the heavens. Everything was in its place; the brushes in their vase, the armadillos on the walls. Only the pile of rags was gone. Though he told himself the housekeeper had finally gotten around to throwing them out, he ran down the stairs for a hammer and nailed the attic door shut himself.

*Dear Gerda,* he wrote in a letter posted on November 20.

*I have told the housekeeper to prepare a room on the second floor. The attic will be too cold for Peter's delicate lungs.*

From among the handful of Jews allowed to remain in Włodawa, Max found a carpenter and a housepainter. He ordered them to paper over the entire upstairs hallway, erasing all traces of the passage that led to the attic. When they were finished, he had them both transported to concentration camps.

*The Führer is right,* he concluded in his diary. *Associating with Jews is dangerous, like an infection. Oh, they might be intelligent, they might be charming, they might treat you like a friend, but once they get under your skin, worming their way into your affections, they twist you all around, making you see things a different way, screwing you up for good. From now on, my relations with them will remain at arm's length.*

Gerda and Peter Haas never made it to Włodawa. Toby was wrong; Gerda wasn't fucking Peter's riding instructor. It was his doctor she was fucking.

Włodawa was liberated on August 24, 1944. Max eluded capture for three full years. He was working as a grocer under an assumed name when one of his former workers happened to step into his shop.

The Americans came for him that night. Immediately, he handed over his war diary, confident that it would vindicate him. After all, didn't the entries prove that he was only a soldier, acting on his superiors' instructions?

The Allies translated the diary into ten languages. With careful analysis, it was estimated that Sturmbannführer Maximillian Haas was present at the deaths of more than eighteen thousand innocent civilians in Russia, Poland, and parts of the Ukraine. He would have hanged but for the testimony of two witnesses: Bianca Lipowa, distinguished for her acts of heroism in the Polish resistance; and Adela Saltzman, his Jewish cook. Max was happy to see them, glad they had both survived.

He was pleased to hear that Adela wanted to meet. He welcomed the opportunity to reminisce about the old days. Visitors were scarce. Gerda had left him, and he didn't want Peter to remember him this way.

She sat across from him at a steel-topped table in the bowels of the prison. Even with the strong overhead lighting, she was stunning, and he experienced a painful cramp of yearning. She had filled out a little since the war; her hair was cut stylishly, and she wore a fitted green coat with a velvet collar that emphasized her curvaceous figure. Her perfume—lily of the valley, the same as Gerda—cut through the stench of carbolic cleaning fluid in the sterile, featureless room.

"It was kind of you to come," he said. He tried an affable smile. "We had some good times, didn't we?"

The hooded eyes believed otherwise. She hadn't bothered to remove her gloves, and now she folded her hands on the table. "My family is dead. I am the only survivor."

"I'm sorry," he said.

The look she gave him was undeniably ironic, but she chose her words carefully. "You may have killed many people, Haas, but you were very good to me. As for Toby, you treated him like he was your son. That's why I came." He dropped his gaze to the table, surprised to find that his eyes were wet. Her words drifted over him like a cloud. "We should pledge our allegiance to the people we love. Not nations, not countries or politicians. I think you understood this, but only when it was already too late."

From her pocket, she slid a yellowed and creased square of paper. "The day of the last *Aktzia* . . . after Toby was murdered . . . I ran back to the villa to collect a few things. I shouldn't have, I had to leave right away, but I climbed up to the attic one more time. It was the only way I could think of to say goodbye to him."

She unfolded the paper and began to read. "'Shayna Mirsky, the miller, and her brother Hersh. Hammer, the tailor. Morganstern, the rabbi's son. Bella Soroka, the saddlemaker's daughter. Adler, whose father owned the bank. Hipsman, the letter-writer. Glincman, who was Falkner's coachman. Katz, whose family owned the lumberyard. All three Pomeranc boys, whose father traded cattle. Szapiro, who collected tolls on the bridge. Tannenbaum, who ran the projector at the movie theater. Wakerman, who raised chickens . . .'"

She went on, but he wasn't listening anymore, her soft, husky voice transporting him back in time to a place where dust motes danced in the sunlight and a thin black scarecrow of a man ravished white walls with blinding color. "'. . . Edelsberg. Melczer. Wizotsky.'" She finished and glanced up at him over the paper. "Do these names mean anything to you, Haas?"

He shook his head.

"You might know their faces. They are the thirty-six people whose likenesses Toby painted on the walls of your son's bedroom, scattered among the patrons of the Café Blue Cockatoo."

She signaled for the guard and rose to her feet.

"Ten thousand Jews from Włodawa went up the chimneys in Sobibór," she said. "But the people in the paintings . . . all of them survived."

# THE PARTIZANS

For generations, Lufts and Hellers had been next-door neighbors on Wirka Street, a polite name for a string of ramshackle wooden cottages at the southern end of Włodawa. Here, where civilization sputtered out before giving way to the deep primeval forests, Zosha and Zev's parents were just the latest in a long line of Hellers and Lufts that stretched from the present back to the early 1700s, two hundred years of eking out a hardscrabble existence, shoulder to shoulder, from the compacted soil behind the rundown houses that sat on the ever shifting border between Poland and the Ukraine.

They knew each other in all the ways that brothers and sisters know each other. At the same time every morning, they set off to school attired in hand-me-downs, Zev's oversize pants cinched tight around his six-year-old waist, Zosha's blond pigtails in disarray; with both parents in the field before dawn, there was no one home to braid them. Often Zev and Zosha would meet on the same errands, to the butcher, the baker, the tobacconist, the newspaper kiosk, dodging the press of older customers in the shopping streets that led to the marketplace. On holidays, Zosha would peek

between the railings of the women's gallery to find Zev
among his brothers on the main floor of the Grand Synagogue, usually in the process of being cuffed by his father for
dozing off. Until Zev turned thirteen, Zosha was taller and
stronger, and she used it to her advantage, secretly tying the
laces of his shoes together under a chair, or grabbing his cap
and sailing it across the muddy cobblestoned street.

After classes were through for the day, Zosha and the
other girls often lingered near the sports fields to watch
the boys play soccer. Damp with sweat, his sharp knees
bruised and dirty below his short pants, Zev would come to
an abrupt stop whenever the soldiers of the local regiment
marched by, rigid and splendid in their green uniforms,
leather boots polished to a high, gaudy shine.

She came to know the features of his face as well as
she knew her own. The straight brown hair that fell around
his ears, the gray eyes that resembled the surface of a calm
ocean. The round cheeks that lengthened and hollowed as
he grew, the tea-with-milk color of his skin. The way his
full pink lips smiled when he teased her. As they entered
the long corridors of adolescence, he grew taller than she
did, and she noticed that, too, the width of his shoulders,
the strength in his hands.

But by all customary measures of Jewish success, Zev
began to fail. In arithmetic, history, and literature, his grades
scraped bottom. At Hebrew school, the rebbe beat him for
restlessness. Instead of praying three times a day like his
brothers, Zev slipped away to play cards with boys his father
called *gangsters*.

It was about this time that the fights came on with
alarming regularity. There were no secrets on Wirka Street;
the windows were open, walls were thin.

*You want another helping? I'll give you another helping!*
Smack! *Your rebbe says you're as stupid as a golem!* Smack!
*Willig says you started a fight with his boy today. Why do I
believe him? Because he's the butcher's son, and you're a nothing!* Smack! *Why are you crying? I'll give you something to cry
about!*

Voices were raised, harsh words flew, the kind that can
never be taken back. Sometimes Zosha heard things break,
or the blows of flesh on flesh.

On those nights, Zosha would find Zev hiding out in
the animal shed, his forehead pressed against the smooth
gray flank of Ferdele, the horse. While the dog slept in a
corner and a few skinny brown chickens scratched for bugs
in the straw, Zev would allow her to slip her hand into his,
and she would tell him marvelous tales of a make-believe
world called Yenensvelt, where clouds were spun from colored sugar and waterfalls ran with milk. Hip to hip on a
tussock of fragrant green hay, they would remain for hours,
safe in the close warmth of the barn.

In the year Zosha turned fifteen, Zev ran away. It was the
end of May, at the height of a glorious spring. During that
azure hour between night and dawn, she was awakened by
the stealthy squeal of the Hellers' front door opening and
closing.

Zosha rolled out of the bed she shared with her younger
brother and went to the window. A man in an old brown
jacket and a soft cap was standing on the porch of her
neighbors' house, his face hidden in shadow.

She had lived alongside him for too long not to recognize the nape of his neck, the loping gait of his step. But
everything else was different. Zev had shed the traditional
knickers and the long black coat of his forefathers, the beard

and *payess* of the pious. Without them, he was changed, unfamiliar.

At the squeak of the floorboards under her feet, he froze. It was cold enough that she could see his breath, a ghostly mist against the gloom. Satisfied that no one was coming after him, he hefted his burlap sack onto his shoulder and set off down the street.

Zosha was afraid to call out to him, afraid she might jeopardize his escape. Instead, she watched him walk away. When he was no more than a small dot on the brightening horizon, she thought she might have seen him turn around and seek out the window where she stood.

His parents wept and moaned, they tore their clothes. Little by little, she overheard details, late at night, when her parents thought she was sleeping. Zev Heller had abandoned his heritage, his religion. He was sleeping with Polish girls, he'd been baptized in the Orthodox Church. It was even rumored that he was eating pork.

In their religion, this was a sin that required mourning, a fate comparable in gravity to death. But Zosha remembered the hurtful words, the bruises, and the black eyes, and thought, *I hope he is happy.*

September 1, 1939, was a Friday.

First the Germans blew up the train station. The day after that, they bombed the bridge that led over the river, barring escape.

Zosha watched as the Deutschen marshaled prisoners in Polish infantry uniforms past her house and down Wirka Street, vanishing into the scrim of trees around the forest. Two days later, hunters found the dead scattered through the marshy underbrush like fallen timber, the leaf litter under their boots saturated with blood.

Watching the silvery bellies of enemy planes fly in tight formation overhead, Zosha felt a tightening in her heart, a sickening sensation in the pit of her stomach, and just like that, she knew. This was the beginning of the end of the world.

It was Reinhart who told them that everything would be all right.

He came one day, in his caramel-colored overcoat and his fancy fedora, filling the people in town with relief. Already, people were saying he was a good German. *There is plenty to do here,* he told them firmly, organizing and dividing the craftsmen around him. *Don't worry.*

Lawyers and philosophers went to work in the woods, teachers and trombonists rebuilt the railroad and bridges. But people in the marketplace whispered rumors they had heard, old men beaten to death for nothing, women forced to clean paving stones with their toothbrushes, beards cut off with bayonets. They whispered other things: entire towns, men, women, and children, taken to the woods and shot after digging their own graves. Others argued; how could this be true? The Germans would be destroying their own workforce. It was absurd.

Gerstein, the butcher, was carried off by a soldier on a motorcycle; two days later, he was found in the woods, cut like a steer into six ragged pieces. Rabbi Morganthau was imprisoned until a ransom could be collected; it was quickly paid, but the Deutschen shot him anyway. The Lords and Masters made a group of merchants do jumping jacks in the square until they collapsed, then shot them where they lay; Korn the fishmonger was among them. On a hunt organized for important visitors from Berlin, the Germans bagged a tremendous red stag, a record for the district; three wild boars; a lynx; and two Jews.

The day it was discovered that there was a shortage of paving bricks, a work detail was sent to the cemetery to pull up tombstones. Berel Holtzmann swore that when he pulled on his own father's headstone, he could feel him pulling back.

On a cold gray morning, Zosha accompanied her mother to the market square. A stranger in a black leather jacket caught her eye as he crossed in the opposite direction.

She lowered her head. By October 1942, Włodawa had already been occupied for three long years. In times of war, women learn quickly that it is best not to attract the notice of strangers.

Despite her best efforts, he slowed, stopped. "Zosha?" he inquired. "Zosha Luft?"

Lifting her head, she took in the strong hands, the sensuous lips. His eyes were still the gray of a calm ocean, but in the years he'd been away, they had changed. Specks of gold inflamed his pupils.

The air smelled of wood smoke and tanned hides. Plumes of vapor rose like spirits between them as they stood in the center of the square regarding each other.

Her mother gave him a scalding glare, tugging meaningfully at Zosha's elbow. She had not forgotten the ugly rumors of pork and Polish girls. He dropped his gaze and thrust his hands into his pockets. At the same time, a man materialized at his side, calling him Wolf, speaking in an unfamiliar dialect.

Zev roused himself, moving like a man waking up from a dream. "This is Baer," he said. This was accompanied by a rueful grin, a self-deprecating shrug. "In the forest, we all have nicknames."

She stared at him, startled by his candor. With those three words, *in the forest*, he had communicated a secret. He was a partizan, a foot soldier of the resistance movement based in the dark heart of the Parczew woods.

"You look different" was all she could think of to say. The child's open face had grown lean, angular, handsome. Embarrassed by the state of her dress, the worn and patched dowdiness of her clothing, she passed a self-conscious hand over her head to smooth her hair, and as if he could hear her thoughts, Zev said, "Leave it alone. It's beautiful."

"I'll see you around," he said finally, before he and the man he called Baer sloped off across the square. As her mother hustled her forward, Zosha stole a glance over her shoulder, just in time to catch him doing the same.

Life went on, much as it had before. Zosha looked after her brother, Shimmy, while their parents went off each morning to the forced labor camp. Only now, wherever she went, Zev was already there.

Walking Shimmy to the bathhouse, she would find Zev loitering in front of the cinema. As she traded table linens with a merchant in return for a few rotten potatoes or a wormy cabbage, she would turn to find him gazing at her, deep in conference with a pack of tough-looking men.

Despite the bitter wind gusting through the cracks in the

drafty wooden cottage, Zosha stood in front of the mirror in her bedroom and contemplated her body, first clothed, and then unclothed. With this act of abandon, her cheeks burned and the hairs on the back of her neck pricked up, as if someone had breathed on them. She experienced pleasure and fear in equal measure, though she could not have explained why.

The knock on the door came late at night, when the Luft family had already settled into bed. Three short raps, followed by the command barked in their harsh language, *Raus, raus, raus!* Zosha and her family were herded into the street by two soldiers holding automatic rifles, where they joined a river of frightened villagers being harassed and harried toward the outskirts of town.

When she looked up, she could see the sky overhead, wide and black and velvety, illuminated by a crisp full moon and tiny white stars. And then they were under the tree canopy, and the heavens hid themselves away from the Jews of Włodawa.

The November wind moaned through the pines as Zosha stumbled barefoot over frozen roots, holding tightly to her brother's hand. Low-hanging branches caught her hair, tore her thin cotton nightgown. She could hear dogs barking, the crude insults of the foreign soldiers, the muddled chanting of men, the frantic cries of mothers and children.

The column of villagers came to an abrupt halt. Zosha shifted her weight from one foot to the other on the icy ground. Off to the side, having a smoke, was a boy who used to play soccer with Zev. His uniform looked new. She caught his eye, smiled. When he recognized her, he turned away.

The line moved forward.

Before her, a clearing opened in the forest. Cleaving it in two was a long pit, jagged and wide. There was Reinhart pacing back and forth, pale and unnerved, his hands clasped behind his back. Two Gestapo men in warm belted overcoats were laughing. Officers chatted among themselves, idly batting riding crops against their boots. Someone's little dog was weaving in between their legs.

An SS major threw down the cigarette he was smoking, crushed it carefully under his boot, and stepped up to address them. *You, you, you, you, you,* he separated out a group of families and ran them at a smart pace to the steep edge of the pit. There, he told them to stop and turn around.

The moon slanted gentle shafts of light into the clearing, allowing Zosha to recognize their faces. The young mother who lived in the house across the road was holding an infant to her shoulder, eyes glazed over with sleep. A woman from the other side of town, a distant cousin, hid her daughter's face in her skirts. A man, shaking so much he could barely stand up, held his hands over his son's eyes.

The soldiers raised their rifles to their shoulders, took aim. There was a sound like firecrackers, and the line of human beings jerked like puppets and fell into the pit.

Zosha's family was next. A soldier screamed in her face, *Lauf! Lauf!* and lashed at her legs with his whip. Still holding Shimmy's hand, she stubbed her toes on rocks and branches, following her mother. When they had reached the pit, she caught a glimpse of the boy who used to play soccer with Zev, raising his rifle to his shoulder, nestling it to his cheek, sighting along the barrel.

The bullet that went through Zosha's throat lifted her up and tossed her backward into the pit. She was aware of the

sensation of flying, then landing on something that was soft
and yielding. Turning her head, she saw her father's face, his
eyes fixed and staring.

Again the sound of firecrackers. Another line of bodies
came skidding down the side of the pit, burying her under
a tangle of arms and legs. She recognized the corpse that
lay on top of her, a certain Mrs. Kimmel, the music teacher.
Fear rose like a fiery bubble to her throat, but she was unable
to make a sound.

The Ukrainian guards noticed it first, a strange lowering
stillness, a dense burden of silence. Uneasy, they swung their
rifles at the trees. Confident in the power that their great-
coats with gold buttons and tall shiny boots conferred upon
them, the Deutschen didn't notice it at all.

A great rush of air rolled towards them through the
darkness, flattening the grass, snaking through the underbrush, growing into a vast, tumultuous roar. It blasted forth
from the trees, boiled over the trench, and screamed up the
other side, overtaking the soldiers where they stood.

All at once the woods were filled with ear-shattering
roars, deafening screeches, wild, animalistic ululations.
Zosha heard the rattle and pop of close gunfire, shrieks of
pain and terror, harsh grunts and squeals.

A bloodied arm ripped free of its trunk fell in the trench,
landing with a thunk. Close behind, a single leg spiraled
dreamily to earth, shod in a cognac-colored riding boot.

Objects were raining from the sky. Dark hunks of flesh
plopped around her with the sound of ripe fruit dropping to
the ground. A hand. A foot. A riding crop. A pair of pants
with something still in them.

There was a heavy thud. From the corner of her eye,
Zosha could see the oblong head of the boy who used to

play soccer with Zev, a look of astonishment grafted to his features for all time.

Something leaped into the trench, landing on all fours with a rippling snarl. The weight of Mrs. Kimmel, the music teacher, was suddenly lifted from her, and a blast of arctic air struck her face.

Zosha didn't know whether she was dead or alive, awake or dreaming. Silhouetted against the light of a full moon was a gray and hairy beast. From the waist up, it was a timber wolf, the most feared animal in the Parczew Forest. Below the belt, powerful human legs were barely concealed by the tattered remnants of an army uniform.

The lean, ferocious head sniffed her with a blunt, tapered muzzle. It bared long canine teeth, displaying black and bloodied gums.

"Zosha, Zosha," it whispered.

At the sight of the wound in her throat, tears collected in the pale wolfish eyes. The creature worked to free her from the tangle of her friends' and neighbors' bodies. Gathering her close to its tufted breast, it sprang out of the pit with as much effort as it would have taken to skip over a crack in the sidewalk.

The wolf laid her down on the dead and yellowed savannah grass, her nightdress billowing like a parachute in the November wind. With remarkable gentleness, it put its arm under her shoulders and pulled her against its chest.

The clearing in the forest had become a battlefield filled with fairy-tale beasts, the stuff of nightmares. A gargoyle with the gleaming feathered head of a falcon held one of the Gestapo men in its talons, its beak buried deep in his guts. A leviathan of a fish, armored with metallic scales and bristling with fangs, was attempting to swallow a struggling lieutenant whole. The earth shook as an ogre with the massive head of a bull pursued one of Hitler's elite guard into the woods, wearing a bloodied butcher's apron and wielding a meat cleaver in its fist. A mammoth red stag used a gargantuan rack of antlers to pinion a brace of SS men against a tree. A hideous, humpbacked behemoth with the bullet-shaped head of a wild boar hurtled through the clearing, an officer impaled on each tusk like a grisly ornament.

The wolf that used to be Zev Heller rested his silky cheek against her forehead. She could feel the warmth of his tears on her face, her throat.

"Baer," the wolf called in an anguished cry, "Baer . . ."

A colossal brown bear was lifting a thrashing storm trooper high into the air. At the sound of its commanding officer's voice, the bear swung around, snuffling in fury. It dropped the storm trooper, snapping his spine over a hairy knee. In a blur of motion, it began to shrink, and suddenly, an officer of the Russian army was running toward them through the carnage, carrying a doctor's black case.

With practiced fingers Baer examined her, probed her wound. She felt light-headed now, the pain was receding. She wasn't even cold anymore. He muttered something to Zev in a low voice, and the wolf nodded, made a choking sound, bowed his head.

She didn't see how it happened, but the man called Baer was growing higher again, as high as the trees, resuming the form of the towering monstrous ursine she had seen before.

"You rest now," the bear said kindly, laying the leathery palm of a giant paw on the side of her face. With a roar of rage, he wheeled around and bounded away.

The wolf who was Zev threw back his head and howled. His men joined him, a victorious cacophony of shrieks, roars, bleats, and grunts that filled the clearing and made the air ring around her.

"Shimmy," she said. Her voice was raspy, guttural, but it worked. "We were running . . . I was holding his hand . . ."

The wolf bent closer to hear her words, his whiskers tickling her nose. "He's fine," he said hastily. "One of my men will lead him over the river to the Soviet side. Life is hard there, but he'll be safe."

The battle was done. Creatures shoveled spadefuls of dirt over the poor souls they had been too late to save, muttering the prayer for the dead over and over.

Zev caressed the hair from her forehead with fingers that were like claws, told her that his unit was expected near Wyryki at dawn. When she reached forward to touch his chest, his muscles twitched, and he sucked air between his sharp teeth with a hiss.

Eyes wide open, she took in the wild beauty of his face, the tilted gray eyes she had always loved, the steep curve of his chest, the silvery pelt that covered his body, lightening across the belly.

The fur fell between her fingertips in furrows, soft and thick. When she told him she wanted to stay with him forever, the wolfish eyes were calm and grateful and grieving all at the same time.

"Of course, Zoshaleh," he murmured, taking her hand. "Of course."

Nowadays, the drab and dreary apartment blocks extend all the way down Wirka Street into the forest. Built in the years of Soviet occupation, the buildings are testimonies to corruption, grim and decrepit.

Among them lies a clearing, green and open to the sky, where no dog ever roams and no child ever plays. No plaque informs tourists of the atrocities that were committed here, no monument graces this quiet square.

It is common knowledge that nothing will grow on this spot except for grass; it is a neat and constant ten centimeters high, despite the fact that no one has ever been known to water or mow it.

The people of the town of Włodawa cross themselves when they pass this place, which is not often, and only by day. They do not speak of it, not even to the priest, but they have not forgotten what happened here in 1942 and who lies buried beneath the peaceful green surface.

Those who have visited the site of the Włodawa massacre by night claim to have seen ghosts. The elders of the town, many of whom lived here during those long, bad years, discourage such wild tales. Let the dead bury the dead, they say wisely.

But the children know. When the anniversary of the massacre falls on the night of a full moon, they gather on the sidewalk to bear witness. At midnight, when the moon is highest in the sky, a strange incorporeal vision can be seen flitting through the trees.

The female wears only a thin white nightgown. Her pale hair shimmers and swims in the wind blowing down from the Russian steppes. The male has the lean upper body of a timber wolf.

Wolves have been hunted to extinction in this southeastern part of Poland, the elders will remind you. One night a year, you can hear still hear them howl.

# THE MESSIAH

A t around two in the morning, my mother shook me awake. The Messiah was coming. There was no doubt about it, he'd been spotted ten miles outside of Włodawa. At this rate, he would be here by daybreak. Get up, get up. We had to pack.

She left me to dress. It was a cold November night; gale-force winds rattled the roof tiles and chimney pots. Reluctant to surrender the warmth of my bed, I shut my eyes tight and snuggled down into the covers to consider this information.

It wasn't as if there hadn't been signs. Strange lights in the sky, unusual weather. An actual golem saving the lives of two hundred and fifty people being led off to slaughter. A whole battalion of Deutschen wiped out by mysterious forest creatures. The news was on everyone's lips. We were in the throes of an epic showdown between good and evil, for sure.

Downstairs, I heard the sound of my mother's voice, hurried, anxious. There would be time for exhilaration later. Now she had to make certain that everyone would have enough food and clothing for the long journey to Eretz Yisroel, the Promised Land.

It was then that I heard it, a tread as light as a cat's footfall. The rustling of cloth, the faintest of sighs. The end of my bed depressed just a bit.

"Get off of my bed, Temma," I said loudly. My sister liked to sneak in when she could. When I was little, I allowed her under the blankets with me, but I was twelve now, almost a man. There was no answer. Annoyed, I stuck my head out from the covers.

A stranger was sitting there in a long white gown tied with a rope around the waist. Over it, he wore a linen robe woven with stripes. On his feet, sandals.

"Hey, kid. Do you mind if I stay here for a minute?" he said. He had shoulder-length brown hair that he wore parted in the middle, and a small neat beard. "It's been a long night."

"How do I know you're the real Messiah?" I challenged him. "There have been a lot of imposters, you know. I'll have to ask you a few questions."

His features had an incandescent beauty to them, like paintings of Jesus I'd seen in school. "Fire away," he said, shifting his staff from one hand to the other.

One by one, he shot down the inquiries on my list. Yes, he was descended from the house of David. Yes, we would still have to keep Shabbos and kosher, he couldn't do anything about that. No, he couldn't raise the dead. Neither would he fly or walk on water. To my vast disappointment, there would be no miracles, no thunderclaps or lightning, no Leviathan feast, heavenly shofar blasts, or voice of God, no giddy ride to the Promised Land on the wings of eagles. He had come to Włodawa on a donkey. Downstairs, I could hear my mother shouting for me.

"I'd better get dressed," I said. "She's getting really mad."

The Messiah made a gesture with one hand. "Don't bother," he said. "You're not going anywhere. I quit."

I stared at him, aghast. "What?" I said, confused. "Do you know how long we've been waiting for you? If you don't get us out of here, the Deutschen will kill every last Jew in Europe."

"I know," he said tiredly, putting his head in his hands. "Don't you think I know? Why do you think I'm here?"

I sat back in my bed. "But you're the Messiah. The rabbis said you were going to rescue us." I am ashamed to report that my voice quavered.

"Not exactly," he muttered.

Downstairs, I could hear my mother and sisters in the kitchen, chattering to one another like birds. His tone of voice made me uneasy. "You're a good little yeshiva boy," he said. "You know all the rabbinical debates. Will the Messiah come on a white donkey? Or after every Jew keeps Shabbos for one week? Will he come in an era of peace? Or will he come at a time of great upheaval, half the world at war with the other half, the Jewish people faced with extinction?"

He spread his long delicate fingers across his forehead. I drew the covers up to my nose. Suddenly, I was seized with a panicked trembling, a shivering I could not control.

"You know the story of Avrohom and Yitzchak," he continued wearily. He didn't seem to be talking to me anymore. "God commanded Avrohom to sacrifice his only son . . . and willingly, Avrohom picked up the knife. Only at the last minute did He stay Avrohom's hand and direct him toward a ram whose horns were stuck in a thornbush."

The Messiah turned his gaze toward me. In my unlit room, his eyes were dark hollows. "The Jews of Europe are the ram," he explained. "Only afterward, when all the bodies have been counted, will there be a Promised Land, the Temple rebuilt, the end of war, peace on earth."

"But—" My throat was dry, it was hard to swallow. "The rabbis promised—the wings of eagles—"

"The rabbis . . ." The Messiah made an impatient gesture, of anger, of despair. "The rabbis will be the first to die." He slid off the bed, got to his feet. With determination, he said, "I've made up my mind. I won't be a party to this anymore."

Then he twitched his head to one side, knotted his brows. "Did you hear that?" he demanded. I had heard, perhaps, the sound of chimes. "He says he doesn't accept my resignation."

"Are—are you—talking to *God*?"

"God? Nah. He's busy running the war. Allow me to introduce you to that *paskudnyak* Gabriel, the *so-called* Angel of Redemption."

My heart hammered against my ribs. "Please, Mr. Messiah," I squeaked. "Don't make him mad."

He shushed me with a motion of his hand. "I don't even know why I'm talking to you!" he hollered at the air. "Where's Melkiel, the angel of the sixth firmament, who stands on the sixth stair of the heavenly throne, responsible for delivering those attempting to escape a besieged city? He's the man for the job." He concentrated for a moment, his hand cupped over his ear. "Oh, *you're* going to deliver the Jews of Europe? You mean the way you delivered Jerusalem into the hands of the Roman Empire? Or maybe you were thinking of the way you delivered the Jews of Spain to the Grand Inquisitor?"

He lunged for the window, threw it open with a bang. A gust of rain sprayed his face. "*No!*" he shouted at the clouds. "I've made my decision."

I thought about this for a minute. "All right," I said. "Let's go tell my mother."

* * *

Mama listened to the Messiah's story, nodding with grim determination. "We'll just see about that," she said, and sent us to talk to the rabbi.

My father was the Chief Rabbi of Włodawa. He listened to the Messiah's complaints, stroking his beard and nodding. Occasionally, he would ask a question, holding up a soft white hand to interrupt. The Messiah recited his story with reluctance, as if he had tired of his burden, wishing only to be rid of it. At the end, my father shrugged.

"Well, then that is our fate," he said. "If this is our role in the redemption, then we must go to it with glad hearts."

"That's what the rabbis say in every town," said the Messiah. "Just before the soldiers turn their machine guns on them."

"Will you stay with us till the end?" my father asked gently, undeterred. "To bring us comfort in our last days?"

The Messiah looked incredulous. "Did you hear anything I said?" With that, he threw his staff onto the floor and stalked furiously out of our house.

There remained the indisputable evidence of the donkey. We put it in the shed, where it shared a stall with the chickens. It seemed grateful for the company.

The next time I saw the Messiah, it was two weeks later. He was leaning on a shovel and smoking a cigarette. Lucky for him, he had been assigned to dig ditches in the frozen earth with one of Chief Engineer Falkner's crews. Lucky, because Falkner protected his Jews.

By now he had traded in his robe for ordinary workman's clothes. "You're still alive?" he greeted me.

I stopped, leveled what I hoped was a superior glare at

him. "You deserted your post," I said sternly, with all the self-righteousness a twelve-year-old boy can muster. "A good leader never deserts his men."

The drainage ditch abutted the empty army camp where, the previous winter, we watched ten thousand Russian prisoners of war slowly starve to death. He blew a stream of smoke out of the side of his mouth. "What's your name?"

"Usher Zelig," I told him.

He rolled my name around in his mouth with the taste of the smoke, blew it into the air over his head. "Well, Usher Zelig. You're a nice kid. I like you. Go home and tell your family to hide in the woods. There, they might have a chance."

"My father will never desert his congregation," I said defensively. "Not like some people I know."

The Messiah grinned, pushed his cap back on his head. I could see he had cut his hair. "You know any girls?" he asked.

"Just my sisters," I said with distaste.

"Any of them pretty?"

I considered them. Eight years old, Suri was all skinny arms and legs, more irritating than any girl had a right to be. Mushka was five, chubby, not old enough to be horrible yet. At seventeen, Temma thought she was all grown up, but she still liked to get in bed with me on cold nights.

"They're all annoying and stupid. But Temma's not so bad to look at."

"Hey!" hollered the guard. "You there, Jewish pig! I'm warning you! Stop talking to that kid before I blow both your heads off!"

He nodded at the guard, threw his cigarette butt down on the cold earth. "Tell your mother. I'm coming for dinner Friday night."

* * *

True to his word, the Messiah showed up after shul that Shabbos. Somewhere he had found a jacket. He had also shaved his beard. When he laid eyes on my big sister, Temma, his eyes widened, and his breath came a little quicker.

"What should I call you?" she asked demurely.

"Call him nothing," said my mother.

"You can call me Shua," he said gently. I don't know if I mentioned it before, he had beautiful eyes, wide and almond-shaped. His breath smelled of oranges and cinnamon.

At dinner, he was polite, almost deferential. My father asked him to make the kiddush, and he did so, in a voice that rang with such sweet celestial beauty that the clocks stopped ticking so they could hear it.

Over the challah, Temma and the Messiah exchanged a few heated glances. My father quizzed me on what I had learned in cheder that week. I recounted the story of the matriarch Rebecca, pregnant with the twins Jacob and Esau, the scholar and the hunter. I also explained the Midrash, the one where the angel tells her that she is carrying two nations within her womb, and that they would struggle against each other until the end of time. I was trying to impress the Messiah with the scope of my knowledge, but I don't think he heard a word I said.

"Where are you staying?" my father wanted to know.

He named a family known to us. The husband was a gambler, the woman augmented their income with gifts from male admirers. "You know," he said to my sister, "I'm not sure how to get there from here."

"I'll walk with you," Temma offered. My mother stared at her, stupefied. So did I. But my father smiled a sad smile, scratched under his beard, and gave them a little wave of blessing. Then they left. They didn't even wait for tea.

Mama made a great clattering din as she attacked the dishes, scouring them clean, stacking them furiously in the cupboard. My father made a tactical retreat to the labyrinth of his studies, then to the labyrinth of dreams. At ten o'clock, when Temma wasn't home yet, I was man of the house.

"Find her," my mother said evenly, but I could see that she was trying not to reveal her real fears. It was already past curfew. "But please, Usher. For Rabboyna Shel Oylam's sake. Be careful." I put my coat on and went out into the night.

Pellets of dry snow assailed my ankles, nested between paving stones. I hadn't gone very far when I spotted them. There was a grassy lane that ran between some of the streets, the houses joined by arches overhead. By daylight, it was pretty. By night, it was dark, private. They were leaning against one of the houses. I recognized Temma by her sweep of glossy hair. Quickly, I hid myself behind the nearest arch. Despite the racket being drummed up by the pounding of my heart, I resolved to spy on them.

The Messiah was standing very close to her. I wondered why her coat would be open on a night as cold as this. The fingers of one hand curved around my sister's waist, while with the other, he smoothed his forefinger over the bow of her upper lip. In disbelief, I watched as she turned her face up to him, like a sunflower seeking the sun. After a moment's hesitation, he bent his head to kiss her. I had to turn away, for on his face was the purest expression of awe.


Two weeks later, they came for us.

With the enthusiastic application of clubs and whips

and guns, we were encouraged along the streets to the Market Square. A *Selektion* was going on, led by SS Gruber, Rohlfe, Hackendahl, and Haas. Falkner and Reinhart were there, too, their workers stowed safely away behind them.

We were being steered toward Haas, who had a reputation as a cold-blooded killer. Today, though, he seemed preoccupied. He kept wiping his eyes with a big white handkerchief. He gave our papers a glance and sent us to the right. Together with seven hundred other Jews, we were hustled at a smart run into the Odeon Cinema.

There's something I didn't tell you about my mother, something I probably should have mentioned earlier. One of her legs was a little shorter than the other, the only remaining trace of the polio she had encountered as a child. It gave a slight rolling pitch to her gait that I found charming; she always reminded me of a ship falling and rising through heavy seas.

But now she couldn't keep up with the crowd; as we ran, she lagged farther and farther behind. I wanted to keep her company, but I was afraid she would yell at me. A guard fell into step with her, screamed that she should run faster. She was really trying; sweat was beading over her brow. The guard, a tall, corpulent gorilla, kicked her to the ground.

The last time I ever saw my mother, she was lying on the cobblestones in front of the Odeon Cinema.

The last time I ever saw my mother, an SS man was bending over her.

The last time I ever saw my mother, she had the slender barrel of a pistol pointed at the back of her head.

Inside the theater, we claimed a section of the floor. Before us, onstage, velvet curtains the color of wine displayed the masks of comedy and tragedy. Above us, tiny white lightbulbs twinkled in a peacock-blue stucco sky.

We sat slumped there for the rest of the day. I kept turning to Mama with questions, then grieving all over again
when I remembered that she was gone. From time to time,
the pop of gunfire would filter in from the street, making
some of the women screech like birds. The world outside
already seemed separate from us, like a scene from a movie
playing in another theater.

I was cold, I was hungry, I was scared. An officer came in
and announced that we were being transported somewhere
farther east, where there would be food and lodging upon
our arrival. People nowadays are surprised that we believed
this.

"Wouldn't this be a good time for the Moshiach to
come?" asked Mushka mournfully. My father pinched the
bridge of his nose between his fingers and began to sob.

I don't know what day it was, or what time, when I
awoke with Temma's fingers over my mouth. It was dark, the
Deutschen in their infinite wisdom had shut off the lights.
The phony stars sparkled away in the faraway ceiling; perhaps they were controlled by a different switch. I struggled,
trying to push her off me. I had been dreaming, and in my
dream, my mother was waking me up for school.

Suddenly, the Messiah was bending over me. He was
chewing gum. "Hey, kid," he said quietly. "Let's get you out
of here."

Gradually, as my eyes grew used to the dark, I saw Suri
yawning and rubbing her eyes, Mushka asleep in my father's
lap. He was propped up against the stage, staring at nothing, like a dead man. When he saw Shua, he revived a little.
"The Messiah," he whispered ecstatically. "He has come for
us after all."

"It's just Shua," he whispered back. "*Shua* has come to

rescue you, and he's not taking you to the Promised Land, he's taking you to the forest. Are you coming or not?"

My father stared at him, then covered his eyes with his hand and began to recite the Viduy, the traditional words of confession before dying.

"Anyone else want to get out of here?" the Messiah offered our neighbors. "This is your big chance."

The other Włodawers shook their heads. "You're going to get them all killed," hissed Motke the Tummler, who told jokes at weddings.

Shua took Mushka from my father's arms. In the dark, we crawled on our bellies like snakes, slithering into the blackness of the orchestra pit. Under the stage, a door opened onto a wide, low-ceilinged room, the control center of theatrical artifice, where various painted scrims, curtains, and scenery were operated by ropes and pulleys along the walls. With perfect faith, we followed the Messiah through the innards of the movie palace, brushing up against ghostly props and costume racks, past posters for movies that were already fading from collective memory. At the terminus of a warren of dingy corridors, we reached our destination, a cement-block staircase ascending to a pair of metal doors. The cellar opened up out of the earth, delivering us into a weedy lot. That was the first miracle.

We walked through deserted streets and alleyways, past houses with shutters closed tight against any knowledge of good or evil. We walked across frozen fields to the curtain of trees at the town's edge. We walked through the earl's forests, towering trunks of spruce and ash. We walked and walked and walked. We didn't stop until we reached what looked like the remains of a small town at the very heart of the Parczew woods. I saw cold firepits with pots still inside them, laundry lines, shelters made from pine boughs. There was more—a smell, a rank unholy odor, like gasoline and burning tires and something else I won't name.

"*Halte!*" came the command, always shouted, never spoken. "*Stillgestanden!*"

Slowly, we raised our hands in the air. Five German soldiers were advancing toward us, already sighting down their barrels. The moon glinted off the silver lightning slashes on their uniforms.

"Looking for your friends?" said one of them, a comedian. "You just missed them. Perhaps you'll find them in the next world."

Temma's lips were moving. I knew she was whispering her final prayers. I grabbed Suri's hand. "Don't look," I said fervently. "Shut your eyes. Say the Shema. Soon we'll be together in *shamayim*."

Only baby Mushka was unafraid, staring at the soldiers with her thumb in her mouth. The comedian didn't like that. "You," he said to me, gesturing with his gun. "Make her stop looking at me."

"Mushka," I said. My tongue was clumsy, stiff. "Come here."

But she dug in her heels as only a little girl can, entranced by the play of moonlight on the soldiers' pips and collar tabs.

"Now!" he brayed. Frightened, she screwed up her face and began to wail.

One of the soldiers seemed uneasy, shifting his rifle from one shoulder to the other. "Shhh," he said almost apologetically. "Please. It's all right, tell her it's going to be all right. Shhh . . ."

His voice faltered, then broke. He was very young, this

soldier. Perhaps he was scared, too. Perhaps, when he signed up for the elite Waffen SS, he didn't know that shooting women and children would be one of his primary duties.

Our imminent martyrdom was interrupted by the Messiah.

"I'm going to do it," he said with determination to no one in particular. "You just watch." His voice grew louder. "Really? That's your expert advice? Okay, here's what I want you to do. You're going to need a pen so you can write it all down. I'll speak real slow. Go. Take. A flying. Shit. In. The ocean."

The Germans found this wildly entertaining. They elbowed one another's ribs, cackling like hyenas, except for the young soldier, who wouldn't look at us. The comedian kicked at a mud-crusted shovel, which skidded across the pine needles and stopped at our feet. "Hey! Jewish dickhead! Shut your hole and start digging."

Shua was still deep in conversation. "Well, you knew what you were in for when you hired me, that's all I can say." Apparently, he didn't like the answer he got, because his next words were "Oh, yeah? Just go ahead and stop me." With his hands still up in the air, Shua addressed the young soldier. "You, German boy," he said calmly. "I'm giving you a chance. Run. Run like hell."

The soldier wavered, then lowered his gun.

"What are you doing, Pagel?" snapped the comedian. "I'm going to report you."

But the boy's gaze was fixed on the Messiah. He took a few unsteady steps backward, turned, and bolted. Cursing through clenched teeth, the comedian wheeled around and leveled his sights at a place between the young soldier's shoulders.

It was at this point that the Messiah levitated into the air over our heads.

The SS men looked up, their mouths slack with astonishment. For a moment he remained there, serenely floating. Then he started to glow like a lightbulb. One by one, each of his fine features was illuminated, as if he were made of frosted glass. Before my eyes, he seemed to spin like a top, rotating faster and faster, rising slowly to the level of the highest branches. A weird humming noise filled the clearing, like the sound of a billion bees.

I hit the ground, pulling Suri and Mushka down with me. There was a deafening crack, as if the heavens had split open, and then something rushed over me, a shock wave of wind and heat and energy, lifting the hairs all over my body to electric attention. I knew I was screaming, but I couldn't hear it. The trees disappeared in a flash of brilliant white light.

Years later, I would read about it in the scientific journals that cover such things, the strange astronomical occurrence that came to be referred to as "The Parczew Event." This is what is known. In the predawn hours of November 19, 1942, the fiery splendor of a thousand suns lit the sky. The subsequent blast knocked down a hundred thousand trees in the forest just west of Włodawa, forming a pattern of tight concentric circles that fanned out over a square kilometer. The energy of the impact has been compared to the atomic bomb dropped on Hiroshima, Japan. The only eyewitness was a young German soldier who happened to be in the forest that night. I've seen footage of the interview, filmed in choppy black and white. The boy shivers uncontrollably, wrapped in a blanket. His hair and eyebrows are singed off. When prodded to tell his story, he jabbers of an avenging angel hurling lightning bolts from the sky.

When I was sure it was over, I hoisted Mushka to her feet, and Temma brushed the dirt off of Suri's knees. Together, we gazed around in wonder at the altered landscape. We were at the epicenter of a shallow bowl, surrounded by the stripped corpses of burning trees. Of the squad of German soldiers, there was not so much as a brass belt buckle.

"I thought you couldn't do miracles," I accused our Messiah as he floated gently back down to earth.

"No, I said I *wouldn't*," he replied sulkily as his feet touched the ground. "Not in the service of the Redemption, anyway. This is completely different." He clapped his hand on my shoulder. "Come on, kid, let's get out of here. In a couple of hours, this place will be crawling with Deutschen."

Eventually, we caught up with the partizans. Eventually, the Messiah would lead us to the Föhrenwald DP Camp, near Munich. Eventually, he would marry my big sister, Temma. Eventually, we would follow him onto a ship bound for Palestine.

Upon reviewing the photographs and the concentration camp log entries, after the arduous, incalculable calculations that added up to six million sacrificial Isaacs, in 1948, the children of Israel were allowed to return to the Promised Land. By then the world had already moved on to the next war. Peace continued to elude us, and the Nations still refused to agree on a God who might love all His children equally. All things the Messiah was supposed to solve before his death, from a bullet that passed through his heart during the lost battle for Jerusalem.

I tried to research him, the man who became our Messiah. He didn't make it easy. It became a game for him, to concoct a progressively wilder tale each time one of us asked about his past. He must have come from somewhere; after all, in our religion, the rabbis say there is a man capable of being the Savior in each generation.

In 1975 I found my answer on the terrace of the King David Hotel in Jerusalem. I was there to promote my new book, *The Orphan's Messiah*. After my reading, a woman approached me and asked if I would meet her for a drink.

We sat at a table that overlooked the crenellated walls of the Old City. Around us, diplomats and politicians murmured, constructing secret deals in many languages over cigarettes and Turkish coffee. She lived in Sydney now, she explained, and was visiting Israel for a bar mitzvah. Her voice was a charming and unlikely marriage of Polish warmth and Australian slang.

His name was Yehoshua Tzedek, she said. He had begun life as a promising student at the celebrated Slabodka Yeshiva. In an escalating cascade of tragedy, both parents died, the money dried up, and the yeshiva *bocher* turned to a life of crime in nearby Vilna. He whored, he thieved, he trafficked in luxury goods on the black market. There was even a whiff of bigamy. When he sold watered-down gasoline to the Soviets, he earned three years in one of Stalin's prisons.

Then the Germans came. One Shabbat in the summer of 1941, right after the Torah reading, the notorious gangster Shua Tzedek entered the Great Synagogue through the main entrance and announced to the astonished assembly that angels had directed him to abandon his criminal ways, shed his modern clothes, mount a donkey, and ride to Jerusalem.

Alas, it was a time when men on all sides lost their battles for sanity. Until she heard my story, the woman from Australia remembered my Messiah as one of them.

I thanked her and paid for her drink. On my way out, I passed through the lobby, stopping for a moment to contemplate the signatures of former guests Golda Meir, Willy Brandt, Elie Wiesel, Lech Walesa, Günter Grass. Waiting for my car beneath a wall of purple bougainvillea, I smoked a cigarette and thought about what she'd said.

Could it be true? Was my Messiah nothing more than an inspired lunatic, and the miracle that saved us a run-of-the-mill meteor? Were my memories real or just the imaginary by-product of a traumatized child's desperate wish for salvation?

There were many Messiahs in those years, coming from nowhere to emerge as heroes for a brief and terrifying time, vanishing afterward into the banality of everyday existence. If an ordinary man can be tapped to be the Messiah, a man as flawed and as human as Shua Tzedek, then perhaps any one of us is capable of bringing about the Redemption.

There are days that I have trouble believing in a merciful God. But about the Messiah, I have no doubt. I know what I saw. Sixty years ago, he got as far as Włodawa. At this rate, he will be here soon.

# THEY WERE LIKE
# FAMILY TO ME

There were two of them, arguing in front of the oblong patch of grass between the decrepit buildings. They didn't look like they belonged there; both of them wore new coats made from fine fabric, well cut and nicely designed, clearly manufactured somewhere else, where people cared about such things. They were holding a map, chattering in a foreign language the old man didn't recognize. One pointed at the map with a gloved hand, while the other shook his head in disagreement.

"Excuse me," said the older one in Polish as he passed by. "Perhaps you can help us out."

The old man was holding the hand of a small child. He was short and fat and out of breath. When he walked, he toddled, just like the little boy. "Are you Jewish?" he said. Though there were no Jews left in Włodawa, he had heard that sometimes they came to Poland to explore their heritage, to reclaim the house their grandfather had lived in, to search cemeteries for distant relatives.

Both men smiled. "No. Not Jewish," said the older of

the two. The old man peered closer. Now he could see the white clerical collar just visible over the lapels of the older man's overcoat. His cheeks reddened with embarrassment. "I'm sorry, Father. It's just . . . in this part of Poland, we don't get many visitors. Usually, they're Jews. I just assumed . . ."

The priest waved it off. "Have you always lived here? In this town, I mean."

"Yes, always. Where are you from? You speak Polish, but I heard you speaking another language with your friend."

"I lived here for a while when I was a kid," he said. "But I live in England now."

"England," said the old man. "I've never been west of Warsaw."

The priest gestured toward the green patch of grass. "Perhaps you can tell me something about this place," he suggested. "On my map, it says something happened here in 1942."

"Oh. Yes. Well . . ." The old man's gaze wandered. "My grandson . . . nursery school . . ." he said vaguely.

"Oh, I'm sorry. Please, don't let me keep you." It was a cold day. For warmth, the priest put his hands in his coat pockets. His eyebrows drew together, and he fished around inside his pocket until he pulled out a chocolate bar. It had a yellow wrapper with a picture of a little girl on it. "May I?" he asked.

The old man nodded. The priest squatted down until he was level with the boy, who accepted the candy in his mittened hand. The priest smiled. The child looked back at him with grave, dark eyes.

"You do this every day?" inquired the priest as he stood back up, brushing off his coattails. The old man nodded. Under his hat, the skin was fragile and thin, like parchment, except for his cheeks and the tip of his nose, which were a startling pink. "You're a good grandfather."

The old man shrugged. "My only grandchild," he replied.

Nothing prevented him from leaving, but still, he lingered. There was something about the priest, his moist green eyes rimmed with long black lashes. It was the face of a man who had heard many sad stories. Just now he was gazing with curiosity at the grassy patch between the buildings.

"It's my own little project," the priest explained almost apologetically. "Well. Obsession, really. I'm traveling around Poland, Russia, the Ukraine, trying to collect stories of what the Nazis did. Before the people who witnessed them are gone. Things that didn't make it into the history books."

The old man's lips compressed into a thin line. "The history books," he said contemptuously, dismissing the entire genre. "All they ever tell you is what happened to the Jews. Never what happened to the Poles." He added hastily, "It's not their fault, of course. What happened to them was terrible, I'm not saying it wasn't. All I'm saying is you never hear anything else."

The priest nodded. Encouragingly, the old man thought.

"The first thing the Nazis did when they got here was round up anyone with a brain. The mayor, Jablonski. The superintendent of the schools, Wygand. The judge, Wiesneski. Slipowitz, who was something important in industry, I don't remember what. Anyone who could think for themselves. They marched them all off to the forest and shot them. But do you see *that* in the history books?"

The priest nodded sympathetically. "Terrible," he agreed.

"The Jews, that was later," the old man continued morosely. "In 1942."

"How can you possibly remember?" said the priest. "You must have been very young. Six? Seven?"

The old man's thin lips curved upward, and then he broke into a dry, shrunken laugh. "You are a flatterer, Father," he said, shaking his head. "I was born in 1927. Eleven years old when the Germans came." He released his grandson's hand so that he could wipe the end of his nose with a soiled handkerchief that he excavated from his coat pocket. Immediately, the little boy turned to the task of making snowballs.

"I remember everything about that day. The sun was shining, turning everything to gold. A soldier came down that road on a motorcycle with a sidecar. He stopped at the pump for a drink of water." The old man sighed moodily. He took off his hat, an old moth-eaten karakul with earflaps, to run a gloved hand over his sparse white hair. "We lived at the edge of town then, next to a Jewish family. The Singers. The parents, Moshe and Maryam. The children, Aron, Cilla, Reuven, Sender."

"You remember their names."

"Of course I remember their names, what do you think? I practically grew up in that house." The priest tipped his head to one side, listening. The old man explained, "My mother died when I was very young. My father worked for the earl, managing his forests. How could he know what to do with a little boy?"

"A hard life," suggested the priest.

"Yes. A hard life, always," he agreed emphatically. He plopped his hat back on his head with a flourish, meaning he had said everything he was going to say.

"Were there a lot of Jews in this town?" the priest asked quickly.

"No more than anywhere else." He squinted out at the

trees beyond the gray Soviet-era building blocs. "It wasn't true, you know, what they used to say about them," he said suddenly. "Not all Jews were rich. The Singers didn't have much. But everything they did have, they shared with me. Sender, the youngest, we were in the same class at school. We used to play together. We were like *this*." He twined the second and third fingers of his left hand together, the fingers thick like sausages. "They saw how things were at our house. Sender used to invite me for dinner. Maryam never said no."

The old man went on now, absorbed in the past. "The father, Moshe. He was a *shoichet*, a Jewish butcher, with a long black beard down to here. Times were hard. The Depression, you know. They didn't pay him with money. He used to bring home the cuts nobody wanted: hearts, lungs, stomachs, brains. Someone else would have thrown them out. But by the time Maryam was finished with them, they were delicious, as fine as anything you'd get at the fanciest restaurant in . . . in *Paris*." He looked at the priest defiantly, as if he expected an argument. Finding none, he went on.

"We used to get in trouble all the time. My father was the keeper of the earl's lands, but it didn't stop us from poaching fish from the stream, or picking apples from his orchards." He smiled wryly with the memory, revealing a series of gaps and gold teeth in his wrinkled mouth. "The lands went on and on. See these buildings?" He waved his hands at the line of gray apartment blocks marching off into the distance down Wirka Street. "This was all forest back then, part of the earl's property."

The old man plunged on, his pale eyes alight with pleasure. "We didn't have fishing poles. We would take Maryam's big wooden bowl, the one she used to knead bread. We'd set the bowl in the river and stand there with our pants legs rolled up, ready with bushel baskets. When the fish came to nibble on the crusts of dough, we'd scoop them up and bring them home.

"This one time we had just finished filling a sack with apples. It was October, the year before the war started. The leaves were just beginning to turn yellow. The harvest was already in. You could see haystacks standing here and there, the tops pointed, like little huts. Anyway . . . Sender was climbing down from a tree in the earl's orchard. Out of the corner of my eye, I spotted my father, running toward us down a long lane of apple trees. He was holding a big stick and shaking it at us. Oh, could he holler! I never saw anybody come down a tree that fast. Sender tossed me the bag, threw himself over the gate, and we ran like our behinds were on fire!"

The old man was smiling again. The priest had the impression that he didn't smile often. "I can still see my father behind the gate, shaking his fist at us and screaming curses. I really caught it when I finally had the courage to come home. He gave me a real licking. Beat me so hard, I couldn't sit down the next day. Sender got two lickings. One for tearing his clothes, one for stealing apples." He shook his head, muttered darkly, "Like the earl would miss a few apples."

"Were many Polish boys friendly with Jewish children?"

"Oh, no. There was a lot of hatred, even before the Nazis came. People were suspicious of the Jews; they said they were Christ killers or spies for the Communists."

"What was it like when the Germans came?" said the priest.

"Like I said, first they made a big show, got rid of the intelligentsia. Then they killed some Jews and passed a lot of anti-Jewish laws, just to prove they were in charge."

"What kind of laws?"

"Let me see . . ." He squinted hard into the sun, trying to remember. "Jews had to give up their businesses . . . couldn't buy food . . . couldn't take streetcars . . . had to wear an armband with a star on it . . . couldn't kill animals the kosher way. Also, the Jewish kids couldn't go to school anymore. That was the end of school for me, too. If Sender wasn't going, neither was I." He smiled, a lopsided, boyish grin.

"For a while, it wasn't so bad. The father, Moshe, now he had to sneak around to do his job, but he was still a butcher, they had what to eat. There were a lot of poor people. Maryam was always sending us over to someone's house, someone with even less. We'd bring them a pot of soup, some stew, a loaf of bread." He glanced down at the snowy ground. "She was a saint, that woman. A *saint*.

"But Sender and me, we still had fun. We were never bored. Not like today's kids. We'd spend hours building forts in the houses that were blown up when the Germans first came, and spend the rest of the day playing war, throwing chestnuts and rotten apples at the other kids. Some days it was the Americans against the Germans, some days it was the Russians against the Germans . . . some days the good guys won, some days the bad guys. There was always something to do. The day we went deep into the forest and came back with berries and mushrooms, Moshe and Maryam treated us like heroes."

The priest smiled. "That was very brave of you."

The old man hunched his coat up around his face, his features almost disappearing behind the upturned collar. "I wasn't so brave," he muttered.

Now his tone turned somber. "In 1941 all the Jews had to move to the ghetto, in the poorest, most rundown part of town. That was when the situation really started to go downhill. They were picking people up off the street and shooting them. I didn't see the Singers so much after that. You could get into trouble for being too friendly with Jews." He lapsed into silence.

"What about you?" the priest prodded him, his forehead furrowing with concern. "You were just a kid. Who took care of you after that?"

"That's when I started hunting," he said. "Rabbits, birds. When the Nazis came, they confiscated the earl's property and turned it into a labor camp. Now my father worked for the Germans. I had to be very careful; you could be killed for poaching on Reinhart's land. He was commandant of the labor camp, all the forests belonged to him. I became an expert at being quiet, at being invisible, like I was a rock or a stump."

"Sounds risky."

"Yes, well, I had to eat, right?"

"Were you ever caught?"

The old man turned his gaze toward the little boy, who was erecting a snowman near a row of cars. He had already collected a large boulder of snow for the base and was unsuccessfully trying to fit a smaller snowball on top of it.

"He's going to be a builder," commented the priest, noting the old man's silence. "Eric, why don't you help him out?" he suggested to the young man accompanying him. Obediently, Eric got down on his knees in the snow.

The priest was sunk in thought for a moment before he summoned up the next question. "Did you ever see the Singers again?"

"They left," the old man replied. "One day I went to the ghetto, asking about Sender. But they were gone. Some people did that. They went to live with friends or farmers, or they just vanished into the forests. Moshe knew his way around pretty well. He had to travel through the woods in his work, going from town to town. I was sad because, you know, they were like family to me. But I knew it was for the best. One day the war would be over, and I hoped they would be all right."

The little boy came over to the patch of grass, looked dubiously at his grandfather. "I'm going to be late," he said. "It's going to be cleanup time."

"Go play in the snow," said the old man. Meekly, the little boy returned to his snowman. "You asked if I ever got caught," he said. His hands were thrust deep in his pockets, he was looking up at the sky. "The sky was blue, like today, and cold. There was snow on the ground. I was in a remote part of the woods, where I used to go with Sender, tracking grouse. No one should have been there. No one."

"Grouse," repeated the priest.

"A kind of game bird," he said. "There were all these tracks in the snow. Hoofprints from boar. Bird feet. Squirrel tracks. Deer, of course. A wolf. Even the pawprints of a large bear."

"A bear!" the priest exclaimed. "Here?"

The old man nodded. "Yes. Not anymore. They were rare even then. But that was when I saw the footprints.

"There was a knoll, a kind of hill, with trees standing on top of it and footprints in the snow all around. Branches scattered near the front disguised an opening. Right away, I knew that someone was living inside there. Someone had made themselves a bunker inside this little hill.

"I was so distracted that I forgot to be careful until it was too late. Angry voices shouted at me in German. I must have stumbled right into one of their patrols. They had me surrounded. Four soldiers were walking slowly toward me, their rifles pointed at my chest.

"They told me to put down my gun, put my hands in the air. I thought, *This is it, they're going to kill me,* and I started to cry. I was only fifteen, you know.

"They looked at my clothes, and the grouse I was carrying, and then they started to laugh. Except for the uniforms, they were just like me, young men out for a hunt on a beautiful winter day. Until they saw the birds, they thought I was a partizan. They *hated* partizans.

"They gave me back my gun, offered me a cigarette, a chocolate bar. They wanted to know where I had found the grouse. I could speak a little German—it's similar to the Yiddish I picked up from the Singers—and this made them even more excited. None of the Poles spoke German except the Jews.

"I was so relieved. And what was more, I had made new friends, important friends. Deep inside, I was thrilled. This could be the start of something big. Maybe they could help me get a job, a good job, that made real money . . . then my father would have to treat me with more respect. I could be a hunting guide or a gamekeeper. I wanted to make myself useful to them. After all, weren't they our new leaders?

"That was what I was thinking when I showed them the footprints in the snow."

He pulled out the soiled handkerchief again. It was very cold. He had to keep wiping his nose.

"One of the Germans kicked apart the branches covering the opening and shouted at whoever was in there to come out. Six people came crawling up out of that hole. They were like raccoons after hibernation, blinded by the light. As they climbed out one by one, the soldiers booted them into the snow.

"To tell you the truth, I didn't recognize them at first. They had wasted down to skin and bones. Their hair was long and matted, their clothes were tattered rags. They had been hiding there for almost a year, living on mushrooms and roots. The Singers.

"The soldiers clapped me on the back, congratulating me on my find. One said, 'Let's kill them right here.' Another one said, 'No. I have an idea.' He said to me, 'Why don't you come with us, this will be fun.'

"So we started walking. We walked and we walked and we walked. All the time, Sender was next to me, whispering in my ear. 'Stefan, why did you tell them? Stefan, how could you give us away? Stefan, Stefan, Stefan, *Stefan!*'" He clapped his hands over his ears as if he could still hear his friend's voice. "I said, 'How was I supposed to know it was you in there? It could have been anyone.'"

The priest nodded, understanding.

"After an hour of walking, we could hear voices, laughter, gunfire. There were trucks and motorcycles, horses, dogs. Important-looking men in shiny leather coats. Officers with medals and ribbons. It was like the circus came to town. Off to one side was a big hole in the ground. A group of Jews being guarded by soldiers stood behind a rope.

"Reinhart was there, of course." The priest's eyelids were lowered; he looked as if he were sleeping. "He was standing with a couple of other officers. He looked very pale. He knew some of the people being killed, they worked for him. He had promised that he would protect them. Either he was lying or his friends back in Berlin had other ideas."

Now the old man fell quiet. He looked over at his grandson. The little boy had found some scraps of coal. Eric had collected branches that they could use as arms. His knit cap was sitting rakishly upon the snowman's round head.

Quietly, the old man resumed his story. "A group of soldiers was smoking and leaning on their rifles, passing around a bottle of liquor. My new friends introduced me to their officer. He seemed happy to meet me; he clapped his hands together and asked if I could help them out. The soldiers were all laughing because I was so young.

"My knees were like jelly, but I did what he said. A line of Jews ran over, stopped in front of us. People I knew. Weissbrot, who used to sell candy and newspapers at a store around the corner from the market square. Professor Schulz, one of the teachers at the high school. Rapaport, whom I used to play soccer with.

"The officer shouted a command. The soldiers put out their cigarettes and lifted their guns. When he gave the word, I pulled the trigger. The Jews fell down into the pit."

"My God," said Eric reflexively. The priest bent him a sharp look.

The old man noticed. His brows lowered in a frown. "What else could I do?" he said roughly. "You couldn't just say no. I had to think about myself, my father's position. What would *you* have done?" Agitated, he took off his hat and rubbed thick, stubby fingers over his pink scalp.

Fearful that Eric's outburst might have frightened the old man into silence, the priest scoured his brain for an innocuous question to get him talking again. But before he could think of anything to say, the old man went on in his dry, papery voice.

"They weren't all dead. Some of them were only wounded, moaning, trying to free themselves. It didn't make a difference; someone scattered sand over them, the officer called for more Jews."

"The Singers were in this next group. Directly in front of me was Moshe, the father. They were ordered to strip. He was standing before me naked, holding his hands over his private parts. I lowered my rifle, I couldn't do it. This man had been like a father to me. But then I saw my new friends watching me. I raised my rifle to my shoulder. When the officer gave the command, I fired."

He was quiet for a long while after that, so long that the priest thought he was finished with his story. He was surprised when the old man's voice stuttered querulously back to life, cracking in the frigid air.

"Why did I look down into the pit? I didn't want to see her dead. I wanted to remember her the way she used to be. But then a powerful fear came over me. What if she was only wounded? What if she was suffering?"

"Her?" the priest was confused. "She? Who are you talking about?"

The old man didn't seem to notice that he was there. "I stepped forward and looked down into the trench. The rest of them had died instantly, thank God. They lay in each other's arms, close together, even in death. Except for Cilla. My darling Cilla . . ."

He broke down, began to weep. The sound was like the parts of a machine grinding together, rusted from disuse. "It was *Cilla* who was my friend, *Cilla* who invited me home, *Cilla* I went fishing with, *Cilla* who got spanked when we stole the apples. My sweet, beautiful Cilla, with her long brown hair and laughing green eyes, the pink mouth I always wanted to kiss . . . When my father beat me, it was Cilla who put her arm around me, Cilla who teased me until I smiled again."

He was staring off into the distance, past the dull gray buildings, the black, leafless branches with their burden of ice. "She was sitting up, holding her stomach with both hands. A bad way to go. It takes a long time to die, and you are in pain the whole way. Even worse, maybe they would bury her alive."

He screwed his hands into fists, pressed them into his eyes. "How could that *szwab* miss?" he burst out bitterly. "*He was five steps away from her.*" For a moment he stood there scowling and shaking his head, an angry old man remembering an ancient hurt.

"They were already shoveling sand over them. I was looking down into the pit, into her eyes, and I saw pleading there. *Help me, Stefan,* she seemed to be saying. *Help me.*

"I am a hunter, I said to myself. I do not let even an animal suffer. So I raised my rifle to my cheek. I aimed carefully. I did not miss."

The priest was staring at him. He had abandoned all pretense of polite conversation. When the old man spoke again, he was calm, almost matter-of-fact. "They brought Jews all that day, and the next day, and the day after that. On the third day, we were finished. There were no more Jews in Włodawa. We were Judenrein."

The priest was finding it difficult to speak. "And where did it take place, all this killing?"

The old man looked surprised. "Right here," he said.

The boy had finished his snowman. It sat at the frozen edge of an undeveloped patch of land between the buildings, the scarf Eric had contributed fluttering in the wind. What was unusual was the grass, a summery apple green even though the temperature was a steady fifteen degrees Fahrenheit and the sidewalk was ridged with ice.

The priest felt goose bumps rise along his arms. "Thank you for your help," he said.

"No, Father, thank *you*," the old man replied, his smile a garish rictus of gratitude. "I've never told anyone that story, not even my daughter. It's good to talk about it after all this time. I should have told you the truth from the beginning. I think I was hiding it even from myself."

This time the wizened cheeks crinkled up into a jovial grin, and the priest caught a glimpse of the boy he must have been before history caught him up in its jaws and twisted him into something hideous, a boy who might have been the lover of a murdered girl named Cilla.

The old man wanted to linger, to talk some more, but the child was tugging at his sleeve. "Maybe there's a reason that you came here today," he suggested with a satisfied sigh. "All these years, I haven't been able to take Communion. Maybe God sent you to me."

"Yes, yes, of course," the priest said automatically. He wanted to get away from him as quickly as possible, as he would from a bad smell.

Only reluctantly did the old man totter away after his grandson. Eric went to retrieve his scarf and cap from the snowman. When he straightened back up, he noticed that the priest was crying, tears falling from his red-rimmed eyes.

"That was horrible," he said.

"Yes," agreed the priest.

"We should report him to someone. He's a war criminal."

The priest, whose last name was Reinhart, wiped his eyes with the heels of his hands. "Yes. We should. But then none of these people would ever talk to us again. We'd be defeating our own purpose."

They began to walk down Wirka Street toward their car,

a battered green Soviet-era Škoda. "I think I have frostbite," said Eric. "I can't feel my fingers. I haven't built a snowman since I was ten."

"Sorry about that."

"Father, I know this sounds crazy . . . but the story he was telling reminded me of something. You know that photograph? The one in the file?"

They had reached the car. Gratefully, the priest slid behind the wheel. Despite the deceptively cheery presence of the sun, it was brutally cold. He took off his gloves to open the manila file that lay on the cracked leather seat of the Škoda. Inside were a few xeroxed pages, accompanied by a grainy black-and-white photograph taken by some anonymous bystander at a mass killing just like this one. The priest squinted at it, trying to imagine it imposed over the present landscape. There was his father, standing with a quartet of officers over to one side. A few soldiers penned in a blurry mass of human beings. In the forefront of the picture, a young man in civilian clothing stood at the jagged edge of a pit, a too-large jacket hanging awkwardly on his frame, aiming his rifle at a girl in the bottom of a trench that was already partially filled with bodies. She was naked; her hands were pressed against her stomach.

The priest had seen all too many photos like this one, but he had to admit, Eric had a point. There was something in the way the gunman stood, a tenderness in the way he cradled the stock to his cheek, something more in the way the girl was looking up at him. The priest shivered.

"Where are we going next?" said Eric, scribbling notes into a loose-leaf notebook.

Carefully, the priest spread out the map of Poland on the dashboard. It was dated 1939, the names of the towns were printed in German. He had to be careful with it; the paper was yellowed and cracking at the folds. It was dotted over with tiny red X's. "There are so many places like this," said the priest wearily. "And these are just the ones my father knew about."

"How can you keep on doing this?" said the younger man. He had finished with his notes and was closing the photo back into the file.

"I have to. It's the only way I can think of to atone for him."

"This guy—we didn't even get his name—did he tell you anything new?"

The priest heaved a sigh. He repeated the old man's words. *He looked very pale. He knew some of the people being killed, they worked for him. He had promised that he would protect them. Either he was lying or his friends back in Berlin had other ideas.*

"That's something," said Eric. Sympathetically. "He couldn't have been the monster they say he was."

"You should have noticed by now," the priest said. "Sometimes a monster looks just like any other man."

He started up the car. After overcoming an initial reluctance, it came juddering to life.

# THE JEW HATER

Pavel Walczak hated Jews.
When the first German soldiers came knocking on the door of his isolated farmhouse, they were just thirsty. Pavel took it upon himself to point out the homesteads and businesses of his Jewish neighbors.

Later on, he would inform upon locals he suspected of aiding Jewish partizans, and after that, he would volunteer the names of farmers he suspected of hiding Jews. Upon sighting bedraggled strangers venturing timidly from the safety of the trees to beg for food, Pavel made a special trip to town to tell the SS where they could be found.

Life had made him that way, his neighbors told each other. A farmer and the son of a farmer, the Lord had seen fit to redeem him from a harsh, unsparing upbringing with the love of a vivacious young girl named Lidia.

After a brief courtship, they were married. They set up house in a low thatched cottage, three kilometers from the market town of Włodawa. That spring, purple wildflowers sprouted from the dirt between the furrows. Gray clouds sprinkled rain over the trembling, heart-shaped green leaves while Pavel built a cradle and Lidia sorted eggs on the porch, her belly growing bigger and rounder with each passing week. They named the baby Kazimir, after the patron saint of all children.

For a year or two, they were happy. Pavel plowed and planted, Lidia raised chickens. The baby thrived, the fields produced. In 1925 the killing flu that had made its presence felt during the Great War writhed one last time before disappearing forever. It took Lidia and Kazimir with it. Shortly after this, the farmer's face closed in on itself, assuming the look it would bear for the rest of his life: cold, hard, with eyes like slits and the mouth no more than a lipless slash, all in muted tones of browns and gray. The less kind among his neighbors suggested that he resembled a potato.

The Depression seemed to bring with it disastrous weather on a biblical scale. Drought stalked the land, followed by the vast unimaginable destructive power of floods. The winding, lyrical Bug overflowed its banks and spread like a five-fingered hand of God over the land, scouring away farmsteads and livestock, obliterating crops. People starved. In church, where the impoverished pious gathered to seek explanation, the priest placed the blame squarely on Communists and Jewish bankers.

Pavel's neighbor to the north was a farmer by the name of Jasinski. When Pavel griped, as he regularly did, that Jewish speculators had started this war, that they had started the last one, and that furthermore, they drank the blood of little Christian children in their religious ceremonies, Jasinski would point out yet again that two of the most trusted merchants in the county, Mirsky the miller and Soroka the saddlemaker, were both Jewish.

While Pavel scowled, Jasinski would bring up an incident that had occurred two years earlier. In June of 1941, tanks

and trucks had rumbled through Włodawa en route to the
Soviet Union. The soldiers of both armies showed no respect
for Pavel's potato fields. They fought there, they died there,
they dug up his seedlings and ate them, they lit fires and
burned his vines and hid in the heavy yellow smoke. Artillery from both sides pounded what was left into muddy pits.

As luck would have it, his ancient wagon harness chose
that particular moment in history to dissolve into dust. The
trip to Soroka's shop was a waste of time. The craftsman
shook his head, saying he could do the repair, but the reins
and bridle were rotted through. Could he fix them? Yes, but
he would feel like he was stealing the farmer's money. Better
to spend his hard-earned zlotys on a whole new harness.

Pavel made some lame excuse and plodded slowly back
to the farm. There would be no money for luxuries like that
this year, even if they were necessities.

To his utter and lasting astonishment, Soroka showed up
the following day with a brand-new suit of leather—reins,
bridles, straps, and horse collars—coiled in the back of his
wagon. Shamefacedly, Pavel was forced to admit that he
couldn't afford it. The saddlemaker shrugged and told him
to pay him back whenever he could.

"Does that sound like a man who drinks the blood of
children at his holiday gatherings?" Jasinski asked, shifting
his smelly cigarette to the other side of his mouth.

Pavel glowered at him. So what, a Jew was a Jew. They
were all cut from the same cloth, greedy, scheming Christ
killers, just waiting for the opportunity to cheat an honest
Pole out of his money. Anyone who thought differently was
either stupid or naive.

\* \* \*

It was like a bad joke, the young man standing in his house, bleeding onto his floor.

At midnight, two men had knocked on his door, rousing him from his bed. Occasionally, he would receive a surreptitious visitor from the AK, the Polish Home Army, asking for food or a place to sleep, and he liked to do what he could to help.

But these men were no Poles. Clearly, they were Jewish partizans based in the nearby forest. The leader was tall and spare, with a handsome hawklike profile, straight black hair drawing back like a crow's wings from a broad, high forehead. Rising from his body were the smells of pine and outdoor living, doing battle with the stink of the smoking oil lamp in the air of the low, cramped hut. He was also armed to the teeth, a modern Russian Mosin-Nagant rifle slung over his shoulder and a rusted World War I–era pistol stuck in a belt around his waist. Even more impressive, he was attired in a Russian army greatcoat. As he stood in the entryway of Pavel's hut, blood dripped slowly from the bottom of the magnificent coat, forming a small pool on the hard-packed dirt floor.

"The Deutschen ambushed our camp," the young man explained, though Pavel hadn't asked. "A lot of our people were killed. They knew we were there. Someone tipped them off." His breathing was labored. Whether it was from his injury or his emotions was unclear. He put his hand to his side and swayed, shutting his eyes for a moment.

"You're wounded," Pavel said. "Good." He spat venomously on the floor. "I hope you die. I hope you *all* die. Poland will be better off without you bloodsuckers."

The young man's eyes were sick with pain, but they could still flame with passion. Pavel found himself staring down the barrel of a German Luger, almost certainly recovered from a dead Wehrmacht soldier. The farmer cowered back in confusion. It had never occurred to him that he might die at the hands of a Jew.

His companion caught his arm, a slight, worried-looking man. "Yosha," he said.

Despite the cold, sweat had broken out on the young man's forehead. "This is why we're here, you prick," he said. "We know you ratted us out to the Germans. Usually, we kill people like you. But today's your lucky day. We're going to give you a chance to redeem yourself."

The partizan moved aside to reveal the little girl hidden behind the skirts of his coat. She was dressed in an elegant navy blue jacket with a velvet collar and a double row of gold buttons. On her head was a matching blue velvet cap that tied under her chin. But for the tumble of red-gold curls that stamped her unquestionably as a Jew, she could have been on her way to church in Warsaw.

"This is Reina. She'll be staying with you for a while."

Pavel couldn't believe what he was hearing. "Were you hit in the head? Anyone can see she's a Jew."

With difficulty, the wounded man got down on one knee and unbuttoned the little girl's jacket. When he lifted up her shirt, Pavel averted his gaze. "Look over here, you bastard," the partizan said between gritted teeth. "You need to know about this."

Under a bandage made from knotted rags was a circular red-rimmed wound. A bullet had passed through the white flesh of the little girl's left flank and out the other side. Despite himself, Pavel caught his breath. What kind of a soldier would shoot a little girl?

"It doesn't seem to have penetrated any organs," said

the partizan. He sounded exhausted. "But it needs to be kept clean, and she needs to rest. Since you're the biggest anti-Semite in the county, no one will suspect you're hiding Jews. We'll come back for her after we set up a new camp. Shouldn't be long. A month or two."

At this, the little girl burst into tears and threw her arms around his legs. Gently, he disentangled himself, speaking to her in the Jews' secret language, stroking her hair. Drip, drip, drip, his blood fell steadily from the hem of his coat onto the floor.

"Is she yours?"

"My sister," he said. "Maybe you knew our father. Soroka the saddlemaker."

A feeling of coldness stole over the farmer's heart, taking him by surprise. "Why can't she stay with him? Isn't he in Adampol, with the rest of Reinhart's Jews?"

The young man bowed his head.

"There is no more Adampol," said the second partizan grimly. "Haven't you heard? Three hundred and fifty people, shot behind the stables."

Pavel was taken aback. Reinhart had a reputation for being a good man, even if he was a German, even if he was a Jew lover.

The wounded partizan, the one called Yosha, was crying, tears glistening on his hawk's face. "I should have gotten them out."

"Stop blaming yourself," the other man said. "We thought they were safe with Reinhart. Besides. Your father is a smart man. For all you know, he's hiding somewhere."

"Then why was she wandering around the forest by herself?" Yosha cried in despair.

This exchange seemed to take the last of his strength. His

head drooped, and the hand he rested on the little girl's neck seemed to be holding on to her for support.

"We'd better be going," said the second partizan. "Someone might have seen the light."

"What will I tell people?" said Pavel desperately. "When the Germans find out, they'll kill us both."

"Say that she's your cousin from Drohobych. Her parents sent her to the country to keep her safe from the Communists."

"I don't have any family in Drohobych."

"You do now."

"Yosha," said his friend, gentle but insistent.

"One more thing," said the young man hurriedly. "She doesn't speak Polish. It'll be easier if you just tell people that she's mute."

Pavel threw up his hands in panicked disbelief. This was really too much. But the young man ignored his distress, instead stooping down to give the girl a soft kiss on top of her head. Then he folded his arms around her in a tight embrace.

Her chubby fingers worked off his cap and tunneled through the waves of his hair. The partizan's eyes squeezed shut, his doomed, dramatic face contracting in expressions of pain and grief; then he straightened up and limped out the door, favoring his left side.

Pavel followed them as far as the gate. "You'll be dead by morning," the farmer jeered at his retreating back. "What's to prevent me from handing her over to the Gestapo the minute you leave?"

The partizan wheeled around, locked the farmer in his feverish, fanatical gaze. "Only this. If anything happens to this little girl—and I mean *anything*, accident, wild animals, act of God—my friend Arno here—Arno the Hammer, by the way—will find you, wherever you are, and burn down your house. With you in it."

Seething with hatred, Pavel watched them leave, killing them a hundred different ways inside his mind, until their forms were liquidated by the black and starless night. He wanted to slam the door, scream curses and insults, but he didn't dare. He closed the gate with an angry click. As he climbed the steps to the hut, his rage mounted in leaps and bounds, looking for an acceptable outlet.

The dog. Where was the dog?

Cezar was the biggest, blackest, meanest, ugliest, smelliest dog in the district, with a blunt, boxy snout and demented red eyes. He had rough scraggly hair like a wild boar and the rabid temperament of a mother bear protecting her cubs. Twice he had snapped at Reinhart when the commandant came to inspect the farm. Pitiless executioner of innumerable cats, mice, rabbits, and weasels, just last week he had killed a fluffy white companion dog as its horrified master looked on, picking it up by the scruff of the neck and giving it a vicious shake. Where had he been during this furtive night visit? Wasn't this the very reason that a man kept a dog? Pavel picked up his walking stick, slapped the thick end of it into his palm. He would beat some sense into the animal's skull, teach him a lesson. At the very least, it would make him feel better. He opened the door, whistling.

There was Cezar, stretched out in front of the fire, his ears pricked up at attention, long pink tongue lolling blissfully from between jagged teeth. The little girl's arms were clasped around his thick woolly neck, her bright head resting on his matted black fur.

*　*　*

Pavel would have liked to keep her in the barn, but he was afraid of what the partizans would do if they found out. So he made her a bed near the stove, a crate of straw covered with a burlap sack and a horse blanket. When he had finished, he crouched over her small body, intending to move her. To his great astonishment, Cezar curled his black lips, emitting a low, threatening sound from somewhere deep in his chest. He was about to club the dog when a random thought popped like a soap bubble in his brain. *She must be starving.*

"Hungry?" he grunted at the girl. "You want to eat?" He made gestures with his hands and mouth, a charade of feeding himself.

But she only stared at him, her eyes round and liquid and dark, like a baby calf's. Pavel had never liked brown eyes; he found them opaque, inscrutable. He went to the cupboard, took out a heel of bread, a hard-cooked egg, a bone with a little meat left on it that he was saving for the dog, and set them before her.

Five little white fingers crept forward like inchworms, snatched the bread as though she thought someone would steal it from her. She ate the egg, too, wolfing it down so quickly, he thought with some alarm that she might choke. The bone, however, she pushed away as if it would burn her. This enraged him further. Meat was a luxury, he'd earned it by the sweat of his labor, what was she thinking, rejecting his offering? And then it came back to him, he must have heard it somewhere—in church? the schoolyard?—Jews didn't eat pigs.

"Not good enough for you?" he barked ferociously. "Fine. Starve."

She flinched at the violence in his voice, looking up at

him through eyes that were fathomless but for a glimmer of raw fear, which he found he rather liked. He seized the plate and stomped outside, scraped it loudly into the pig's trough.

*How dare they do this to me,* he thought bitterly as the sow grunted happily, crunching on her treat. *Me, who hates Jews more than anyone, who gives their fighters away to the Germans even though they're part of the resistance.* His self-pity swelled, made him feel righteous in his anger.

When he skulked back into the house, he found that the girl hadn't moved from her place before the fire. Why didn't she go to her box already? Was she able to walk, or would he have to do everything for her? What about the toilet? Could she use it, or would he have to change her diapers like she was a baby?

"The toilet is outside," he growled. "You understand? Through there." He thrust his chin in the direction of the kitchen door.

No response. Cursing, he hefted the small, light body into his arms and carried her across the room, the dog padding silently after them. When he lowered her onto the straw, the beast circled three times, then lay down beside the crate. *He's guarding her,* thought Pavel, with amazement and some annoyance.

Disgusted, he turned away from the sight of her. He kneaded the sore spot at the back of his neck with calloused fingers, chafing under the noxious burden of having to care for the Jewish child in his house. He even thought he could smell her, an odor of forest floor, of bog and fungus and rotting vegetation. How dare they? The girl was an affront to everything he believed in: his religion, his politics, his sensibilities. The injustice of the situation rose up and overwhelmed him.

"You pee outside!" he roared. "*Outside!* Understand?"
The child recoiled from him, her eyes glittering with tears. Satisfied, he extinguished the lamp, got into bed, and turned toward the wall.

The next morning dawned raw and ugly, a thin rain hurling itself at the windowpanes. Pavel rolled out of bed, went outside to urinate. Only half awake, he contemplated the dream he'd had the night before. Partizans in his house, threatening his life, leaving a Jewish child in his care.

Returning to the warmth of the kitchen, he was confronted with the crate before the stove. His heart sank.

But the girl had vanished. She wasn't under the bed, or in the cupboard, or in the other room. Only the dog greeted him, tongue hanging out, wagging his stringy tail.

Had she run off to join her brother in the forest? Was she gone? Could it be? He hardly dared to hope. He sat down at the table, covered his eyes, laughed weakly with relief. Joyfully, he felt the anxiety of the night before evaporate into the air.

Throwing himself at the door, the dog began to bark.

Pavel knew all of Cezar's barks. The sharp yelp he made when he hit him with the stick, the soft gurgle announcing that a deadly attack was imminent, the full-throated protective baying that heralded visitors or meant *keep on moving*. The savage, deep-chested burst of rabid, frothing vitriol that meant *danger*.

This bark was a combination of the last two categories.

Buttoning up his fly, Pavel went to the door. Though it was barely eight in the morning, his visitor smelled of alcohol and was already in need of a shave. "Heil Hitler," he said.

A chill glided down the length of his spine, clutched the pit of his stomach in its fist. If the little girl chose to reappear now, they were as good as dead.

Once upon a time, Lothar Hahnemeier had grown beets. But the beet farmer had come up in life since the arrival of the German panzer battalions three and a half years ago, though his leadership of the local Volkdeutscher organization was apparently not important enough to warrant a uniform. He'd made do by augmenting the sleeves of his civilian overcoat with red swastika armbands. Pavel knew him well, for it was to Hahnemeier that he carried his tales of partizan movements and sightings of Jews straggling furtively along the pitted road.

"Come in, sit down," said Pavel, stuffing his shirt into his pants and pulling up his braces to hide the fact that his hands were shaking.

"No, no, just passing by," Hahnemeier puffed with a trace of self-importance. Still, he stepped eagerly out of the piercing wind into the warmth of the room. "Our soldiers cleaned out a nest of partizan snakes yesterday, just where you said they would be. There were upward of eighty Jews living in that forest behind you! And not just partizans, either. Old men, women, children. A whole village." He brayed out a laugh. "Well, they got what they wanted, their own village. In heaven!" He reached into the pocket of his thick overcoat. "I have something for you, Pavel. A gift. Something special."

Pavel wished he would keep his gift and just leave. "I don't suppose you have a tractor in there, do you? This farming business is for the birds."

Hahnemeier guffawed, his small, piggy eyes squeezed closed by pockets of fat. With reverence, he set a squared-off bottle of clear spirits on the table. "Real slivovitz," he said worshipfully. "None of the local bathtub junk. Rohlfe was grateful, very grateful."

Pavel gave a terse nod. He wanted Hahnemeier out as quickly as possible. But the Volkdeutscher wasn't moving; Pavel realized he was hoping to be offered a taste. "Well, what are you waiting for?" he said immediately. "Let's crack it open."

"At this hour? I wouldn't think of it," Hahnemeier said. A smile broke across the shining fat face. "Who am I kidding, I thought you'd never ask."

The rush-bottomed chair squealed under his weight. Pavel found two glasses, poured the customary finger's depth in each. After a moment's hesitation, he filled the second one to the top. *"Nazdrovia,"* he said.

*"Proste,"* Hahnemeier replied, then downed the slivovitz. His face grew red, with a grimace of his livery lips. "Oh, that's good," he wheezed. "That's very good."

"Have some more," said Pavel, tipping the bottle into Hahnemeier's glass.

"What are you trying to do, get me drunk?" he said sternly, avidly following the movement of Pavel's hands. Afterward, he sighed with satisfaction and sat back in his chair with a loud scraping sound. He wiped his lips, his forehead, and then his nose with a white handkerchief. "You're all right, Pavel," he said cheerfully, cramming the handkerchief back in his pocket. "Not like some of your neighbors, smiling to your face but helping those AK murderers behind your back." His voice turned emotional. *"You* know what it means to be a friend."

Hahnemeier's unfocused eyes roved muzzily around the room. Had he given the man too much schnapps? Pavel wondered. He looked as if he were going to pass out. In his heart, Pavel cursed the dark-haired partizan. He had no experience with this sort of thing. Who did they think he was, anyway? He was just a farmer, a plainspoken workingman.

Slowly, the Volkdeutscher's gaze came to rest on the girl's box before the stove. "What is that?" he said, squinting. "Looks like a bed."

Desperately, Pavel tried to think of a lie through the haze of plum brandy, hoping the partizan was already roasting in hell. "It's for Cezar," he blurted. "My dog. I think he has arthritis."

At the mention of his name, Cezar padded across the room, stopping only to lift his lips in a sullen growl. Pavel kicked him in the ribs, silently wishing upon him a painful and lingering death.

"He looks fine to me."

"You should have seen him yesterday."

Hahnemeier looked at the dog, the box of straw, then at Pavel again. "You know," he said slowly, laboriously selecting his words, "if it was anyone else, I'd think they were hiding something. But you . . . I think I would believe that you were fucking my wife, *and* my mother-in-law, *and* my best nanny goat, before I believed that Pavel Walczak would have anything to do with Jews."

It must have been the tension, or maybe it was the schnapps. Simultaneously, they burst into whinnies of giddy, sodden laughter. Hahnemeier was beating his fists on his knees; Pavel, sliding off his chair, grasped at the table for support. The Volkdeutscher wagged a knowing finger at him. "Pavel, Pavel. That dog is smarter than you are. What will he have you doing next, wiping his bottom for him?" He leaned conspiratorially across the table, his earnest puffy face damp with sweat. "Let me tell you what I think. I think you need a girlfriend, a girlfriend with a nice, soft ass and nice, big tits—"

Here, he broke off. Hahnemeier had actually known Pavel's wife; they'd all been in elementary school together. Perhaps he'd sobered up enough to see that he had said too much. Perhaps it was the expression on Pavel's face. Whatever the reason, he leaned back in his chair again and clapped his hand over his heart like he was taking a vow. "It's not good for a man to be alone. That's it. That's all I'm going to say." He put his hands flat on the table and swayed to his feet. "Well, I'm off. I want to see the place where the Jews had their village. Sounds like it was quite a battle; we lost three men. Of course, the Communists are arming them."

Pavel knew where he was going. It was always the same. When Jews were taken away, their neighbors dug up the yard and pried up the floorboards, looking for valuables. It was an undisputed fact that all Jews were rich. Maybe these had time to hide their bags of gold in hollow tree trunks or bury it under roots and leaves.

At the door, Pavel gave Hahnemeier the name of someone he suspected of hiding Jews, his neighbor to the west. It was a precautionary measure; truthfully, he had no idea whether they kept Jews or not. If so, they deserved whatever they got. If they didn't, the *szwab* might search their barn, shake them up a bit, but they'd be all right.

The door safely closed behind him, Pavel leaned his stubbly cheek against the rough wood and experienced a dizzying wash of relief. At every moment, he'd expected the Jewish child to pop up from some cupboard or sashay through the door. He glanced at the clock over the fireplace. Already nine, the cow would be bursting. He clambered into his boots and pulled on his corduroy jacket, whistling for Cezar, but the dog had disappeared again.

The wind was coming from the east, blustering across the barren fields. Head down, he slogged his way across the muddy courtyard and hauled open the barn door.

There was the dog, lying astride a mound of hay in the far stall. When he saw Pavel, his stringy tail thumped steadily on the floor. With his tongue hanging out, he looked as if he were smiling.

"Hey there, you son of a bitch. How did you get in here?" Pavel greeted him. Frowning, he checked the doors and windows, counted the animals. Had there been thieves during the night?

In answer to his question, the haystack heaved, began to stir. The little girl emerged, first her head and then the rest of her, thistles and seedpods rooted in the wool of her Sunday coat, blades of dried grass sticking at wild angles from her hair.

His heart froze inside his body. If she had said one word, made one sound while Hahnemeier was in the house . . . But then it came to him, she was the master and he was the student here. She had been hiding from people like Hahnemeier all of her short life.

Her eyes were frightened and teary. He let his hand fall on the small shoulder. "All right, all right," he said stiffly. "You've been a good girl, a very good girl. How about some breakfast."

As winter turned to spring, the little girl lay in the bed of straw he had made for her before the stove. Mindful of the partizan's threats, Pavel washed and rebandaged her wounds, smearing on a salve of Lidia's invention, made from honey, butter, beeswax, and the resin of a particular pine tree. Within a few weeks, new pink skin grew over the site, leaving nothing but a dip in the skin the width of a fingertip.

To him, she said nothing; when he gave her directions, she obeyed, her eyes expressionless like the bottom of a grave. But he would catch her conversing in her language with the dog, manipulating the toes of his front paws in mysterious, complicated finger games. At the sound of her whispery voice, Cezar would cock his brutish head to the right as if he understood every word.

Months passed without any sign of the partizans. Pavel was restless; it was time to be out working the soil, hoeing and raking, plowing and fertilizing. There could be no putting it off. This far to the east, the growing season was short.

But what would he do with the little girl? She could hardly be out in the fields. The Gestapo had eyes everywhere, no one knew that better than he did. Her appearance was certain to provoke unwelcome interest from the local farmers and their workers.

He decided it would be more prudent to leave her in the cottage. Despite the fact that she would be alone from dawn until dark, he persuaded himself that she would be fine. Jews were so resourceful. Everyone knew that.

The sun was setting in a fiery display behind the treetops as Pavel stumped up the road leading his horse. He had been shoveling manure over the eastern field since dawn, and he was bone-tired, his shoes, his clothes, his face, his hands coated in a fine brown dust. As he neared home, his heart swelled painfully inside his chest. Silhouetted against the vastness of the sky, a figure was standing on the road in front of the cottage.

Quickly, he reviewed the lie the dark-haired partizan had suggested. *My sister's daughter, a city girl from Drohobych.* Behind him, the horse's hooves went clip-clop, clip-clop; a murder of rooks stalked through the rows, pecking at his seedlings. When he made an angry gesture, they launched themselves halfheartedly into the air, black crosses against a turbulent sky.

The silhouette gained shape, definition. He recognized the proportions of the widow Michalowa, from the nearest neighboring farm. Next to her sat the little girl. Pavel's feet grew heavy, for Marina Michalowa was the name he had given Hahnemeier.

He stopped in front of the porch. "*Dzien dobray,*" he said carefully.

"*Dzien dobray,*" she replied. Her fists were planted on her hips, never a good sign in a woman, he knew. "I was checking on my field, the one close to the road, and what do you think I found? This little one, digging up my potato plants. I think she's hungry. She belong to you?"

He couldn't meet her eyes. "My sister's daughter," he mumbled.

"I wasn't born yesterday, Pavel Walczak." She nodded brusquely at the golden-orange curls. "Only Jews have hair like this."

As she waited for an answer, Pavel's mind raced through the possibilities. Did she know that he had given her name to the SS? Was this revenge? Would she turn him in?

Cezar bounded up to her, barking ferociously. "Call off your bastard dog, Walczak," she said impatiently. "I can't stand the sight of him. He's already killed two of my cats."

He whistled, but the dog wouldn't leave her alone, his stringy tail batting against Michalowa's potato-colored skirt. He butted his nose against her hand until she was forced to pet his ugly head. When she smiled, she looked pretty. Casually, she addressed the little girl. "What's your doggie's name?"

He opened his mouth to reply, but the little girl beat him to it. "Fallada," she answered promptly. Pavel stared. It was the first word he'd heard her speak.

"That's a nice name. Like in the fairy tale." The girl nodded. Thoughtfully, the widow scratched the dog behind his ears. "Who is she?" she asked.

"I told you. My sister's daughter. From Drohobych." Drohobych was a big city, with oil refineries, wide boulevards, fancy architecture with angels and columns and vines. Men wore suits, ladies dressed themselves in the latest fashions. Surely, there one could find women with red hair.

"Oh, come on, Walczak. You forget whom you're talking to. You don't have a sister in Drohobych. Your sister is married to a forester in Lubień."

He would never know why he relented. Was he tired of living? Was it exhaustion after a long day's work? Was it the way she tied her apron, white with tiny flowers, in such a way that it clasped enthusiastically her small neat waist? Or was it her eyes, a clear lake gray that made Pavel feel as if she could see right through to the back of his head and read his private thoughts?

"Soroka's daughter. You know, the saddlemaker. She's been living in the forest." He decided to lie about the partizans. "I found her hiding in my barn."

"Soroka's gone?" She pressed her hand to her cheek. "Was that your handiwork? Did you give him away?"

Pavel felt stung. Just last week he had whittled the Jewish girl a toy, a baby doll, even bequeathing her one of Kazimir's precious little shirts to use as a dress. Didn't that count for something? "No," he said. "He was in Adampol."

For a long moment, she looked out to the horizon, where the sky met the land. And then she folded her arms, bent a fierce gaze upon him. "Look, Walczak. You can't leave a little girl alone in the house all day. It's not safe. Not for her and not for you."

"What am I supposed to do, hire a babysitter? The fields won't plow themselves."

"Put her to work! That way she's not in the house, waiting to be discovered by the first *szwab* soldier who gets it in his head to knock on your door looking for a free breakfast. Why don't you send her out with the animals? The dog seems to like her. Put a babushka on her, and no one will know the difference." To demonstrate, she whipped off her own shawl, a faded black square embroidered with flowers that must have been red once, and knotted it under the little girl's chin. The transformation was breathtaking; without the accusatory distraction of the telltale orange curls, she could have been anyone's child.

Standing shoulder to shoulder with the widow Michalowa, Pavel became aware of a sweet smell wafting through the night air. A flowering vine? Clover? Whatever it was, it danced on a tightrope between honey and vanilla, seducing him into noticing her uncovered hair, a miraculous glamour of lights and darks, pulled away from her face in long, smooth braids. Inside himself, he felt something perceptibly move. He wanted nothing more than to loosen her plaits, to feel the satin strands falling through his fingers. Catching himself, he almost laughed. His nails were caked with mud, and he was crusted in a contiguous layer of soil and manure from head to toe. He was even dirtier than usual.

Cezar ran his tongue around his black lips, leaned his bulky body in to Michalowa's skirt. As she patted his scarred head, his red eyes closed, and his right leg pawed the ground in frenzied ecstasy.

"She can keep that babushka," she said, scratching under the dog's chin. "Don't worry. Once they take a look at this monster, I promise you. No one will want to go near her."

In the spring of 1944, Pavel Walczak counted among his possessions a horse, some chickens and geese, a cow, and a pig. In the past, he had enlisted the help of a neighbor's boy to drive them to pasture. Did he dare to let the girl do it? Michalowa had a point, it was smarter to hide her in plain sight than to lock her up in the house. She spoke no Polish, but she understood it well enough. If she met up with other shepherds, she could do as her brother had suggested, pretend she was mute.

Pavel walked her to the pasture to show her the way. They made a curious parade. In front, the geese and chickens strutted proudly, like politicians showing off their ribbons. The dog galloped ahead, periodically doubling back to nip at the cow's straggling hooves. The pig trotted briskly alongside the little girl, snuffling and wagging her bristly head with every step.

At the meadow, Pavel handed her a sack with some lunch, told her to stay put until he came back for her. She regarded him with those dark eyes, black and shiny as coffee beans. Then she took the staff and sat down beneath the spreading boughs of a chestnut tree.

He worked feverishly all that day and deep into the evening. After all, he was only one man, and already two weeks behind schedule. By the time he returned for her, it was late, stars twinkled in the cornflower-blue sky, dusk gathered in the dips and hollows of the pasture. Beyond the patchwork of fields, past the bell towers of St. Adalbert's, there was a fading band of aqueous light. The animals had spread themselves thinly over the meadow, he could barely see them. Bustling toward him on stubby legs, the pig grunted inquisitively, clearly baffled at being kept out so late. The geese bobbled forward to form a circle around his feet. He was irritated when he found the cow knee-high in a stand of onion grass. The milk would taste of onions for days.

But where was the girl? He was surprised by the fear that tightened like a chain around his heart. Gradually, as his eyes grew accustomed to the low light, he could see the malevolent shape of the dog, his demonic eyes glowing crimson, awake and alert. Swathed in Michalowa's babushka, she had fallen asleep among the broom and wild marjoram.

To wake her, Pavel rapped on the bottom of her feet with the staff, scolded her for nodding off. If the animals wandered into someone's field, there would be hell to pay. That was when he noticed the holes in her shoes.

On the way back, Pavel considered his options. He couldn't very well waltz into the shoemaker's shop and order her another pair. People talked. By the time he left the store, one half of Włodawa would be telling the other half that Pavel Walczak was hiding Jews.

He decided to try something else. After dinner, he traced the outline of her foot on a chunk of lumber he fetched from the woodpile. By the oily light of the lamp, he began to shave long curling strips of wood onto the floor. A pair of wooden clogs took shape. He spent hours rubbing the insides with sand until they were smooth as glass.

She accepted his gift with appropriate solemnity. With a child's agonizing slowness, she took her time removing her broken boots and arranging them just so at the side of her mattress. Equally slowly, she wiggled her little pink toes into the wooden shoes. Finally, she looked down at her feet, turning them this way and that way, like a lady in a shoe store.

"Well?" he burst out. "Do they fit?"

Emphatically, she nodded her curly head up and down, once, twice.

"Good," he said. "Now go to bed."

The matter was finished. But the feeling of satisfaction he took from this accomplishment would last him through the end of the season.

Pavel was preoccupied with harvesting new potatoes, that's what he told himself. Though it was only July, he could tell it would be a good year. Not a bumper year but a solid one just the same. He would be forking potatoes out of the ground through October. Perhaps he was feeling cocky, that was why he told the girl to drive the animals home by herself.

She was late. Pavel paced back and forth on the road in front of his small cottage and peered uneasily into the distance, trying to see past the blackened foundation of a manor house shelled to rubble during the invasion. It was almost curfew, the sun was setting fast. At seven-thirty, as the sun dipped behind Jasinski's rye field, he hurried up the path toward the pasture.

He didn't have far to go. Just beyond the ruins of the

manor house, a man on a horse came into view, taking shape against a coppery nimbus of clouds. Before the horse stood a child in a babushka that was too large for her. Pavel whipped off his hat, trembling; every farmer in the province knew that particular prancing chestnut mare.

"Is this your shepherd girl?" inquired the Reich Regional Commissioner of Agricultural Products and Services, frowning. "What's the matter with her? She won't talk to me."

The babushka was askew, revealing a froth of orange curls on her forehead. Pavel found he couldn't speak—his mouth was dry, his tongue cleaving to his palate—so he just nodded.

Reinhart tilted his head, surveying the girl with critical green eyes. People called them hypnotic. "Jewish?"

Pavel's fingers kneaded the cloth of his cap. "No, sir. My sister's daughter, sir. From Drohobych, sir."

Reinhart dismounted, looked down into the diminutive round face. Pavel thought he was going to faint. True, people used to say that Reinhart was a Jew lover, but somebody's signature had to be on those orders to shoot the Jews in Adampol. "She's Catholic, then. Say the Lord's Prayer for me, little girl."

The girl stared into the green eyes. "I don't have to say my prayers for you. I say them for God," she snapped.

Reinhart stared back at her, stunned. And then he guffawed, an exhilarated belly laugh so deep and so unexpected that he dropped his riding crop. Pavel, standing to the side of the road, smiled uncertainly, too terrified to laugh.

After wiping tears from his eyes with pearl-gray gloves, the German officer bent down, his hands on his knees. "I know who you are," he said to her in a soft, steady voice. "You're Soroka's daughter."

And then he swooped her up in his arms. To Pavel's everlasting astonishment, the German officer was pressing his cheek tightly against hers. The babushka slipped down to her shoulders, revealing the rest of her hair in all its sunset-colored glory. His next words were almost lost in the thicket of curls. "Don't worry," he said gently. "Your secret is safe with me. And when you see your father . . . tell him Reinhart says hello."

Cezar sat down at Reinhart's feet and began to gnaw contemplatively at his own hind leg. Pavel was mystified. Six months ago, this same dog had launched himself at the commandant, slavering as if he were made of raw meat.

Reinhart let the little girl slide out of his arms. He wrinkled his nose, made a face. "I remember this dog. God, what a stink! What do you call him, Cezar? Tried to rip my throat out once. He's a hound from hell. I don't know why you keep him."

"His name is Fallada," piped the little girl.

The commandant's eyebrows arched up in mock surprise. "Fallada? But that can't be! That's the name of my horse!"

Fondly, she stroked the dog's hairy neck. He pressed his boxy muzzle against her chest and sneezed, nearly bowling her over.

Reinhart put his foot in the stirrup, swung himself back up on his horse. She snorted like a prima donna and shook her lovely pedigreed head, the long tawny mane falling coquettishly across one eye.

"You're the potato farmer, the one who's such a good friend to Hahnemeier," he said.

Pavel nodded, relieved. That should buy him some goodwill, he thought.

But Reinhart's face was expressionless when he turned

the horse around and said, "Be careful, farmer. We are living in dangerous times."

Michalowa was waiting for them at the door. She was holding a heavy iron pot; she had taken to cooking for them.

Pavel had accepted the widow's attentions with reluctance. Every time she knocked on the door, he felt ashamed all over again. She'd never mentioned any kind of trouble with Hahnemeier's Tartars; perhaps, sloshed to the eyeballs, the Volkdeutscher had forgotten the name Pavel had slipped him. He took a guilty pleasure in her visits, though they were a measure of her regard for Soroka, whom she had liked, not for him, Walczak the collaborator.

He explained why they were late. After setting the pot on the rings of the tiled stove, she sat heavily down at the table, put a shaking hand to her forehead. Had it been any of the other local Reichsleitung—Rohlfe, Haas, even Hahnemeier—they'd be dead by now, lying beneath the soil of the rye field. Michalowa, too, because Pavel would have been tortured until he cried out her name.

After dinner, the little girl went to sleep, the dog curving himself into a U around her box. Michalowa rose to her feet. Pavel racked his brain for a way to keep her there just a little longer. "Who's Fallada?" he said.

She sat down across from him again, giving him another chance to admire the high round cheeks, pink at the center, her skin the color of an apple after he'd cut into it. "You don't know *The Goose Girl*? A princess goes to a faraway land to marry a prince, with only her maid and a talking horse for company. On the way, the wicked maid forces her to trade places. When they arrive, the maid marries the prince, and the princess is put to work as the goose girl. The talking horse knows everything, so the fake princess has it slaughtered. The butcher hangs the head outside his shop. Every time the goose girl passes, it says, *If your mother only knew, her heart would surely break in two.* The horse's name is Fallada."

Why did he have goose bumps up and down his arms? "How does it end?"

"Oh, you know. Everyone lives happily ever after. When the prince finds out he's been fooled, he tricks the fake princess into coming up with her own punishment." She was readying herself to leave, rearranging the babushka around her shoulders.

"What is it?"

"She's stripped naked. They put her in a barrel lined with nails. Horses drag her through the streets until she's dead."

He shuddered. Those old fairy tales could really be gruesome. Her hand was already on the doorknob when he said shyly, "You know, you don't have to go."

As she stood there deciding, Pavel moved quickly. He brought out the slivovitz, plunked down two glasses.

"Real slivovitz!" she marveled, holding the bottle up to the lamp to test its clarity. On the opposing wall, a kaleidoscope of rainbow-colored lights chased each other across the plaster.

By the light of the smoking lamp, Pavel gazed into Marina Michalowa's clear eyes and saw the world as it used to be, a world run by the seasons, not by soldiers with machine guns. With harvest dances and girls who wore flirty, flouncy skirts, singing as they spun flax in their parents' parlors. Where neighbors helped one another instead of running to tell tales, where people made an honest living working the land of their fathers, where it was against the law to kill another man's children because of how they worshipped or the color of their hair.

Over the slivovitz, she confessed: Two of her sons were fighters in the illegal Home Army, she hadn't seen them in months. She feared sleep. When she slept, she dreamed, and when she dreamed, it was always the same thing, her boys screaming, tortured by SS butchers, or torn open in a ditch somewhere, crying out her name.

This was why, when she discovered that Pavel was hiding the saddlemaker's daughter, she wanted to help. While her sons fought for Poland by stealing arms and sabotaging troop trains, her battle was waged in a two-room hut at the edge of a potato field. She would fight to keep a single Jewish child alive.

Pavel felt a pang of shame. His motive was self-interest, pure and simple; he was hiding the girl because the dark-haired partizan had threatened to burn him alive. Before Michalowa's innate altruism, he was touched by an almost religious awe. He had never met anyone who could be so good, so righteous, and still so beautiful. She was like one of the saints painted on the walls in St. Adalbert's, like the Blessed Virgin herself. Had Lidia lived, she would have been just like this, he was sure of it.

For the first time in many years, he uttered a private prayer. *May the Holy Mother care for Michalowa's sons in the same way that the widow cares for the child of a lost saddlemaker.*

The dog barked and barked. Pavel roused himself from sleep before dawn to the sound of someone knocking at the door.

It was a firm knock, an authoritative knock, the kind of knock that announced that the person delivering it would not allow himself to be ignored or denied entrance.

Panicking, Pavel glanced at the girl's crate. She was gone. "All right, all right," he groused loudly, pulling on his trousers.

It was Hahnemeier, looking sober and upright, his hands clasped behind his back. Today his eyes were a cold cluttered gray, not unfriendly, but the eyes of a tyrant just the same. "Looks like you're a little behind with the harvest, Walczak. We expected to see your potatoes a week ago."

"Sorry," he said, pulling up his braces. "I'm just a one-man operation here." Fear clawed at his heart. This could not be the real purpose of his visit. The Reichskommissar did not send Volkdeutscher officials to friendly farmers' cottages at this hour of the morning to remind them that they were late with their taxes.

"How's your dog?" Hahnemeier said. He was peering past, trying to see into the dark house.

"I don't know," said Pavel. "I haven't seen him this morning. Probably out hunting somewhere."

"I thought you said he has arthritis."

"You tell a dog not to kill rats."

"Come on, Pavel. Don't keep me waiting out here. Aren't you going to offer me a coffee?"

Reluctantly, Pavel opened the door. Hahnemeier hobbled in, his alert gaze darting here and there, oozing over each object in the room. Pavel followed every move of the small, piggish eyes, fearing the discovery of a nightshirt, a shoe, the doll. His gaze came to rest on the drain board. "An extra cup and bowl, I see!" he said jovially. "Company?"

Prickles of heat burned Pavel's cheeks. He'd never been

so frightened in his entire life. Visions of a painful, violent end swam before his eyes. Would he have to dig his own grave before they shot him, like the Jews they marched off into the woods? Would he be clubbed to death, hanged? Would they drag it out or make it quick? How much would it hurt?

"Yes," he mumbled. "I mean, no." He felt, rather than saw, the fat, inquiring face turn toward him. His head was pounding. How much slivovitz did he have last night? He buried his face in his hands, awash in an agony of contradictory feelings. *I'm no good at this. I'm a farmer, I'm just a farmer.*

"Please, Lothar. In honor of our long history as friends," he finally blurted.

Hahnemeier drew a short, sharp breath. "I can't make promises like that. I represent the law here," he said sternly. "What is it, Pavel? You have a guilty conscience, it's all over your face."

The farmer swallowed hard, his Adam's apple bobbing visibly up and down. Then he expelled a long, sorrowing sigh. "All right," he said quietly, surrendering. "You're going to find out anyway. I might as well tell you. Michalowa—"

"Ja, ja, ja, Michalowa." he said crossly. "My boys already paid her a visit. She was clean. You have something new for me? Communists? Partizans? Black-marketeers? Jews?"

Pavel dragged a heavy hand across his damp forehead. "Oh God, no, nothing like that. The cup, the bowl . . ." he stammered. "They're Michalowa's. She stays over sometimes, that's all. Please don't tell anyone, Hahnemeier, I'm begging you. She's a crazy person when it comes to privacy. You know how people talk. If this gets out, it's all over. She'll kill me." He felt sick at drawing Michalowa into his lies again, but it was all he could think of on the spot.

With a fat pinkie finger, the Volkdeutscher official went excavating inside one large, whiskery ear. "That's it? That's what has you all nervous and sweaty like a kid with his first prostitute? You have a *girlfriend*?" He saluted, clicked his heels together, made a *my lips are sealed* gesture with his right hand. "So you took my advice after all! Don't worry, Comrade Walczak, you can tell Michalowa that her secret is safe with me. Come to think of it, don't tell her anything. I know that woman. She *will* kill you. But what a way to go!"

It was another hour before he left. So that his visit wasn't a complete waste of time, Pavel fried up some eggs and sausages with tiny new potatoes, and together they had a big country breakfast. Hahnemeier had to open the top button of his trousers. While they debated this year's crops and whether signs indicated a hard or easy winter, the farmer wondered queasily about the girl's whereabouts. Was she in the toilet, just outside the kitchen door? Was she in the fields, on her way home because she smelled breakfast? Had she taken it into her head to drive the animals to pasture herself? And where was the dog?

The sun was just breaking through over the potato fields, flooding the gray landscape with tender lavender light. As Hahnemeier settled himself onto his overburdened horse, Cezar came bounding out of the barn, barking viciously, saliva flying from his black jaws.

"You don't keep your barn door locked?" he said, unperturbed. "You're too trusting, Pavel. In times like these, you really should." The Volkdeutscher kicked his horse in the ribs and cantered off toward town.

Not until his guest had disappeared into the morning mist did Pavel whisk open the barn door. Illuminated by long slanting sunbeams, the dust kicked up by his boots flared like sparks as he hurried past the animals to the last stall.

"Reina!" he called in an exaggerated stage whisper, but there was no answering movement from the pile of hay. He realized he had never used her name before, addressing her only as *you* or *girl.* Slowly, he scratched the stubble on his chin, screwing up his face in thought. If he were a little girl, where would he hide?

Of course. The answer was right in front of him. How many times had he run from his father's rage, escaping to the cozy gabled space under the rafters? Cautiously, he climbed the creaky ladder into the hayloft and stuck his head through the trapdoor.

She was right there, her few items of clothing rolled up in a ball, huddled like a baby bird in a nest. He became aware of the presence of an unfamiliar sensation humming along his nerves and throughout his body, a rapturous tingle of well-being.

"It was very clever of you to hide here," he said. "How did you know he was coming?"

"Fallada told me," she said.

"You mean he barked?" He must have been really drunk if he'd slept through more than a minute of the dog's deep-chested, full-throated alarm.

"No, he *told* me," she repeated in her lispy, hesitant voice. "He tells me things all the time. But this morning was different. When he woke me up, he said to hurry, the Deutschen were coming up the road, I had to hide in the hayloft."

"The *dog* said that?" Earnestly, she nodded, making the orange curls bounce and shimmer. "That's impossible. Dogs can't talk."

Her eyelashes were a pale golden color, almost invisible with the sun coming through them. "Fallada can. He told me to hide last time, too."

Someone had filled her head with fairy tales. They would have done better to teach her something useful, like cooking, sewing, digging potatoes out of the frozen ground. "Fine, fine, Fallada tells you everything," he grumbled. "Maybe he can make us breakfast, too. Don't just stand there, come down and have something to eat. You're safe for now, and the animals are waiting."

It came that night, the banging on the door, the sound of a motor, raucous shouting in German. Terrified, Pavel leaped out of bed with a glance at the crate. Empty. How did she know? He unbolted the door to find Hahnemeier glowering on the top step, a gun in one hand, smelling of alcohol. "Where are they!" he roared.

The headlights were blinding. Pavel raised his arm to shade his eyes. "Who?"

"Your *Jews*, you fucking *polacke*! You think I'm an idiot? You're hiding them in the barn! You've been lying to my face for months."

Outfitted like Hahnemeier with red swastika armbands on the sleeves of their civilian coats, a gang of Volkdeutscher militiamen stood on the road in front of the cottage with torches, guns slung behind their shoulders. The flames popped and crackled over the rise and fall of the crickets' song.

"What are you talking about?" Pavel shouted back furiously. Maybe he could bully his way through this. "It's me, Lothar, your friend Pavel Walczak. The Jew hater. How many times have I told you where to find their partizans? How many times have I told you which farmers were hiding Jews? You know me. I hate those filthy *zydzi* more than you do. Someone sold you a bill of goods. Forget about this. Come on in, your men, too, let's knock off the rest of the slivovitz."

Hahnemeier turned to his men. "Set the barn on fire," he instructed them. "Shoot anyone who comes out."

The men touched their torches to the roof. With a whoosh, the thatch exploded into a fireball, clouds of gray smoke barreling high into the starry sky. Suddenly, the night was alive with the screams of animals, the cow bawling, the horse trumpeting its panic. "*No!*" Pavel cried, running toward the barn.

Inside, the roof was already engulfed in flames. Fiery yellow tongues lapped and sucked and gnawed at the rafters, howling like some monstrous wolf. Outside, he heard high-pitched squeals, then a gunshot, and realized they had shot the pig. He threw open the horse's gate and smacked its rump. It started forward and galloped out the door. In the next stall, the cow was paralyzed with fear, squeezed into a corner, where she remained immune to his slaps and entreaties.

Coughing, he passed an arm across his forehead. The fire was gaining on him; it had overtaken the open area where he stored the tools and feed sacks, voraciously consuming the aged wooden furnishings and the dry burlap bags. *The hayloft. Get to the hayloft.* It was only a few steps to the ladder, but the heat grew more intense at every rung. He wasn't halfway to the top when part of the roof collapsed, dropping into the cow's stall and setting the straw alight.

Flames eddied all around him now, licking at him from

feed troughs and bales of hay, from the thick blanket of straw scattered on the floor. Fire bayed at him from the rafters, from the old-fashioned covered buggy with the sprung seat that had borne his parents to church and now bore only roosting chickens, from the baby crib he'd never been able to give away, from the good strong walls nailed together a century earlier by his great-grandfather's father.

The flames paused for breath, then doubled in size. A beam fell, whizzing past his head. He clenched his teeth and ascended another rung, and then he was at the top.

Through the trapdoor, he could see into the hayloft. The cozy hiding place under the rafters was an inferno, exhaling heat like the mouth of a giant furnace. Even the floor was on fire. Pavel flung one arm up to protect his face, breathing through the fabric of his sleeve, and felt for the form of a small girl near the opening.

That was when the ladder gave way, dropping him to the floor of the barn. He couldn't see; the smoke was thick and dirty, it was like breathing a physical entity into his lungs. Blinded, he groped his way forward, feeling his way along the wall until a rush of air struck his face. The doorway. With the fire shrieking like a freight train behind him, he hesitated. Hahnemeier's men were outside, he had ordered them to shoot anyone coming out of the barn, but it had to be better than burning to death. Pavel threw himself forward.

They knocked him to the ground, wielding fists, kicks, and truncheons, and when they tired of that, they employed the butts of their guns. Pavel curled up in a ball, trying to protect his face, his belly, his groin.

"*Enough.*"

Backlit by firelight, a breeze stirring his thin hair, the

former beet farmer looked like he was leading a political rally. Pavel blinked up at him through a haze of blood.

Just then something streaked out of the barn, like a meteor, or a falling star. One of the geese, trying to escape the flames burning along its back and wings. A militiaman swung his gun to his shoulder and fired. With an abbreviated squawk, the goose tumbled to the ground, rolling head over heels like a fiery pinwheel until it came to rest in the tall grass beyond the courtyard. To his horror, Pavel saw that it wasn't dead; one flaming wing was raised against the black sky. Another gunshot and it was still.

Hahnemeier leaned over him. "Your clothes were on fire," he explained. "My men had to put you out. Maybe they were a little too enthusiastic. You should see yourself, Pavel. You look like hell."

Behind his head, flames were blasting up out of the hole in the roof like a broken gas jet. Finished for the night, his men were hopping back on their truck, each with a souvenir. One carried the dead pig over his shoulder, another held a brace of flapping chickens by the feet. A third, his eiderdown quilt. A fourth, the goose.

"I should shoot you, my dear Pavel," Hahnemeier said reproachfully. "The laws are very clear on that point. But up until now, you've been a very good friend to the Reich. A very good friend." The Volkdeutscher winked. "So I'm giving you a second chance. You can keep the horse and wagon. After all, we still need you to bring in the harvest. But please, Pavel, you have to promise me. No more of this nonsense. Michalowa stays over sometimes . . . Come on. I'm not an idiot." He wheeled around and strode off, swinging himself up into the passenger seat of the truck. He waved his hat in farewell, bellowing, "If you had told me a year ago that Pavel Walczak would have anything to do with Jews . . ."

There was an ominous groan, then a protracted sizzle from the interior of the burning structure. The barn shifted, tilting toward the left, and then the walls shivered. With a whoosh, they crumbled into the foundation, sending up a fiery vortex of orange sparks.

Pavel rolled onto his stomach, felt the rough packed earth of the yard scrape his cheek. There was a sharp ache in his chest. He had failed, he had utterly failed, he had stood by and watched as the little girl suffered a lonesome, hideous death. A choked sob burbled out of his scorched throat. He pressed his hand to his mouth, trying to keep it down, but there was no stopping it, tears were spurting out of his reddened eyes, coursing down the sides of his blackened face. He wiped them away with the backs of his burnt and blistered hands, wishing that Hahnemeier had killed him after all.

*Walczak?* someone whispered. He didn't recognize the voice, there was a roaring in his ears. *There you are. Don't move, I'll get you home. And another thing, Walczak. Don't worry about the girl. She's fine.*

Someone, he didn't know who, half carried and half dragged him into his house. Strange hands cut off his clothing, bathed him, applied something warm and soothing to his skin while he drifted in and out of delirium, sometimes in excruciating pain, sometimes feeling a benevolent goodwill toward all.

When he came back to consciousness, he was in his own bed. It was nighttime, the lamp was lit on the table. Beside him, darning a basket of socks in the yellow light, was the incomparable widow Michalowa. By the fire, the girl sat with the dog.

Pavel began to cry again, tears leaking tiredly out of his eyes. "It's all right," Michalowa assured him, brushing back his hair. When she bent over him, he smelled honey and vanilla. "She was at my place the entire time."

"But how?" he croaked. "How?"

"Shhh," she said. "Don't talk." She helped him to a sitting position and fed little sips of water through his cracked lips while she told him what she knew.

Hahnemeier's men must have been on a rampage last night. Earlier in the evening, they'd raided Jasinski's farm. Glancing at the little girl, she lowered her voice to a whisper. They had discovered an entire family hiding in his barn. At gunpoint, Hahnemeier had forced them to wade into the cold river, deeper and deeper, until it was over their heads. "His wife and children, too . . . the ones who didn't drown, he shot." She crossed herself, wiped her eyes. "Except for Jasinski . . . him, they buried alive."

Pavel turned his face away from her. *How many homes did I send Hahnemeier to? Five? Six?*

"A little soup?" she said. "You haven't had anything to eat since last night. You need to keep up your strength."

Impatiently, he shook his head. He didn't deserve her kindness. At ten o'clock last night, she said, there was a quiet knock at her bedroom window. Hoping it might be her sons, Michalowa tiptoed to the kitchen door, opened it a crack. In the sliver of light between the door and the steps, she saw Reina in a nightshirt. At the same time, she noticed a revolting stench, a cross between skunk spray and a rotting corpse, and she realized that the dog must have accompanied her; in the dark, all she could see of him was a pair of fiendish red eyes. She hustled her into the kitchen, wrapped her in a blanket, gave her tea to ward off the chill.

According to the girl, Fallada had roused her from a deep sleep, poking his cold, wet nose under her arm and licking her face until she opened her eyes. When he saw that she was awake, and these were her exact words, he explained that the Deutschen were coming, and this time, instead of her hiding in the hayloft, he would lead her through the fields to Michalowa's house.

What did it mean? the widow asked Pavel. Could there be any truth to this story? The little princess had never been there, how did she know where to find the house? Was the dog some kind of a ghost, a spirit? Or had she made the whole thing up? As for herself, she told him, she didn't care if Satan himself had brought the girl to her place. She was just glad she was alive.

Her gaze shifted downward to study her hands as they smoothed out invisible wrinkles in the pressed white sheet. There was more. She thought she knew why Hahnemeier had been suspicious. Several times she had ordered the girl who did her cooking to make a big pot of potato soup for the widower Walczak. Without considering its significance, she specifically told the girl not to use meat. This must have been the tip-off; who, except for Jews, ate soup without meat? The cook had a boyfriend with a suspiciously shiny new bicycle. Only collaborators had shiny new bicycles.

With effort, he pulled his hand out from beneath the covers, wrapped to the elbow in white gauze. He rested his bandaged hand on top of hers. "Don't be so hard on yourself," he said earnestly. "Who knows how it happened. The day before, with Reinhart, out in the open, we could have been seen by anyone. A poacher, another shepherd, someone sleeping in the haystack, an extra hand hired for the harvest . . . There are eyes everywhere. I should know."

She gave him a tremulous, grateful smile. To his immense surprise, she leaned over, kissed him on the forehead, the tips of her hair brushing against his chest. It happened so quickly, he hardly had time to enjoy it.

Pavel leaned his head back into the soft pillow. There was so much he didn't understand. He should be in despair over the loss of his barn, he should be in a white-hot fury with the cabal of international Jewish bankers for bringing so much trouble down upon his head. Instead, a strange feeling came creeping over him, an ineffable notion of well-being, of satisfaction in being part of a cause greater than himself. Something like love fluttered in his heart, and gratitude that his little stitched-together family was safely together under one roof.

Marina—from now on he was to call her Marina, she said—was still talking, but he had to close his eyes. He was on morphine for the pain, she explained. A Home Army medic had left it for him. There were superficial burns on his face and arms, and his throat would hurt for a while, painful but not life-threatening. The main thing was to keep his wounds free of infection. If he could do that, he would be digging potatoes again in no time.

Pavel felt himself ebbing away into unconsciousness, but before he fell asleep, he directed her toward the cupboard that held Lidia's salve and instructed her in its use. She opened the jar, sniffed, dipped a finger into it, looked doubtful.

He turned his head to look at the hearth. The little girl was playing with the dog's toes, singing the song from an old children's game, *the old bear is asleep in the woods, when he wakes he'll eat us up!* And then he fell into a deep, druggy torpor where, in his dreams, he was holding hands in a circle with Reina, Lidia, Kazimir, Reinhart, Marina, her two sons, the dog, and sometimes the dark-haired partizan. Over and over, the bear awoke with an angry roar. Over and over, the circle broke, the children scattering in all directions.

Looking back on it, Pavel would realize that Hahne-meier was always the bear.

The Russians liberated Włodawa in August of that same year. Finally, the partizans emerged from the trees. For a while, they could be seen everywhere, driving around in jeeps with the Soviet and Polish military authorities, sporting new army uniforms covered in decorations. Quickly, a government sprang up. Pavel's barn wasn't the first to be rebuilt, but it wasn't the last, either.

Now was the time for revenge. With trepidation, people who had taken over the homes of their Jewish neighbors waited to see what would happen upon their return. But only a few stragglers ever showed up, seeking news of missing family members before moving on. Pavel trembled as local collaborators were pointed out to the Russian soldiers, who arrested them on the spot. Miraculously, no one pointed at him.

Marina's boys returned, whole, healthy, with tales of bloody battles and wondrous escapes in the Parczew woods. Marina couldn't stop touching them, needing to reassure herself that she wasn't dreaming, they had really survived, they were actually there, sitting at her table, eating eggs and bacon.

Days went by, then weeks, but no one came to claim the

little girl. In church, there was a new priest, young, from Lvov. Anyone harboring Jewish children could bring them to the convent in Chełm, he announced. The nuns would care for them until their parents were found or other arrangements could be made.

Something in Pavel rebelled against this. An idea began to grow in his mind. *What if she just stays here?* Why should he give her away to strangers? Didn't he have as much a right to her as anyone else? He could care for her as well as any old nun. In the fall, after the crop was brought in, he would sign her up for school. Maybe he would even get her measured for a new dress, buy her a real pair of shoes.

When Pavel apprised him of these plans, the priest looked at him with pity, then shook his head. "No, Pavel. She belongs with her people. What if she has family somewhere?"

He should have known better than to trust the priest. A few days later, an officer in a Free Polish Infantry uniform drove up, hopped off his vehicle, told his driver to wait. From the corner of his field, where he was forking straw over a conical heap of potatoes in advance of the first hard frost, Pavel had observed them zipping down the road from town. Funny. Before the war, there had been two cars in all of Włodawa. Now they were everywhere.

It was a beautiful fall day. In the strip of forest that bordered the edge of his land, the leaves were turning red, bronze, caramel, and gold, like the colors in the little girl's hair. Looking around, the officer spotted him, a gray man in gray work clothes against the rich palette of autumn. He shouted in four different languages, trying to get his attention. Pavel pretended not to hear.

Carefully, the officer stepped over rows of straggling potato vines, trying not to muddy his shiny shoes. A mimeographed paper fluttered in his right hand. Pavel threw another forkful of straw over the potatoes.

"Hey, farmer," the officer said. "We meet again. Remember me?"

Pavel looked into his face. The stars on his shoulder boards identified him as a captain. On his breast were pinned various ribbons alongside the Cross of Valor. No, he did not remember him.

"Maybe you'll remember this," the officer said. "You're the biggest anti-Semite in the county. My friend and I left a little girl with you. My name is Captain Arno Hammer."

Pavel concealed his shock. This decorated war hero in the peaked cap, starched uniform and ribbons, he was the same creature as the ragged resistance fighter who pledged to burn him alive? "Where's your friend?" he asked, stalling for time. "The one with the dark hair. The brother."

The captain gazed off into the distance, studying, perhaps, the changing leaves at the edge of the forest. "Yosha," he said stiffly. "You were right. He died before morning." Pavel saw the muscles of his jaw clench. "Before he died, I made a promise."

Inside the cage of Pavel's heart, fear opened its wings. With one wrong word, he would lose her. He couldn't bear to imagine his hut stripped of her bed with the flowered quilt, or the dish drainer without her bowl and spoon resting next to his. Fear turned to rage, sparked through his system all the way down to his fingertips. So what if the captain had made a promise? Reina belonged to him now, a gift from the dark-haired partizan. Hadn't he earned the right to a little happiness?

He rested his hands on the handle of his pitchfork. "Then I'm sorry to have to tell you this," he said, carefully weighing his words. "You should have come a month ago. The little girl was sick. She had a bad fever. She didn't make it."

At first he was frightened by the blaze of emotion in the officer's eyes. *If anything happens to this little girl . . . and I mean anything . . .* But the man formerly known as Arno the Hammer simply looked down at his paper, absently rubbing his thumb over the typed words. With a little sigh, he folded it back up, slowly, lovingly, and tucked it in the pocket of his uniform. Then his face crumpled. Suddenly, he looked ten years older.

"Sorry for your trouble," he said, the life gone from his voice. He got back into his vehicle and said something to the driver. They drove away.

As Pavel watched the jeep disappear in the distance, he felt elated. So, happily-ever-after could happen for liars and collaborators just as it happened for princesses and frogs. He did a dusty little victory dance right there in the furrows, with his pitchfork for a partner. Nothing would change. Life would go on, a man and his adopted daughter eking out a quiet country existence at the edge of a potato field. She belonged to him now, only him.

She came back before dark, like a good girl. Pavel let his hand light on her head as she passed, then told her to put the animals in the barn. The dog loped behind her, his tongue hanging out.

The fever started after midnight.

He was wakened from a sound sleep by the noise of her teeth chattering. When he put his hand on her forehead, he was astonished by the amount of heat it generated. He fed her an aspirin, laid a cold, damp cloth on her forehead.

She vomited four times in the space of an hour, twisting and churning on the white metal bed for which he had exchanged a bucket of eggs and three chickens. He sat by uselessly as she was assailed by pains that seemed unfairly outsize for such a pitiably small being.

In the last episode, her convulsions brought up only bile. "There, now you'll feel better," he told her encouragingly, patting her on the back. "Sleep it off." Privately, he cursed his own stupidity. In speaking with the partizan, he had invoked the wolf, and the wolf had come; he never should have allowed those four words, *she didn't make it*, to leave his lips. As long as he was already lying, he should have said she'd run away. He made her drink some weak tea, then went to his own bed in the other room. He had to get up early. After all, there were still potatoes to dig.

He was wakened by a wet nose snuffling in his face. He pushed the dog away, sat up. From the other room, he heard moaning, a gibberish of Polish and Jewish. Glancing at the clock, Pavel saw that it was three in the morning.

With a soulful grunt, Cezar rested his muzzle on the sheets near her pillow, his demonic red eyes shifting anxiously between the man and the little girl. Pavel began to worry. She had sweated through the covers. This time, when he asked her how she felt, she didn't answer; her eyes were glassy, half open, he couldn't tell if she was awake or asleep. He found the thermometer exactly where he had left it in 1925, behind the glasses at the back of the top shelf in the cupboard. The mercury reached 106 before it stopped rising. The little girl needed a doctor. His heart began to thump heavily.

Pavel took the small limp hand in his, turned it upward to kiss the soft pink palm, held it to his cheek. He had presided over this scene before, first with Kazimir, then Lidia. Slowly, he collapsed to his knees, watching the thin chest fight up and down, then buried his face in his hands. The minutes dragged by, one rasping breath after another, until he lost track of time.

Outside, there was a blinding flash, followed by a loud crack, the sound of something crumping into the earth. Lifting his head, he could see that the atmosphere in the room had changed, the shadows subtly altered. He glanced out the window. There was a light in the barnyard. Squinting, he tried to make it out. Could it be a firefly? Not this late in the season. Was it someone with a lamp, trying to signal him? If so, he didn't know the code.

Curiosity got the better of him, luring him outside. The moon was a silvery disk in a gray and hazy sky, illuminating the stubbly fields where workers had already finished harvesting corn.

The light was on the move now, floating up the road toward the pasture. Up and up he climbed, into the low foothills. As he drew closer, he was surprised to see the little girl, her hands cupped around a softly glowing orb.

"Where is your shadow?" she demanded. She was wearing only a thin white nightshirt, barefoot in the cold mist. "Are you a demon? You have no shadow."

He looked at his feet, bewildered. What was she talking about? She must be delirious. But it was true. Though the moon shone directly overhead, he cast no shadow. He shivered. "Let's go home, princess. You belong in bed. What are you doing out here? You're going to freeze."

The orb pulsed, shooting rays of light to all points of the compass before dying back down to a spark. "I have to get this star back to heaven before it goes out," she fretted.

"See, it's already fading. If I don't get there in time, the sun won't rise, morning will never come, and this night will go on forever and ever. Lend me your wings."

"I don't have wings," he said helplessly.

But a rustling noise from behind gave him away. She was right, rising from his shoulders was a magnificent pair of gray feathered wings. Without hesitation, he wrenched them off and fixed them to her back. Delightedly, she tried them out. They made a fierce flapping sound, stirring up a strong breeze.

She beamed at him. Her face was radiant in the star's flickering light. "Thank you, Pavel," she said. The wings beat the air. She soared straight up into the night, then vanished. On the earth where she had been standing, he saw the little wooden shoes he had made for her.

Pavel scanned the black sky. Far above his head, the morning star dazzled to life, steadfast and bright, and he knew that her mission had been successful. He sighed with relief. It was cold. Now the long night could finally end. Hugging his arms around himself, he waited for her return.

The sky began to lighten, the stars to wink out. It was almost dawn. What was taking her so long? And just like that, he knew. A sharp pain transfixed his heart. She was never coming down.

Dark clouds scudded over the sky, lightning lashed the horizon. A sonorous voice came from above, addressing him. "Pavel Walczak!" it thundered. "You have My thanks."

"No!" he shouted hoarsely. "Give her back! She's *mine*!"

"Pavel, Pavel," it chided him sadly. "Don't you trust Me?"

No, Pavel certainly did not trust Him. The Voice had taken Lidia and baby Kazimir, Marina's husband, Jasinski and his family, the saddlemaker and his son the dark-haired partizan. All the poor souls he had betrayed to Hahnemeier, the thousands shot in the forests and cities . . . the ones who died in battle and the ones who'd been gassed, beaten, buried alive, and starved . . . as far as he was concerned, the Voice had a lot of explaining to do.

Pavel bent down, searching for rocks he could hurl up at the sky, but the Voice was done with him, it had said its piece. Slowly, the clouds began to revolve, to rotate, a swirling phantasm of dancing green light that broke apart into the aurora borealis.

When he startled awake, weak winter sun was filtering in through the glass. There was a patter of rain on the dirty windowpane, and a rumble of thunder sounded softly in the distance.

Mercifully, the little face was turned away from him on the pillow. He was still holding her hand. With a dry sob, he pulled the small, light body into the cradle of his arms, upsetting a glass of tea standing on the night table.

Her eyes flew open. When she saw what he was doing, she smiled. "I had the nicest dream," she said.

Within the week, an unfamiliar wagon came toiling up the road, the driver taking the last rise before the farmhouse like he'd been doing it all his life. Pavel hardly recognized the saddlemaker, decked out in a new fedora, a smart overcoat, a suit, a tie. The last time Pavel had seen him, he'd been dressed like a farmer. Despite the years of tragedy and hardship, his pale eyes were friendly under the wide brim of the soft hat.

"Good to see you, Walczak," he said. He stuck out his hand to shake, and then his face broke into a wide grin. "I believe we are even for that harness I made you."

They had survived after all, hiding with a farmer near Okuninka. On one bad night in November 1943, a detachment of German soldiers had descended upon the Adampol work camp, collected all the Jews from their homes, and began prodding them toward the trees at the edge of the outlying buildings. Someone got word to the commandant; when he caught up with them, he was out of breath, as if he'd been running.

They all stood around and listened. *What are you doing? These are my best workers!* they heard him shout at the commanding officer.

He ordered the soldiers to wait there while he returned with the officer to the castle and made a phone call. An hour later, they'd returned, amid much laughing and backslapping. *All right, then, I'll see you next week. You won't believe the size of the boars we're bagging!*

Just like that, the crisis was over. Reinhart had turned to them, raising his hands above their heads as if he were bestowing a benediction. *It was a misunderstanding, all a misunderstanding. Everything is fine. Go back to bed,* he announced with a look of triumph and relief on his handsome face. Side by side, the Jews and the SS men who were supposed to shoot them turned around and trekked quietly back toward the castle.

Who knew if Reinhart's magic would work next time? The following night, the saddlemaker and his family filed out the kitchen door and into the sheltering arms of the forest. They were headed toward a farm a couple of kilometers away, run by an old friend who owed him a favor. Dawn was breaking before they realized that the little girl was missing. She was such a wee thing, only seven; perhaps she had fallen asleep or gone right when the rest of them went left.

They couldn't go back. Someone might have noticed they were missing or heard them calling her name. Besides, they had to reach the farmhouse before the sun came up. So, the saddlemaker made a decision, a decision no parent should ever have to make. They would keep moving forward.

Oh, did the Mama cry. He'd gripped her shoulders. *God will send an angel,* he had told her.

Here, the saddlemaker broke off. He took a handkerchief out of his pocket to wipe his eyes.

"Your son brought her here," said Pavel gravely, cautiously. "A handsome boy. A brave boy."

It was early in the afternoon, unusually warm for an October day. Though she wasn't expected back until sunset, a speck appeared on the horizon, a tiny toy shepherdess at the center of a toy flock.

At the top of the ridge, she stopped. For a moment she stood absolutely still, then broke into a wild run. Past the bombed-out foundation of the manor house she ran, babushka flapping like a flag behind her. Past a scarecrow guarding the stubble of a razed cornfield, past a thatched wooden hut set in an ocean of rippling grass, past the dawdling creek that was a tributary of the Bug. Past Pavel.

The saddlemaker swept his daughter up into his arms. They stayed that way for many minutes, hugging and crying and whispering to each other in their secret language. Desolation settled like a flock of crows onto Pavel's shoulders. Ahead of him, he thought he could see the future, a bleak gray landscape of loneliness stretching onward for the rest of his days. Overcome with longing, the potato farmer turned away.

Misunderstanding, Soroka let her slide out of his arms. "Come on, get your things," he urged. "Mr. Walczak has done enough for us."

Inside the cottage, Pavel had her all to himself for a few precious minutes. Odd how she was already packed, her clothes neatly folded and waiting in a moth-eaten suitcase that she must have scavenged somewhere. In wordless sorrow, he watched as she added a single item, her nightshirt; it joined a three-tiered embroidered skirt that was almost new, a flowered apron trimmed with ribbon, warm wool stockings. Finally, she donned a pink coat with a real rabbit-fur collar and a pink cap. Since the end of the war, he had been able to trade for some pretty things.

He helped her snap the suitcase closed, buckled it securely. "What made you come home so early today?" he asked, already knowing what her answer would be.

"Fallada," she replied in her lispy voice. "He said, 'Tati is waiting for you at the farm.'"

There was nothing left to do. He tied the pink straps of the cap in a bow under her chin. He wanted to stoop down and give her a kiss, but he lacked the courage. In the end, all he did was lay his hand on her shoulder as he carried her suitcase to the porch.

"Did you say thank you to Mr. Walczak?" Soroka said, taking the suitcase and putting it in the wagon. Suddenly, she was bashful, hiding her face in her father's coat. She released him only to slide down to her knees beside the dog, to bury her face one last time in his matted, mangy coat. Cezar sat very still, his wolfish tongue lolling between his teeth, his stringy tail beating against the saddlemaker's trousers.

As the wagon bearing her clattered away, the dog trotted behind until it crossed over the property line. After that, he sat down on the road and watched until they disappeared.

\* \* \*

For three days, Pavel didn't come out of his house except to care for the animals. The cow, lowing for the meadow, could be heard from half a mile away. At the end of the third day, there was a knock on his door. Marina was there, bearing a pot of potato soup, this time with meat. She stayed in his bed that night and every night after that. They were married before Christmas.

Cezar lived on for another five years, undistinguished in every way. The biggest, blackest, meanest, ugliest, smelliest dog in the district continued to be a loyal and indefatigable shepherd, snapping at strangers, pitilessly executing mice, rabbits, weasels, and the occasional companion animal, even after it hurt him to walk, his joints grown stiff with arthritis. If he was indeed blessed with the power of speech, he never shared it with his master. Sometimes Pavel addressed the dog, hoping he would speak. But Cezar merely looked at him, then dug contemplatively behind his ear with his hind leg. He died in his sleep on a cold wet winter night, stretched out before the fire, like any other dog. Pavel buried him under a tree behind the house.

After burning herself one morning on a hot frying pan, Marina reached into the cupboard for Lidia's salve and was impressed by how speedily it worked. She sniffed it. "What's in here, anyway?" she asked him. "I smell honey."

He told her the ingredients and the method for making it. Marina turned the jar over and over again, thinking.

The next week she made a big batch of Lidia's recipe, put it into clean jars, and wrote *Lidia's Magic Cream* on the lids. Wrapping them carefully in old newspaper, she put the jars in a wooden apple crate, loaded the crate into the back of the wagon, and drove to the market square in Włodawa. Marina sold three jars that Thursday and twenty jars the following Thursday. The cream healed burns, soothed dry skin, made scars, wrinkles, and age spots disappear. Within weeks, she was selling a hundred jars a day.

In 1955 Marina formed the Lidia's Magic Cream Cosmetics Corporation. The jar of salve made from beeswax, honey, and the resin of a particular pine tree could be found in medicine cabinets and cosmetics cases all across Europe. Which was a good thing, because after fifty years of digging potatoes, Pavel needed a rest.

One sunny August day in 1989, he received an official-looking letter with a government seal on the envelope. It informed him that a museum in Israel called Yad Vashem had designated him, Pavel Walczak, as Righteous Among the Nations, for hiding Reina Soroka Wilks on his farm from 1943 to 1944, despite considerable risk to his own life. In two weeks, there would be a ceremony on the steps of Town Hall, with members of the family, the mayor, representatives of both the Polish and Israeli embassies.

At the age of eighty-seven, Pavel could only shake his grizzled head. Imagine, the biggest anti-Semite in the county receiving a medal for this act that had seemed so repugnant to him at the time and had ended in bringing him every good thing.

That was when he finally told Marina that he had passed her name to Hahnemeier in an effort to distract him from the presence of the little girl he was protecting against his will.

"I know," she said. "Of course I knew."

He looked at her, dumbfounded. She explained, "Three soldiers knocked on my door, pointed their guns at me, said they had information that I was hiding Jews. It was just daybreak, I was still in my nightgown. I remember how they kept staring at my breasts. It wasn't true, I wasn't hiding anyone, but my boys had buried a box of ammunition in a pit under the barn. If they found it, I was dead. The soldiers made a big mess, turned everything upside down. It ended only when I offered to make them breakfast."

He hid his face behind his hands. Gently, she pried them away, pulled her husband's craggy head between her honey-scented fingers. "That was a different man," she said firmly. "That Pavel Walczak died a long time ago. The night his friends burned down his barn for the crime of protecting a little girl."

Half a lifetime had gone by, and he still couldn't believe she had chosen him. He took her hand, turned it over, and kissed it. "Thank you, *kochanie*. For all of it. For coming to find me, for getting me home, for taking care of me. Me, Pavel Walczak, who deserved it less than anyone. All on a night when monsters walked the earth."

Her eyebrows shot up, she opened her mouth to protest. He held up a hand to stop her. *Not yet.* It had taken him forty-five years to get to this point, he wanted to finish. "But most of all, thank you for your forgiveness. That means more to me than everything that came before."

"I didn't take you home," she said, surprised. "After bringing Reina to my door, Fallada ran off, I couldn't stop him. At midnight he showed up again, whining and scratching. He wouldn't stop barking until I followed him. You were already in bed, barely breathing. Perhaps you should have thanked the dog."

It was a warm evening. There was a horse-drawn hayrick over in the field closest to the strip of forest; this far east,

things didn't change so fast. Over the rise and fall of the ci-
cadas, he could hear a dog bark, a telephone ring, the chants
of children at play.

He caned himself out to the edge of his field. From the
barn, he could almost hear the lowing of a cow, the con-
tented cluck of chickens. But that was impossible, there
were no animals in the barn; for years now, it had been given
over to the production of Lidia's Magic Cream.

A breeze stirred the hair on his forehead, stirred the trees
at the edge of the old potato field, currently leased to someone who grew sunflowers. Across the road, the corn was
high, almost over his head. In another few weeks it would
be harvesttime.

A dog emerged from the corn. As big as a mountain,
black, with a blunt boxy snout and eyes that glinted red in
the sunset, it sat down on the edge of the road and looked
at him. The long scraggly tail thumped the dirt.

It was followed by a little girl, bursting from the rows of
cornstalks. "There you are!" she scolded him, grabbing his
collar. "Bad dog." She was dressed for a party in a frilly pink
dress and black patent-leather shoes, pink ribbons woven
into her braids. Unmindful of her party clothes, she plopped
onto her knees and buried her face in the dog's neck, whispering to him as she stroked his thick fur. When she noticed she was being watched, she blushed, turned bashful.
Together, the girl and the dog vanished back into the corn.

Marina came outside, leaned against the porch railing.
"Almost harvesttime," she said, echoing his thoughts.

Just above the tree line, the sun was sinking into a pil-
lowy stack of cumulus clouds in shades of turquoise, pink,
amber. He smiled, thinking of the first time he had seen her
standing there, silhouetted against the sunset.

# THE GOLEM OF ŻUKÓW

The Russians and the Germans pummeled the Polish army all through the harvest season of 1939, trampling golden fields of shimmering wheat, fertilizing the earth with their blood. When it was over, Poland divided neatly between them, the Russians withdrew to their side of the Bug River and advised the Jews of Żuków to leave their homes and come along with them.

The supply officer was Jewish. "You think Stalin is bad?" he murmured to Shayna. Momentarily alone in the office as his troops piled bags of flour on the back of a truck, he caught hold of her wrist. "Listen to me. *You have no idea.*"

Shayna ignored him. Warnings like this had been sounded before, in voices thick with foreboding. Politicians would rattle their sabers, shout threats, demand impossible things. Young men would shoot each other dead in near and distant fields. Life would go on. Everyone needed flour.

Shayna and Hersh's parents were the third generation of Mirskys to inherit the farm. As the proprietors of the only grist mill in a province famed for its endless fields of wheat and rye, they worked hard during their short lives, wearing themselves out before they turned forty. When their father was killed in the first week of fighting, their mother had already been in the ground for five years.

There were many farmers willing to take advantage of the new orphans. After all, there was a Depression going on, the son was young and a dreamer, the daughter, just a girl. Offers for the mill rolled in, preceded by phrases like *People say I'm too generous* and *As a favor to your parents*. But Shayna's black eyes crackled with a fierce intelligence, her tongue was quick and sharp, and she soon put an end to all that.

It was true that Hersh loved to read, but the dreamy exterior concealed a calculating mind. While Shayna ordered the hands around, made sure the wheels ran true and the gears mended, he stayed late in the office, poring over bills and receipts.

As he totted up their totals, Hersh told the farmers tall tales of forbidden feasts presided over by demons, many-headed dragons destroyed by their own teeth, sly foxes outwitting greedy wolves. Slapping heavy bags of flour on the backs of their wagons, they shook their heads, regarded him with lined faces burned by the sun, hard flinty eyes. Life was brief and brutal and pitiless, they told him. Fairy tales were a waste of God's own time.

When the Germans finally arrived, it lacked a certain drama. A lone soldier putting down the rutted road on a motorcycle, followed by a few camouflage-colored trucks. Soon afterward, a guard was installed at the mill, armed with a helmet and a Mauser.

Nothing much changed. Farmers came in with grain, Shayna made deliveries to town. Apples, rye, and wheat still came in from the Earl of Zamoyski's estate, though now that his hereditary lands had been confiscated, SS Kommandant Reinhart's name was stamped on the bags.

Shayna treated the Nazis as she would any other client: She saw that the job was done well, weighed accurately, bagged securely. Achim, the soldier the Germans installed at the mill, was a farm boy. After a week of watching the millstones turn, he put down his rifle, rolled up his sleeves, and went to work alongside the hired hands.

On a cold Thursday in October, Shayna drove the wagon to the nearby town of Włodawa. The horse's name was Toni; she flapped the reins over his back to make him go faster, but he had his own idea of how long it should take to get there.

It was market day. Farmers had arrived before dawn to set up their booths, and the air was filled with the sounds of women haggling, the smells of dung and cabbage and smoke. Shayna waved at the woman who sold eggs, a friend of her mother's, a big woman with high pink cheeks and a generous body.

Shayna pulled up in front of the bakery. A squat, square-headed man emerged in a cloud of steam, wiping his hands on an apron dusty with flour. A stranger.

"Where's Handelman?" she said.

"Not here," he said.

"Let me talk to Fania," she said. The baker's wife.

He apprised her with pale blue eyes. "Gone, both of them. Resettled to the east. I'm the baker now."

She felt a chill pass over the hairs at the back of her neck. Once he had finished unloading the bags, she chirruped to the horse, shook the reins over his gray shoulders. But the new baker blocked the road in front of the horse, putting his hand on Toni's bridle.

The baker's skin was pasty and scarred, his eyes flat, his expression unreadable. A light sheen of perspiration beaded on her forehead, though there was snow on the ground and the horse's breath came out in white gusts. It took her a moment to realize that he wasn't looking at her.

In the market square, five men performed jumping jacks, presided over by an SS officer and three laughing soldiers. As she watched, one of the men collapsed. With a start, Shayna realized that she knew him. Korn the fishmonger. Still laughing, the officer took out his pistol, aimed carefully.

The horse, startled at the gunshot, would have bolted if Shayna hadn't been holding the reins so tightly. The baker released Toni's bridle, averting his gaze to the bags of flour on the cobblestones.

"Same time next week," he said. She heard herself agree. "Be careful," he muttered, then stepped away.

Her heart pounding, she clucked to the horse. Reassured, he set off down the street that would lead them out of town and away from the blood tracing a delicate spiderweb pattern in the cracks between the cobblestones.

They sat in Shayna's bedroom, the walls papered with tiny flowers.

"We should leave," said Hersh. "Disappear into the forest. Join the partizans."

"And leave the mill? The mill that's supported our family for generations?"

"It's not our mill anymore, Shayna. It's the Deutschens' mill."

"You, with a gun," she said, amused, dismissing the idea. "The Germans will kill you on your first day. I can see it now.

You have them surrounded. Someone asks you a question. Next thing you know, you're blabbing away, telling them the one with the flying rabbi and the demon with the stretchy arms, and *bang.*"

"The *widow* and the demon with stretchy arms," he reminded her sulkily. "Were you even listening? It was the midnight before Rosh Hashanah, and a widow was on her way to synagogue for *selichot.* A stranger carrying a prayer book asked if he could walk beside her. It was a dark, moonless night, so she was glad for the company. When they reached the shul, the lights were out, and it was cold and deserted. She went upstairs to the women's gallery to wait, but as she took her seat, she saw him staring at her, his eyes like red coals burning in the darkness. And then he reached out to her, like this, and his arms stretched and stretched, like *this,* all the way up to the—"

"Okay, Hersh. That's enough."

"There's nothing to tie us here," he said. "We should go."

"Reinhart likes you," she said.

It was true, Reinhart did like Hersh. The commandant had visited last summer, and Hersh had shown him the grounds: the waterway that ran the mill, the stone storehouse, the giant gears, the pitted stones. At the sight of the great waterwheel paddling in the stream, the German officer had smiled like a little boy.

And because he was Hersh, he told the commandant a story. At least it was a good one, with a midwife, a tabby cat, and a treasure. Clapping Hersh's slight shoulder, Reinhart guffawed and said that no one had told him a bedtime story since his grandmother died. Then he winked at Shayna, climbed into his big black Mercedes, and drove away.

"When the time comes, he'll kill us anyway," said Hersh.

"They need the mill," she reminded him. "As long as Reinhart's happy, we're safe."

"I'll bet Korn thought he was safe, too," said Hersh, and the discussion was over.

That night was cold, colder than it had been in weeks. It was still dark out when Shayna was awakened by a noise.

She bolted upright, her heart thumping. *Pok. Pok. Pok.* The sound was coming from outside. As her heartbeat slowed, she realized it was the front gate, banging in the wind. Someone must have had left it unlatched.

She settled back into the warmth of her feather quilt. She had been dreaming, and in the dream, her mother, the woman who sold eggs in the market square, and a tabby cat were perched on the end of the mattress, encouraging her to find a suitable young man. Shayna had been explaining to the cat that she liked her independence, a husband would insist on doing things his own way. She was grateful that the noise had roused her. Her jaw was sore from grinding her teeth.

She smelled him before she saw him. As her eyes adjusted to the dark, she saw that someone was standing before her bed. Completely naked, he towered over her, long ropes of muscles bunching and shaking, smeared in filth from his hair down to his toes. His hands were clasped together over the place between his legs.

Seeing that she was awake, he leaned forward. "You called me, Rabbi?" he said urgently. "It's me, Yossel." And then he fainted dead away.

* * *

Two things they established immediately. One, the young man was Jewish; standing before them stark naked, it was impossible to miss. Second, and this was important, he was crazy.

"What's your name?" Shayna asked him again.

"I *told* you," he answered plaintively. "Yossel."

"What are you doing here?"

"You called me. You said you'd call me whenever the Jews were in trouble. Don't you remember?"

Hersh stared at him, wide-eyed. "My God," he said, in a voice choked with laughter. "He thinks he's the Golem."

She looked at him fiercely. "Real life going on here, Hersh. Not one of your stupid stories."

"You know this one. It was just before Passover, and Rabbi Yehuda Loew, the Maharal of Prague, got wind of an evil plan. Someone was going to tell the peasants that Jews used the blood of Christian children to make their matzo. It was a lie, but it always worked; angry mobs would storm through the streets where Jews lived, killing everyone they found, destroying everything they touched. So, the Maharal made a man out of clay that he dug from the riverbank. His sole purpose was to protect the Jews from danger." He corrected himself. "Not a man. A monster. The Golem of Prague." He smiled sweetly at his sister. "If he's the Golem, I guess that makes you the rabbi."

They washed him off in the barn. Whatever he was covered in stank of dead fish and decay. Despite repeated applications of soap and water, the color of his hair remained the same, a muddy brown, like the sticky clay they used to scoop out of the land near the river when they were kids.

He was built like a laborer, with a deep wide chest and big sinewy arms. Blank, stony eyes stared out at her from shadowy sockets. From the trunk in the attic where they kept Papa's clothing, Shayna loaned him trousers, a jacket, a shirt. Before she handed it over, she saw Hersh surreptitiously slide a tiny paper scroll into the jacket's inner pocket.

"It's the Shema," he explained sheepishly. The prayer Jews chanted each morning, at bedtime, and before dying. "The Golem wears it next to his heart. It's how the rabbi brought him to life. Don't look at me like that. He asked."

"That's ridiculous," said Shayna. "Fairy tales."

Hersh and his stories. Before his bar mitzvah, Papa had made arrangements for him to learn Talmud with a doe-eyed rabbinical student who bartered lessons for flour. Dutifully, Hersh had mastered the intricate legal discussions constituting the body of the Mishnah. But when it came to the myths and legends of the Midrash, his eyes took on a misty faraway look, and he would ramble on about the pious ox who refused to work on Shabbos, or the exact number of plagues that befell Pharaoh and his chariots in the Red Sea. This was undoubtedly their mother's influence. Until he was eight, Hersh was confined indoors with weak lungs. To entertain him, Mama had filled his head with talk of dybbuks and demons, fireflowers that conferred mystical powers, enchanted talking bears. Folktales she'd heard from her mother or from the Polish women who cooked and sewed and cleaned for them.

Shayna gave in. "Fine, he's the Golem," she said. "He must belong to someone. Tonight he can sleep in the barn."

The next morning Hersh took the wagon to town. No one seemed to be missing a confused young man. Shayna asked the farmers waiting for their flour, receiving terse shakes of the head in response. But when the guard, Achim, went outside to open the sluice, one of the farmers relayed a terrible rumor he had heard: all the Jews in the town of Lubień marched into the Parczew Forest, massacred. Shayna dismissed it. All these *bubbameinsas* about atrocities. Propaganda warmed over from the last war.

"We can't send him away," said Hersh. "He doesn't have any papers. If the Germans don't get him, someone else will."

She put her hands on her hips, pursed her lips in a frown. Another dreamer she had to be responsible for. "All right, then. If he's going to stay here, he has to work."

"You can't give a Golem an ordinary job," said Hersh. "The Maharal was very clear about that. You have to save him for something really big. Like helping the Jews in their time of trouble."

"He's helping this Jew," she said. Turning to the young man, she made sure to speak very slowly and clearly. "We need water," she enunciated carefully, handing him a bucket. "Fill up the barrel outside the kitchen door."

The young man gripped the handle, never taking his eyes from her face. Curiously, she studied the even features, the blank expression. Something flickered in the darkness behind those hollow eyes. Was it yearning? A memory?

Not that it mattered. The commandant's rye was not going to grind itself. Shayna returned her attention to the millstones. As it turned out, one of the gears was off, and the waterwheel wouldn't turn. Lost in the repairs, she forgot about Yossel until dinnertime.


The sunset painted the clouds in bands of rose and aquamarine. With work over for the day, the farmhands were grouped around for a smoke outside the kitchen. Shayna's feet ached, her back ached, her fingers, too, as she trudged across the footbridge toward the house.

It didn't register until the mud reached her ankles. The courtyard was flooded. A steady stream slopped from the barrel down to the barn and clear across the road. Whorls of silty water gurgled at the kitchen door, lapped gently at the bottom step of the storehouse.

Yossel labored past her under the weight of two over-flowing buckets. As she watched in disbelief, he emptied his pails into the barrel, turned around, and headed back toward the well.

"*Stop!*" she shouted, running at him. He halted midstep. "Give me that," she said harshly, grabbing the pails from his fingers. "What are you, an idiot?"

Maybe he flinched a little. The men tittered. Fuming, she stomped into the house.

Behind her, the hands filed in for dinner. While they wolfed down their borscht and pierogi, Yossel remained outside, rooted in place. When Achim left to visit a girl at a neighboring farm, the conversation changed course, the men talking in low voices about people who had vanished, news of the war. By the time they pushed themselves away from the table and ambled toward their huts, it was ten o'clock. Yossel was still in the yard, exactly as they had left him, mud setting like cement around his boots.

"You have to tell him what to do," said Hersh. "Tell him to come in for dinner."

"No," she said savagely. "He wants to be a Golem? Let him stand there all night."

She was sure he was pretending. Looking out the window of her bedroom as she shook out her braid and brushed her hair, she could see him, as lifeless as a slab of granite, shivering in the cold.

The next morning a stiff rain pelted down from an angry sky, pounding the hardened earth. Shayna joined Hersh at the kitchen door. Water was running off the peak of Yossel's cap, dripping from the hem of his sodden cloth coat.

"This is ridiculous," she said to her brother. "Even animals know enough to come in from the rain."

But Hersh was staring at him, watching the rain fall drop by drop from the end of his nose. "The Golem doesn't have any will of his own. He only does what the rabbi tells him to." He threw open the door, hollered to him over the clatter of the rain. He might as well have shouted at the waterwheel; Yossel didn't move. Hersh turned to his sister. "Well, Rabbi," he said. "He's your Golem. You try."

She could hardly see him through the long, slanting rays of rain, barely distinguishable from the sea of mud around him. "Come in, you jackass!" she yelled.

He trained his vacant eyes on her, stirred his frozen limbs. Pulling his feet from the sludge with a sucking sound, he lumbered stiffly forward, up the steps, and into the house, where he stopped in front of Shayna, dripping on the kitchen floor.

"Look," said Hersh. "It's not enough to tell him to fill the water barrel. You also have to tell him when to stop. You can't just say 'Come in.' You've also got to tell him to take off his boots, change into dry clothes, sit down at the table, have something to eat."

"He's not a baby," she said in exasperation.

She told Yossel to wait in the pantry behind the kitchen while she fetched him dry clothing. He disrobed as if she weren't there, allowing her to pass curious eyes over his bare body.

Shayna had never seen a man naked, not even Hersh. Tipping her head to one side, she inspected the width of his shoulders, the angles of his rib cage, the way his muscles lapped forth over his narrow hips. She observed other things, too: the kite-shaped plate of muscle at his back, the upside-down triangle of sinew above his buttocks, the shape outlined by the patch of hair between his thighs.

"What is it, Rabbi?" he said. His voice had a gravelly, unused quality.

Reluctantly, she did as Hersh suggested. "Put these on. Then come to the kitchen, sit down at the table, and have some breakfast."

She caught her breath at the play of muscles across his chest as he thrust his arms into the sleeves of the shirt. When he turned away from her to pull on the trousers, she withdrew, quietly shutting the door to the pantry behind her.

Thursdays, Shayna delivered flour to the bakery in Włodawa. She left shortly before dawn. She had planned on making her escape before Yossel rose; if he saw her leaving, he would follow on foot behind the wagon, trailing behind her like a wraith for the rest of the day.

Frost lay between the furrows, whitened the stubble of cornstalks razed knee-high in the frozen fields. She flapped the reins over the horse's shoulders just as the sun burst in a pink and orange haze across the horizon. She raised her chin and closed her eyes, letting the early-morning sun warm her skin. She'd been looking forward to this time away from home, where Yossel dogged her every step.

The second job they had given him was impossible to screw up, or so they had thought. All he had to do was carry flour sacks from the warehouse to the wagon that went to Reinhart each week. Yossel managed to heap them into a rickety tower twenty feet high before anyone noticed. Next he was given the unenviable task of mucking out the animal shed, shoveling shit and dirty straw. By the time she stopped him, he had dug himself into a hole five feet deep. When she let him feed the animals, he piled the troughs to the rafters with drifts of hay and filled the henhouse knee-deep with cracked corn. The day she ordered him to top up the samovar, well . . . She could have sworn she told him to stop when it was full.

When properly supervised, Yossel was a good worker; he did whatever he was asked, promptly and without complaint. The other men hissed at him as they passed; he was making them look bad.

She discovered by accident that he'd been sleeping standing up. One night there was a tumult in the barn, someone had left the door open, and a fox made off with two hens. As she pulled the door shut against a wasting wind, she saw him in an empty stall, head down, swaying on his feet.

"What are you doing?" she had asked, unnerved by the sight.

At the sound of her voice, he came to life. "Does the rabbi need me?" he said.

"No," she said. "And stop calling me Rabbi."

"What does the rabbi want?"

"The rabbi wants you to lie down and sleep," she replied firmly, wincing at her own use of the title. "Tonight. Every night."

He dropped like a stone into the straw. Within moments, the deep chest was rising and falling with the steady rhythmic breathing of sleep. He must have been dreaming. His feet twitched as if he were running, and he brushed at wet eyes with the back of his hand.

It was midmorning by the time she entered Włodawa. Expertly, she maneuvered the wagon through the maze of crooked streets, the rows of poplar trees like columns, past the pastel-colored houses and the onion-domed basilica. Toni flicked his ears back at her, harrumphed white vapor from his velvety nose. In the market, tables were laid out with potatoes, cabbages, mildewy clothing. Merchants stood around fires lit in rusted oil drums, stamping their feet, slapping their arms to stay warm. A squad of German soldiers crowded together in a circle, laughing with an officer.

One of them glanced up, catching her eye. Shayna looked away, remembering the way the fishmonger's blood had pooled around the cobblestones, but it was too late; the soldier separated himself from his comrades and blocked her way.

"Good morning, miss," he said, as if he were delighted to see her. He assured her she wasn't in trouble, it was just that he and his companions had a friendly little competition going. Which of these ladies could do the most push-ups, they wondered. Could she help them out?

Beaming benignly, another soldier took the horse's bridle, stroked his head as Shayna climbed down from her seat. Maybe she wasn't moving quickly enough, maybe he didn't like the look on her face. He smashed the butt of his rifle into the side of her head, knocking her off her feet.

The soldiers parted to make room for her to pass. Inside the circle, three women were waiting on their hands and knees on the cold paving stones. The place he guided her to was already occupied by a steaming pile of horseshit.

*I'm dead,* she thought, tears stinging her eyes. *Will Hersh ever know what happened to me?*

The soldier leaned close, smiling confidentially. "Go on. You're younger than the other ones. I'm betting on you." He winked. "Don't let me down."

Shayna lowered herself onto the pile of manure.

The officer's cap was pushed back on his head, his cheeks flushed with excitement and the cold. He held a stopwatch in his hand as he counted off *eins, zwei, drei.*

For the first set of push-ups, she held her breath, almost blind with the pain and odor. But with the deprivation of oxygen to her muscles, she soon found her arms weakening, her pace slowing. It was suicide. Giving in, she gasped great lungfuls of stinking air. The stench filled her nostrils, made her light-headed, made her eyes water.

*Up, down. Up, down. Up, down.* She was careful to keep her face blank, expressionless, but her injured eye leaked continuously. For a while she kept track of the numbers, and then she lost count.

The woman to her left collapsed first. Shayna was conscious of the harsh wheeze of labored breathing as a pair of polished boots clicked slowly to a stop behind her head. There was a moment that felt like forever, and then a gunshot exploded near her ear, the report ricocheting off of the buildings surrounding the square.

The woman beside her jerked violently, lay still. When the boots had clicked away to a safe distance, Shayna dared a glance. Recognizing the staring blue eyes, the astounded round mouth, she went weak in the knees, her pace slowing.

"Come on," the soldier's voice was nearby, encouraging her. "You can't stop now! One down, two to go."

Her chest was on fire, her head throbbed. *Up, down. Up,*

*down. Up, down.* Every movement an agony. It wouldn't be long now.

A pair of cognac-colored oxfords stopped at the edge of her field of vision. The soldiers stiffened to attention. With the sound of Reinhart's hearty voice, she felt tension spark and fizzle in the air. He made a crude joke, the soldiers laughed knowingly, and then the crisis was over, the soldiers drifting apart, strolling away.

Shayna swayed to her feet. She put a hand to her forehead, recoiled from the stink of her own clothing. Her bruised eye had swelled shut.

Reinhart was standing right in front of her. "Mirsky?" he said softly. Incredulity, followed by rage, blazed in his bright green eyes, hidden under the wide brim of his fedora. Then the expression was carefully tucked away, the clean-shaven face urbane and bland and smooth again. "You should see a doctor."

"I'm fine, Herr Kommandant," she said stiffly. "I just want to go home."

He nodded toward the corpse on the dirty cobblestones. "Who is she?"

"Zimmer. She sold eggs in the marketplace." Her voice wobbled. "She knew my mother."

Reinhart averted his gaze. "Don't come back here anymore," he said in a low, tense voice, just loud enough for Shayna to hear. "You understand? Don't come back."

With a swirl of caramel-colored coattails he strode off, instructing the soldiers to unload the bags at the bakery and escort his miller and her horse safely out of town.

It took a staggering amount of effort to climb back onto the seat. The soldier who had struck her was now as polite as could be. Shayna struggled to keep her composure as he cheerfully unloaded the flour, then swung himself up into the wagon. She could hear him whistling as they rolled away. At the edge of town, he swung back off.

"I still think you would have won," he said, grinning engagingly. "And what a prize I had waiting for you!" He winked. Shouldering his rifle, he stopped to light up a cigarette, then strolled at a leisurely pace down the road that led back to town.

Shayna lashed the reins over the horse's shoulders. Toni leaped forward, almost tossing her out of the seat. In a frenzy of fear, she whipped the reins against the horse's neck until he was going at a full gallop.

When she reached home, the courtyard was empty. Shayna uncoupled the wagon and led the horse into the barn. He gave a sympathetic whinny and nudged his big head into her side. Exhausted, her head throbbing, Shayna finally dared to look at herself in a cracked vanity mirror hanging from a nail next to Toni's stall.

She was covered in shit from head to toe; it was caked in a solid coat across her thighs, her chest, her sleeves. Stench rose around her like a cloud of carrion birds. Her injured eye seemed unable to stop weeping.

They were all Golems now, the Jews of Europe, forced to commit the same acts again and again like machines, free choice a dim memory. Automatically performing their duties until told to stop, easily replaced, their lives in the hands of the men who called themselves their Masters. The first helpless sobs burst from her throat.

Yossel was in the empty stall, watching her. Something moved in the blank face, struggled for life in the shadowy eyes. With the tip of his index finger, he traced the black and purple stripe that crossed the orbit of her eye and ran down her cheekbone.

He left the barn, moving quickly and with purpose. Her stink had chased away even him, she thought dully. But he returned with pails of hot water, sloughed them into a washtub he set in the straw. Steam curled lazily into the air as he pushed the shawl back from her face.

His long fingers worked the buttons of her coat, undressing her as if she were a child. He unpinned her hair, shaking out the plaits of her braid; freed, it splashed down her back like a puddle. He unfastened her sweater, then her skirt, letting them slip down around her ankles. With great care he untied her boots, sliding the muddy, hobnailed things from her feet as if they were holy relics. He went down on his knees to roll the thick wool stockings down her legs.

When she was stripped down to her underwear, he lifted her, carried her to the tin washtub. Dipping a cloth into the water, he washed gently around her blackened eye, rinsing away layers of blood and muck until she was clean.

With the washcloth, he massaged along the nape of her neck, down the length of her arms to the tips of her fingers. He made slow, lyrical circles on her back, sweeping the flannel over her belly, her thighs, her knees. Emotions dawned one by one across the planes of his face, shaped by the liturgy of flickering shadows. There was a ragged catch in his breath as he passed the cloth over the swelling of her breasts, down the slope of her bottom.

He made her close her eyes as he poured the last of the warm water over her head. Clean water ran in rivulets from her hair, down her body, draining away into the dirty straw.

Steam rose from her skin in the cold of the barn. Yossel towered over her, massive in the yellow light of the kerosene lamp.

"Shayna," he wondered in his dusty, disused voice. Putting his hands on either side of her face, he kissed her.

He laid her down in the hay. She didn't see when he took off his clothes. Then he was kneeling over her, his skin pale and smooth and smelling of green fields and mowed grass and children's games and summertime. His chest was so deep and broad, she couldn't reach all the way around him. She buried her face in the curve between his neck and shoulder and gripped him between her thighs, and for just a little while, everything was all right.

It was already dark when the soldiers came for Achim, the German farm boy. His chair made a scraping sound on the floor as he pushed away from the dinner table. A few minutes later he reappeared in the kitchen, dressed in his uniform. There was a moment of awkwardness, as if he wasn't sure which group he belonged to anymore. "All right, let's get going," he said sheepishly, gesturing with his rifle.

They were walking to Włodawa, where they would meet up with other Jews from the Lublinskie province. From there, they would get on trains for resettlement. No need to pack food or belongings; everything would be provided at their destination.

Shayna's fingers shook, making it difficult to button her coat. Fear bled through every thought, the way frigid air bled through the seams of her clothes as she shut the kitchen door behind her.

The nine occupants of the Mirsky mill joined the convocation of Jews waiting outside, collected from the many little towns nearby. They were quiet for such a large crowd. There must have been two hundred and fifty of them, shepherded by five soldiers with rifles. As they tramped down the road, Shayna peered back toward the place that had housed her family for generations, the mill a landmark in these parts, but it had already been swallowed up by darkness.

The barren fields along the road were a ghostly white in the moonlight. Dogs barked at them from each shuttered farmhouse they passed. Shayna had no illusions about where the Jews of the Lublinskie province were headed. She couldn't bear to look at Hersh, pale and frightened, his face sunk deep in the collar of his coat. If she had listened to him, they might have been safe in the forests with the partizans. His birthday was next month, he was going to be eighteen, a man. This year he had finally managed to coax forth a blond wisp of beard. Tears leaked continuously from her injured eye. All those tales of miracles and wonders, did they give him comfort now?

The column of Jews wavered, came to a halt. Word passed down the line. They were turning off the main road, into the Parczew Forest.

To her left, Yossel grew agitated. She could see him trying to glance ahead and then behind them, his breath gusting out in great plumes, like Toni when something disturbed him. She took his hand and wove her fingers through his, hoping to calm him. Hersh's jaw dropped open in surprise.

From somewhere far ahead they could hear commands shouted in German, a burst of caustic laughter, something that popped like a string of firecrackers. The guards looked relieved. German soldiers disliked the forests around Włodawa, rife with saboteurs and partizan activity.

A corona of green light dawned in the night sky. Shayna caught her breath. The aurora borealis was rarely seen this far south. For a few minutes, it undulated gently among the stars. All at once, the great green ribbon flushed red.

A frenzy of strange sounds discharged all around them. A muffled whine. The screeching of birds, wheeling through the trees just overhead. The roar of an attacking bear grew in volume, then receded as it bounded through the woods. Branches shook as some huge beast galloped past them, just out of sight.

The Jews muttered among themselves, the guards glanced at each other uneasily. All down the line, they held their rifles at the ready, swinging their flashlights wildly at the underbrush.

To Shayna, it seemed like an opportunity. She whispered to Hersh, "They're distracted. If we're going to make a run for it, now's the time. There are only five of them."

Hersh hissed furiously. "Are you crazy? He'll shoot us." He jerked his chin in the direction of the soldier guarding them.

"They're going to shoot us anyway," she said.

Sweat was making rings in the armpits of Achim's greatcoat. Breathing heavily, he swept his rifle at the woods, at the prisoners, at the woods again. In the flashlight's beam, Shayna could see that his eyes were round and fearful. She almost felt sorry for him.

Yossel followed Achim's movements with a troubled expression, his muscles jumping and straining under the skin. Perhaps he was frightened. Turning toward her, he laid his hand on the side of her face. "Shayna," he said in his gravelly voice.

All the tenderness in the world resided in that one word. He leaned over, rested his head on top of her shining hair. Then he separated himself from her and launched himself at their guard.

Taken by surprise, Achim wheeled around, bringing up

the barrel of his weapon. He managed to squeeze off a solitary burst before Yossel struck him to the ground. As if he were taking a toy from a child, Yossel took the gun out of his hands. With a single killing blow, Achim was dead.

Yossel climbed to his feet. He seemed to grow larger before her eyes, the muscles of his arms and legs and shoulders and chest rippling and swelling as if he were a giant in one of Hersh's stories. "Run," he said.

A line of bullets drilled across Yossel's chest as he hurled himself at the next guard. The Jews fled, scattering in every direction. Hersh grabbed Shayna's wrist and dragged her into a thicket, where they lay flat in the underbrush.

They heard men shouting and pleading in German, the staccato rat-a-tat-tat of gunfire. The creak of leather boots running frantically back and forth, fewer at each pass. The snap of breaking branches, or was that bone? The desperate cries all creatures make when they're wounded. Shayna buried her face in the shoulder of Hersh's coat, put her hands over her ears.

The shooting grew sporadic, then ceased altogether. Eventually, so did the moaning. Quiet settled over the woods, more dreadful than the sounds that had preceded it.

Men came fanning through the brush now, calling furtively in Yiddish and in Polish. Soldiers of a Jewish partizan unit, seeking survivors. A man in the uniform of the Soviet army helped Shayna to her feet, told her she was safe. They had to move quickly, he said. The forest would be swarming with German soldiers by morning.

"We have to go back," she told him urgently. "We left someone behind."

"We've all left someone behind," he said.

Her hair blowing wild around her face, she started back

through the forest. Swearing, he followed her back to the place where they had last seen Yossel.

They found the first German soldier hanging from the fork of a tree. Loops of his entrails dangled to the earth like ribbons.

The second one was missing his fingers. Another had lost his nose and both ears. The third soldier had his throat raked open. He had no face at all. The last one had no skin.

"What did this?" the partizan breathed in appalled awe.

They found Yossel on the riverbank. He lay on his back, half in and half out of the water, the current tugging gently at his body. Though his eyes were closed, his chest struggled up and down with the effort to breathe.

At the sound of Shayna's voice, his eyes flew open. With nerveless fingers, she prised open the flaps of his jacket, then sat back on her knees.

A dozen bullet wounds tracked in a curved line across his chest. There were more stitched across the flat stomach she had kissed, stab wounds where the bayonets had found him. She couldn't believe he was still alive.

Yossel was looking up at her. His face was knotted with pain. Shayna took his hand. When he breathed, it made a wet, syrupy sound. "Shema," he whispered.

"Shayna?" she said, with a calm she did not feel. Tears were blurring her vision. "I'm right here."

"Shema," he begged. With an effort that was painful to watch, his hand crept slowly up to his chest.

Beside her, Hersh drew a sharp breath. "The Shema," he blurted. "He wants you to remove the Shema." His voice was unsteady. "The Golem can die only when his mission is complete. When the rabbi removes the name of God from over his heart."

Inside his jacket, she found a pocket. Her fingers closed around a tiny scroll of paper. The Shema Yisrael, washed in blood.

She put the scroll in his hand, curled his fingers around it. Gratefully, he smiled. He turned his head a little so that it rested against her lap, and then he was still.

The town of Żuków, located halfway between the Parczew Forest and the Bug River, has a thriving tourist industry. At least once a week in the warm months, a taxi arrives at the hotel, bearing American Jews who are seeking their Holocaust roots, or a family whose grandparents came from Żuków before the war, or college students with grants to study the partizan activity that flourished in the area.

Żuków even has its own mascot, the Golem of Żuków. A bronze statue of the Golem occupies a place of honor in the center of town. You can buy a small reproduction cast in tin, or a picture postcard of the statue at sunset, at any of the stores and kiosks around the square. The partizans who witnessed the results of the Golem's rage carried his story throughout the region.

Since no photograph of the Golem exists, the sculptor leaned heavily on artistic license, carving him with a huge barrel chest, short legs, and exaggerated, dull-witted features. On the pedestal, a Stalinist-era plaque describes in Polish and bad English how the Golem of Żuków saved two hundred and fifty innocent civilians from death at the hands of the fascist enemy forces in the winter of 1942.

There is a hotel named after the Golem, and a café. For a modest fee, a taxi driver will drive you to the Mirsky mill, now nationalized, or to the riverbank, where a shrine sprang up to honor his memory.

After the fall of the Soviet Union, new records surfaced that shed some light on the identity of the so-called Golem. Late in October 1942, the Jews of the town of Lubień were herded into the forest, where they were stripped, machine-gunned, and buried in a mass grave, a story tragically familiar throughout Eastern Europe. By some miracle, the barrage of bullets missed David Turno, oldest son of the rabbi of Turno, a respected authority on the Maharal of Prague. Later that night, he must have dug himself out of the tangle of bodies, physically unharmed but mentally shattered, and wandered through the freezing darkness until, too tired to go any farther, he stumbled into the home of Shayna and Hersh Mirsky. One of the partizans who buried him was from Turno. He recognized the rabbi's son.

In 1990 a reporter tracked down Shayna Mirsky, now the owner of a kosher bakery in Chicago, Illinois, looking for an interesting angle. All this time, he asked her, did she honestly believe she'd been saved by a Golem? Did she really believe in magic?

Obviously, she had given it some thought over the years.

"Love is a kind of magic, too, isn't it?" she said before hanging up the phone.

# A DECENT MAN

He arrived in Włodowa on a wet Wednesday in April, at the start of a muddy and riotous spring. Seven months earlier, Russia and Germany had divided Poland between themselves, and his first job was to negotiate the movement of Russian, Ukrainian, Volkdeutsch, and Polish farmers across newly drawn borders to their proper territories. Willy Reinhart was very good at this, earning praise from all sides.

Within a year, he was the Reich Regional Commissioner of Agricultural Products and Services, administering over the districts, towns, and villages of the Włodawa sector. He was directed to take up residence in Adampol Palace, a white baroque villa belonging to the Earl of Zamoyski, recently relocated to Paris. Nestled in the heart of an ancient wood, the villa had been used as a hunting lodge; the earl had invited aristocratic acquaintances from all over Europe to shoot red deer, elk, boar, bison, wolves, lynx, and bears.

A starchy, thin-lipped wife arrived from Breslau with two dark-haired boys and was duly installed in the castle. It wasn't long before the trunks were loaded back into the wagon, the wife and boys deposited at the station. No one could explain this mysterious turn of events—until the cook's beautiful daughter was spotted riding around town in the back of Reinhart's black Mercedes.

His first act as Regional Commissioner was to summon the estate manager to his office. The manager was a frightened young man in his twenties, with a raft of sandy brown hair and a prominent Adam's apple that bobbed up and down whenever he swallowed hard, which he was doing now. His thin, spidery fingers roved nervously over the account books he was carrying. Obviously, he was going to be shot. So many Poles in positions of responsibility had already been killed, he seemed to expect that it was his turn.

Reinhart was opening and shutting the drawers of an eighteenth-century desk with an Italian marble top. Instead of the customary SS black, he was attired in an umber suit with pinstripes. His tie was a satiny bottle green topped by a Windsor knot, his shoes polished a deep, glassy obsidian.

Finally, he found what he was looking for, a wooden box of cigars. With a little sigh of contentment, he put one between his lips, held a match to the tip until it glowed, then leaned back into the leather cushions of a Louis XIV chair. When he was almost completely enveloped by a cloud of blue smoke, he spoke. "What's your name?"

"Drogalski." The manager's voice was shaking.

"Drogalski," said Reinhart, firmly taking hold of the name. "I have a little job for you. I want you to make me a list of the craftsmen around here. But Drogalski, one moment, please. I want only the best. The best tinsmith, the best blacksmith, the best stonecutter, the best carpenter, the best tailor, the best miller, the best saddlemaker, the best shoemaker . . . I'm very easy to please, you see, Drogalski. All I want is the best of everything."

When Reinhart smiled, all the witnesses would later

agree, you believed exactly what he said, that everything
was going to be all right. The corners of the sensual mouth
angled up, the green eyes squeezed down to a jovial glint.
The smile twinkled encouragement: *Come on, it's not so bad.*
The smile promised that it knew your secrets and would
keep them safe. The smile wanted to tell you a dirty joke, to
buy you a drink, it wanted you to stop worrying. The smile
threw its arm around your shoulders and called you friend.

Reinhart walked him to the door of the office, a hand on
his shoulder. "You married? Wife, children?"

Drogalski replied reluctantly. "Wife. One daughter."

"I'll have to meet them," Reinhart said. Another smile
creased the handsome friendly face. "And one more thing,
Drogalski. Stop looking so anxious. You're making me
worry. Everything is going to be fine."

As Drogalski compiled his list, he told the men whose
names were on it: *This German, Reinhart. He seems to be a
decent man.*

The Gestapo was quartered on Staromiejska Street, on the
market square. Reinhart was directed to an inner courtyard,
where he found the police chief, an Obersturmführer Otto
Streibel, standing in a sea of Jews, reading from a typewritten list. As he called out names, men moved to the right or
to the left.

Streibel looked up from his clipboard just long enough
to put the fear of God into him. A youngish man, perhaps
in his middle thirties, who took himself very seriously, with
hair shaved to a line above his ears and remote, mirthless
eyes. "This is impossible," he grumbled irritably. "I can't even
pronounce half of these names."

Reinhart introduced himself. He never went anywhere empty-handed; a case of Hennessey was unloaded from the trunk of his car. It was acknowledged with a flicker of pleasure across the stony face. If you didn't have business with the Gestapo, it was good policy to stay as far away from them as possible. If you did have business with them, it was wise to bring gifts.

Streibel granted him a cold, professional smile. "We're having a little get-together, a Beerfest, at the SS club later tonight," he said. "Your driver will know where it is."

Reinhart nodded enthusiastically. Of course he would be there. Had he met anyone else in the local administrative hierarchy yet, Falkner, Rohlfe, Haas, Gruber? No, but he certainly looked forward to it. Did he like to hunt? They often held shooting events, and they hoped to use the Adampol Palace as an unofficial officers' hunting lodge. Marvelous, a splendid idea, he would be happy to host, nothing would give him more pleasure.

The meeting over, Reinhart strode back through the corridor. A blond secretary carrying a set of files sashayed toward him, her breasts jiggling perkily under the blouse of her uniform. Just the way he preferred his ladies, with a tiny waist he could put his hands around, a curvaceous behind, long legs. She smiled as she drew near, he smiled back. Reinhart liked women. No, that wasn't entirely true—Reinhart *loved* women, he adored them, he worshipped them. His first sexual experience had come when he was just fifteen, with the mother of one of his school friends.

One of Blondie's files went swishing to the floor. Was she making a pass at him? Despite her anxious clucking, he dropped chivalrously to one knee to pick up the scattered papers, taking the opportunity to enjoy a closer look at her rounded calves. She smiled and murmured her thanks, pushed a strand of hair back behind one pink ear. Reinhart continued on his way, stealing a glance over his shoulder to see if she was still watching him. That was why he nearly tripped over the man sitting to the right of the duty officer's desk.

Reinhart almost apologized, the words already escaping his lips, when he noticed the white armband on his jacket. Dejectedly, the man raised his head. He looked miserable. Who would look any different, confined to a bench in the Sicherheitspolizei headquarters? The Jew's eyes were as light as the sky, set deep in a sunburned, leathery face with a square, determined chin. A strong, honest face, a face you could trust. Reinhart wondered what he was in for.

Quickly, the Jew dropped his gaze back to the floor. Looking directly at the Deutschen could get you beaten, maybe killed. With a glum sigh, the Jew removed his cap and furrowed his fingers through his hair, which was a sunny orange.

A woman flung open the door to the building. Her eyes were fierce and black under eyebrows drawn down together in an angry vee. Like the other village women, she wore a flowered apron over a heavy shapeless skirt, her hair swathed in a long shawl. In her fist, she clutched a blackened frying pan. "There you are!" she shouted, marching up to the man on the bench. "So it's true! They said I would find you here!"

To Reinhart's immense surprise, she began flailing the frying pan at the red-haired man's head and shoulders. "You *bastard!* I've been looking for you everywhere!" *Thwack.* "Where have you been?" *Thwack, thwack!* "Never came home last night!" *Thwack!* A good one to the side of the head.

One by one, the German administrators turned their heads to watch the show. "Do you have a girlfriend? Tell me, you louse, you lazy bum! Where were you all night? You were drinking with that shit-for-brains Jablonski, weren't you? When the kids are hungry and begging for bread!" *Thwack, thwack, thwack, thwack!*

By now, the place rang with laughter. People stuck their heads out of their offices to see what the commotion was about. The man held his arms over his head, beseeching her to stop, pleading for forgiveness, babbling excuses, swearing to God and the devil and anyone else who was listening that he would never do it again. The furious little babushka gave her husband another corrective blow with the frying pan, grabbed him by the earlobe, and dragged him out the front door. The German officers shouted encouragement: *You tell him, little mother, again! Give it to him good!*

Reinhart glanced hopefully down the corridor at the secretary, her red lips parted in a lovely blond laugh. He took the opportunity to ask for her name, and would she be interested in seeing his castle. Of course she said yes; he would send his driver for her later.

The show was over, work was waiting for him back at the castle. He pushed open the door to the outside. It was a fine May morning, the cherry trees were in bloom, silky pink petals swirled around the cobblestones at his feet. He stopped to admire his sleek new automobile, idling at the curb. It was market day. He could smell horse manure, rotting vegetables, smoke. The square was packed with wagons, tables and booths, tradesmen sharpening knives and scissors, selling pots and pans, old clothes, live chickens. Merchants hawked their wares, villagers milled around tables, voices were raised in haggling. Reinhart smiled. He'd grown up near a town like this, and though he'd left it to attend university in Breslau, it still felt like home.

That was when he spotted them, the angry little wife and the hapless workman, making their way through the vendors. At the other side of the square they halted, dared a glance behind them in the direction of the Gestapo Headquarters. When they saw that no one had followed them, the wife dropped the frying pan on the cobblestones, and the couple embraced. They stayed that way for a long moment, arms wound tightly around each other, bodies pressed together as if they were dancing. Then the man took his wife's face between his two hands and kissed her hard on the lips. After that, they melted into the crowds flowing down Rynek Street, and out of his sight.

The next time he saw the red-haired workman, Reinhart was standing in his shop.

Reinhart was in love. He had just purchased, for a song, the girl of his dreams, a Polish Arabian mare by the name of Fallada. A feminine, sweetly arched neck, a tapering, dish-shaped face with a muzzle no bigger than a teacup, eyes that were the icy blue of a skating pond, and a luxuriant coat the color of bittersweet chocolate. But it was her mane and tail that made people stop and stare: long and wavy, with strokes of mahogany, ochre, copper, and caramel, like a painting by a Renaissance master. She had a pedigree as long as his arm, the horse trader assured him; her parentage could be documented as far back as 1813, to the great stallion Bairactar.

He would need a new saddle, of course. An exquisite beauty like Fallada deserved it, the way a bride deserves a white dress. He was directed to a man named Soroka, the best leather artisan in the region, according to Drogalski, with a shop on the market square across from the grand old synagogue, which had been refurbished by the current administration into a stable.

A bell tinkled when he opened the door. "One moment, please," a voice called from the back room.

The room smelled like leather and neat's-foot oil. Reinhart inhaled happily. His father was a farmer, and his grandfather before him. Not a peasant attached to some nobleman's turnip field, but a real *Landwirt*, a man with his own farm. Millions of cabbages had paid with their heads for little Willy's university education, where he was supposed to study hard and make something better of himself. He'd wanted to pursue architecture; his father had wanted him to become a judge. He became a lawyer, arbitrating settlements between warring heirs, petty criminals and the state, men and their wives. The money was good, it had won him a pretty bourgeois wife with a small inheritance, but he was bored beyond belief. He'd never really purged the land from his soul. When war came, and with it, the offer of a Party job arbitrating between farmers and the Reich, he jumped at it.

A man came to the counter, wiping his hands on a rag. With a shock of recognition, Reinhart realized that he knew him. "Remember me?" he said with a smile. "Last week I nearly fell into your lap. I should have bought you dinner first."

Soroka froze. Reinhart could practically hear the questions rocketing through his brain. *What does he mean by that? Should I run? Should I lie? Will he turn me in? What should I do?* A stack of hides lay on the table. Reinhart ran his fingers appreciatively over the smooth leather. "What did they want you for, anyway?"

The saddlemaker lifted his shoulders in a shrug. "Who knows. My name was on a list."

"I'm Willy Reinhart," he said. "Regional Commissioner for Agricultural Products and Services. My manager tells me you're the best saddlemaker in all of Poland."

"Thank you, Herr Kommandant, he's too generous." He hesitated. "Hahnemeier told you that?"

"No, my manager is Jozef Drogalski. Who's Hahnemeier?"

"He was the manager under the earl."

"Oh, him. Volkdeutscher. Used to be a beet farmer. Fired for stealing, I heard."

Soroka pursed his lips and nodded. Reinhart had the sense that he was being appraised, evaluated.

"Let's have a look at your horse."

He walked Fallada into the yard behind the house. Soroka unbuckled the saddle, turned it over to inspect the padding, then placed it carefully on the table. Next he ran his fingers expertly over the dip in her back. The horse flinched. A whinny of pain escaped her. Angered, Reinhart felt his fists clench.

But Soroka was grimly shaking his head. "That's what I thought. Feel here." He directed the commandant's hand to a place on the horse's back. "And here."

The horse trembled at his touch, flicked her gorgeous tail. Under his fingertips, he could feel scabs, welts, raw skin. Bearing his weight must have been torturous, but she never showed it. He felt ashamed. "Poor girl. I didn't know."

"Of course you didn't know." The saddlemaker's lips were pressed together in a thin line. He rummaged in his pocket, found a sugar cube. Fallada nosed daintily into the palm of his hand like the fine, highborn lady that she was. While Soroka stroked her neck, he murmured to her in Polish, and she dipped her pretty head against his chest. "Before you, she belonged to Forster." He muttered in an undertone, "He always knows better than everyone else."

A shockingly incautious statement. A Jew could be shot for this, the crime of being critical of a German. He looked curiously at the saddlemaker. Was it deliberate? Was it a trick, a trap?

*No*, he decided. The man was just being honest. Reinhart understood that he had found something of value, something that was in short supply here, a man who would say what he really thought.

"Anshel!" called the saddlemaker.

A boy bounced through the door. Resting his chin on the counter, he gazed with wonder at the stranger in his father's shop, at his clean-shaven handsome face, his unimaginably fine coat, his hat with the feather in it.

Soroka leaned over, spoke in Jewish. The boy nodded and skipped back into the other room. Moments later, he returned with a glass jar.

"Go on," his father persisted, nudging him forward. Hesitantly, the boy put the jar into Reinhart's hands.

"Let her rest for a few weeks, no riding, nothing on her back. Rub this into her sores every day." Curious, Reinhart unscrewed the top, grimacing when the smell hit his nostrils. The saddlemaker chuckled. "I know. *Es shtinkt!* But it works. Don't worry, Herr Kommandant, she'll be fine."

The German officer reached down, clapped the boy's thin shoulder. "Call me Reinhart," he said.


"No!" she gasped. "*Not yet!*"

With her long thighs wrapped around his hips, Petra was rocking fervently up and down, her eyes closed, like she was having a religious experience. Only when she had squealed to a finish, collapsed on top of him did he take his turn.

Afterward, they shared a cigarette. With one finger, she made slow circles in the scruffy hair on his chest. He crinkled a smile, slapped her curvy bottom. "How about getting us a drink?"

She threw aside the covers. He admired her creamy skin, the mole on her right shoulder, as she walked naked to the dresser. Pretty Petra, his marvelous chef's marvelous daughter. Just nineteen years old, she was the village beauty, an angel in the kitchen, and a fury in the bed. With little formal education, she knew three languages and was delightful in each one.

He linked his hands behind his head and watched smoke rise in lazy rings over his head. Women always did as he asked, he was thinking. Men, too, though what he asked from them was more complicated and infinitely more risky than climbing into his bed.

Except for a certain knack with the ladies, he'd led a fairly ordinary life: a good student but not spectacular, decent enough on the playing fields but not a standout. After Germany and Russia blew through Poland, borders shifted, farmers on all sides had to leave their ancestral homes, and this was where he really shone. The transition went smoothly. The farmers thought he was fair. Men in power said nice things about him.

Publicly, he protested that he was just doing his job. Privately, he was immensely proud of his efforts on behalf of his country. He saw himself as a kind of ambassador; in his own small way, he was bringing the German sense of justice and fair play to a dangerously uncivilized part of the world.

In November he witnessed his first massacre.

It was almost incidental. A meeting with a local SS honcho, like a hundred other meetings. Only this one was scheduled in the woods outside of town. A routine matter; could Reinhart fix it so that Farmer X, a cousin to the SS man, received the land of Farmer Y, who had, shall we say, moved elsewhere. Also, could he join the major and his wife for a dinner party at their villa.

Reinhart tried to focus on the officer's moving lips. In the near distance, among the slim white trunks of birch trees, wave after wave of naked human beings filed into a pit, knelt on the bodies of their neighbors, and were shot in the back of the neck. Bearded old sages passed him, young girls trying to hide their breasts, mothers gripping toddlers by the hand. The shooters were German soldiers.

Later that night, Reinhart had sat with the windows open, smoking cigarette after cigarette, trying to vanquish the smell of death that filled his nostrils. Was it in his hair? His clothes? It wouldn't go away even after he'd bathed.

Reinhart had no stomach for the Party's racial rants. He'd fought as an infantryman in the last war, where he'd seen enough bodies, blown up, bayoneted, or riddled with bullets, to know for certain that in Death's opinion, all men were created equal. He'd always known Jews, and as far as he could see, they were no different from anybody else. Back home, there had been Jakobowitz the livestock trader, whom his father treated like a brother. At school, there'd been Lemberg, who let him copy his notes, Perlmutter, who listened to his girl troubles and made him laugh.

There were places, secret places, where people who found fault with National Socialist policies were taken. Willy Reinhart was the son of a farmer and the grandson of a farmer. He knew the value of keeping his mouth shut and fixing his gaze on the horizon. Still, the next day he asked his secretary for a map. In the privacy of his own bedroom, he drew a tiny red X over the Bydgoszcz woods.

After that, his rise was of the sort commonly described as meteoric. As crosses metastasized over the face of his map, colonels and generals sought out his company, laughed at his jokes, competed furiously to fulfill his requests. It didn't matter what he wanted—more workers, more wagons, an airy apartment in the best neighborhood, a vacation villa on a lake, placement in elite schools for the boys—he was never refused. It was like he had some kind of power over them.

Within months, he was the lord of Adampol Palace. Ruler over a Polish fiefdom, he had a thousand laborers at his command, and his word was law. Behind his back, people whispered that he was a sorcerer, or perhaps Hans Frank's brother-in-law. As if being related to the German governor of Poland could be the only explanation for his dazzling good fortune.

He rolled onto his side, stubbed out the cigarette. The truth was too mundane for them, he thought, that he was just good at his job. Or was it a gift from the angels?

Petra returned from her quest. As she put his glass down on the bedside table, her shirt gapped open, revealing one perfect pear-shaped breast. Though it was so soon after the last time, he felt the stirrings of desire. He slipped his hand inside her shirt, rubbed his thumb over her nipple. She closed her eyes and caught her lower lip in her teeth.

When he reached up to turn off the lamp, she stopped him. "No," she breathed. "Leave it on. I want to see *everything*."

\* \* \*

"Excuse me, sir," said a mournful voice from the doorway.

He blinked, rubbed his eyes. He'd nodded off over the ledger that tracked each farmer's assets, from how many chickens they kept down to the last milk cow. He put his finger on a column of numbers so that he wouldn't lose his place. "What is it, Jozef?"

"The tailor, Hammer. He finished repairing the uniforms."

"How do they look?"

"Perfect. Like new."

"Wonderful. Was his wife there? How did she look today?"

"She was wearing the green dress. The one with polka dots."

"Ah, Dora. You're killing me. Anything else?"

"Yes. We need more workers to bring in the wheat harvest. An experienced crew, please."

"I'll tell Haas. He's the new Chief of Employment."

"One more thing. Mirsky delivered the flour earlier than expected."

"Good. Excellent. What else?"

"Jasinski. He says his cow died."

"Hm. Too bad. Tell him he has to bring it here before we can mark it off."

The pallid face registered horror. "You want him to bring his dead cow? Here?"

"Tell him to leave it around the back. Near the stable or the rabbit hutches. It stinks so much already, a dead cow can only be an improvement."

"Excuse me, Reinhart. But what do we want with Jasinski's dead cow?"

"How can I be sure it's really dead? For all I know, he

sold it on the black market." He went back to the books. "By
the way, you're doing a spectacular job with these ledgers.
I could never be this organized. Take an extra bag of sugar.
Go on, you've earned it. Tell Manya it's from me."

"Speaking of Manya, she sent you something special."

Reinhart liked Drogalski's wife, a pale, freckled farm girl
with apple cheeks and straight, sandy hair. She came now
and then to bring the manager his lunch, accompanied by a
cherubic flaxen-haired daughter. "What is it?"

"*Topielec.* Poppy-seed cake. Old family recipe."

"How did she know? My grandmother used to make
poppy-seed cake. Thank her for me, will you? And stop
looking so anxious. You're making *me* worry." This was a
running joke between them, but today the manager wasn't
smiling. "Come on, what is it? Money trouble? Girl trouble?
Your secret's safe with me."

The manager's prominent Adam's apple bobbed up
and down. He chose his words with care. "You remember
Hahnemeier?"

"Sure. Volkdeutscher. Used to be the manager. Fired for
stealing."

Drogalski shifted from one muddy boot to the other.
"Well, since I started here, he's been talking to people. To
our farmers. When I see him, I tell him to leave. He says he's
just visiting friends. But what I'm hearing, it's worrying me."

Reinhart massaged his forehead. After spending a whole
day in the manager's close office, reviewing ledger entries
scrawled in a neat, upright hand, he had a piercing headache. Also, there'd been the letter from his wife today; she
wanted him to come back to Breslau for summer vacation,
the boys hadn't seen him in months, they needed to spend
time together as a family, etc. etc. "What are you hearing?"

"Well . . ." He looked uneasy. "For years, Hahnemeier lied to the earl about how much the estate was bringing in. He would say this farmer had a bad year or that one came up short. Then he would sell the difference and pocket the profits. When I started here, that was the end of his business."

"What does that have to do with you? He was a bad thief, he got caught. He should have been more careful."

The Adam's apple bobbed up and down a couple of times before he spoke. "He says I'm taking food out of his children's mouths. He says something might happen to make me sorry I ever met him."

Reinhart burst out laughing. Drogalski looked startled. Affectionately, he squeezed the younger man's shoulder. "Do you really think he would dare to hurt a hair on your head, you, Jozef Drogalski, manager of Adampol Palace, assistant to the Reich Regional Commissioner for Agricultural Products and Services? Come on. He'd spend the rest of his life in jail, if he wasn't shot! Sounds like tavern talk to me. He's just blowing off steam, trying to make himself look important. Now, cheer up. Have some of your wife's poppy-seed cake. And explain to me what happened to the rest of Walczak's potatoes."

His vacation was planned for July, it couldn't be helped. He left Adampol with a heavy heart, turning around in the backseat of the Mercedes for a last glimpse of his glorious castle before it disappeared behind the curtain of trees, just in time to see Petra wave goodbye to him, heartbreakingly beautiful in the yellow square of light that was their bedroom window.

At the lake, he parceled out gifts, swam with the boys, lay in the sun, made dutiful, docile missionary love to his wife.

While the boys quarreled, his wife bombarded him with mind-bendingly dull trivia; the neighbors were impossible boors, the cook had purchased the wrong roast, they were invited to Judge Koenigwasser's for a luncheon, she volunteers with Winter Help, he's a big shot in the local civil administration. In his heart, he was riding through his forest on the back of his beautiful Polish Arabian mare, Fallada.

On the fifth day, he received an official-looking telegram. Lotte, watching him read it, saw him pale and lean against a wall for support. Then he summoned the car, bid his family a hasty farewell, and sped back to Włodawa.

"How did he die?"

The doctor bent over the body. "Clearly, he was badly beaten. You can see for yourself, there's massive bruising on the chest and stomach." He pointed to the blackened marks mottling the thin, sunken chest. "And, of course, there's the large wound here, on the side of the head. It looks to me like he was hit with a shovel."

For a moment the only sound in the room was the accusatory buzz of busy flies. Someone thought to bring in an electric fan; the reek of decomposition in the small hot room was almost overwhelming. By the time Reinhart had the body exhumed, it had been in the earth for a week.

With shaking hands, he took out his handkerchief, held it over his nose and mouth. He'd been wrong about Hahnemeier, terribly, irredeemably wrong. The Volkdeutscher had confronted Drogalski on Sunday, right after church. In front of his wife and daughter and a whole host of farmers, he'd promised to kill him in such a way that no one would ever know, and no one would ever find the body.

The doctor was examining the wound, black with earth and clotted blood. "The trauma to the head is bad, but it wasn't enough to kill him. See his hands, the way he's holding them over his chest?" He sighed, stroked his little pointed beard. "I'm sorry to have to tell you this, Kommandant. These men, whoever they were . . . in my opinion, when they buried him, your friend was still alive."

It was late in the afternoon when Reinhart's Mercedes pulled up in front of Soroka's shop. The worst heat of the day was over, the sunset was painting the gables of the Great Synagogue across the street in shades of jade and tangerine. Emerging from the back of his car into Włodawa's market square, Reinhart felt like he was swimming through swamp water.

He dragged off his hat, wiped the sweat from his brow with the back of his arm. He should eat something, he thought dully. When was the last time he'd eaten? He didn't remember. The droning of flies in the saddlemaker's yard reminded him of Drogalski's corpse, and he was almost sick right there on the doorstep.

Inside, an adolescent girl was rocking the baby. He was crying, a thin, reedy sound. She rattled a halter trimmed with sleigh bells, but it wasn't working. Even in his current state of distress, Reinhart still noted her soft-looking mouth, her high breasts, the simmering mass of hair.

"Why is he crying?" he said.

"He's sick."

"Maybe he should see a doctor." Reinhart took a step toward her. She paled and clutched the baby tighter. He knew why. There were too many terrible stories about SS men and crying babies. "Kitchy-kitchy-koo," he crooned.

The baby gripped the proffered finger in his little fist and regarded him with dark, serious eyes.

"He's warm," he said to her. "Where's your father?"

She was so surprised that she forgot to answer. Soroka materialized in the doorway, wiping his hands on a rag.

"Haskel," said Reinhart. He was having trouble controlling his voice. "You probably already know. My manager, Drogalski . . . someone killed him."

The saddlemaker's eyes were red. "His father is one of my oldest friends," he muttered. "Jozef was a good boy. A very good boy."

They were quiet for a moment. Reinhart spoke first. "I know you, Haskel," he said heavily. "People tell you things. What do you know about this?"

Soroka hesitated, then bobbed his head. A forester, going through the woods on his regular rounds, had seen it all from start to finish. Drogalski, already bleeding as he stumbled over roots and stones. Drogalski, sobbing as he dug his own grave. Drogalski, on his knees, begging for his life. And right behind him, Hahnemeier, drinking and laughing, delivering the final blow.

Perspiration rained down Reinhart's back, and the world began to go out from under him. One Soroka fetched him a chair, another Soroka laid a cold wet cloth on his forehead, a third Soroka passed him a glass of something clear and fortifying.

"He needs air," someone murmured, and opened the shutters with a bang. A shaft of light streamed into the room. It fell across his face, warming one side with an amber glow.

He had to save them. All of them. His workers, their families, their friends, people he'd never met and would never know. Too many decent, unremarkable folks were losing their lives, destroyed by men committing unforgivable crimes in the name of his Fatherland. Why the war in Eastern Europe turned men into monsters, he couldn't say. What he did know was this: Someday the frenzy of killing would end, and the rule of law would return. Until then, Willy Reinhart would save everyone he could.

The baby started to fuss again. Soroka's wife took him in her arms, clucking to him in a silly singsong voice. But nothing worked; the little red face was screwed up tight, and his tiny fists were white-knuckled as they pumped the air.

A memory. His son Matthias, the sweet smell of him after a bath, swaddled in a downy yellow quilt. "May I try?" said Reinhart. "I used to do this with my boys."

Gently, she deposited the youngest Soroka on his shoulder. The bramble of soft black curls tickled Reinhart's nose. After a very few pats, the baby gave a loud, satisfying *braaaaaaaaaap!* His eyes flew wide open, as if he had surprised himself.

He didn't know who started laughing first, maybe it was him. But then Haskel joined in, and then everyone was doing it, they laughed and laughed until the force from their laughter shook the walls, rattled the dishes in the cupboard, pushed against the ceiling.

Carefully, he handed the wiggling baby to the lovely daughter. Got to his feet, passed his hand over his hair, dropped his hat back on his head. Tipped it just so. And then he climbed back into his Mercedes and drove away.


There was no trial. The police went to Hahnemeier's house, picked him up, and threw him in jail. After two weeks, he was out again.

Reinhart had to shout over the orchestra. "Perhaps there's been a mistake. This man is a murderer."

"Really? They gave him two whole weeks?" Streibel burst out laughing, pink and effusive on Reinhart's brandy. "Come on, Willy, he killed a fucking *Polack!*"

In the ballroom of Reinhart's castle, corks popped, jewels sparkled, women laughed, couples danced. Someone's girl sang sentimental pop songs. There was a buffet of boar and venison, goose and wood pigeon, shot earlier in the day by the guests and prepared to perfection by the palace chef. On all counts, the hunting party was a smashing success. They'd bagged two boars, a bear, a timber wolf, an enormous stag with antlers half the width of the room, an entire aviary of game birds. More important, his beloved Fallada had performed magnificently, sure-footed, always a lady, soaring effortlessly over gates and streams. Soroka's saddle was such a sublime fit, it was as if horse and rider were fused into one supreme mythical being.

"Who painted those murals?" said Haas. Thorough and humorless, behind his back the others called him "The General of the Jews."

"I don't know. It was done in the twenties, I think."

"I could use a good housepainter," he mused. "I'd like something like that in my dining room."

"Are you married, Haas?" asked Falkner from across the table. Younger than Reinhart by ten years, he had a topknot of dark hair, a pale elongated face, and soft, surprised-looking brown eyes. He was the brains behind the drainage project, a massive network of scaffolding and canals meant to turn the swamps around Włodawa into fields of waving grain.

"Yes. To the most wonderful woman in the world. She's joining me here in two weeks." Haas's eyes shone.

"A lovely idea," agreed Lina Falkner. Her voice was polite, but her grave gaze lingered disapprovingly on Petra's décolletage. She didn't approve of the way Reinhart flaunted his mistress in public.

A fire crackled in a medieval fireplace big enough to roast an ox on a spit. Reinhart drew a gold cigarette case from his dinner jacket, lit one for himself and one for Petra. She was a knockout tonight in a bouffant of silver silk the color of moonlight.

There would be no justice for Drogalski, he knew that now, not as long as the Nazis were in power. To replace him, Soroka recommended a big, steady fellow named Wysocki to oversee the farming, and a Jew named Friedman to handle the books. Reinhart liked the Poles, and he could tell they liked him. Conscientious, respectful, hardworking people, a thousand times more honest and dependable than the psychotic pigs he served with. After the atrocities he'd witnessed, he had no illusions left about the superiority of the German character.

Just yesterday he'd visited the gristmill, a real jewel of a business, a marvel of efficiency, run by an orphaned-brother-and-sister team. The boy, so young he didn't have a beard yet, told a story he'd heard last at his grandmother's knee. One dark and stormy night, a midwife was called to deliver a demon's baby. An incredible coincidence, the demon's wife turned out to be a stray tabby cat the midwife had been feeding. Though the demon's cave sparkled with gold and jewels, the cat advised the frightened woman not to accept any food or presents no matter how hard she was pressed. Taking the cat's advice, she was led safely home. Upon waking the next morning, she found piles of treasure heaped in every corner.

Reinhart glanced at the inlaid long-case clock next to the fireplace. It was a hundred years old, at least, maybe two, from the now-defunct pharmacy of a certain Pinchas Grinstein. By the time he asked Haas if he could have the pharmacist installed at his castle, Grinstein had already been shot for some infraction. But Reinhart's eye had fallen upon the clock, and later that day he'd sent a wagon for it. It wasn't stealing if the owner was already dead, was it?

The table laughed at something Hackendahl said. "*Aktzia*," Gruber was shouting to Haas across the table, but his eyes were following a bosomy, honey-haired girl around the room. "Saturday morning."

Reinhart frowned. "What *Aktzia*?" He leaned forward. "What about my workers? We're in the middle of hay season. Without them, it's going to rot in the fields. Nobody told me anything about any *Aktzia*."

Gruber, his eyes still on the bosomy blonde, put a fat, conciliatory hand on his arm. "All right, all right, don't get your panties in a bunch. They're not taking essential workers this time. Just children, twelve and under. Now, will someone pour me another brandy?"

The solution was obvious. He had a castle. The castle had stables, a henhouse, storehouses, workshops, sleeping quarters for seasonal field hands. His Jewish workers could stay with him until the current madness blew over.

The trick was getting the wives and children to Adampol. Technically, what he was doing was hiding Jews, and everyone knew how that ended, a bullet in your brain, a trip to a concentration camp for anyone you'd ever said hello to. He couldn't just have them waltz past Streibel's men, saying,

"Excuse me, can you let us through, please, we've been invited to stay at Reinhart's castle."

Alone in his office, under a painting of an eighteenth-century Zamoyski ancestor surrounded by hunting dogs, he buried his head in his hands. It was already Thursday; he had only one more day to come up with a plan.

Images of Soroka's daughter kept interrupting him. Could it be a coincidence that her hair, which she kept in a long thick braid that reached to her waist, had all the same autumnal tones as Fallada's tail, mahogany, bronze, a rusty gold? He shook his head, irritated with himself. This was getting him nowhere. He pushed himself away from his desk and went to the window.

From his corner office, he could look out to the front of the house, at the vast trimmed expanse of lawn that rolled on and on until it disappeared into a fringe of old-growth forest. Most important, he had a view of the drive, the better to see which farmer was coming in with his produce—or which Party big shot might be paying him an unexpected visit.

The castle looked its best in late afternoon, he thought, when the sun washed her white pavilions in gold. Rising squarely from the flat Polish landscape, the baroque facade was dramatic, spectacular, complete with towers, a crenellated turret, wide sandstone steps leading up to a domed portico ringed with enormous ionic columns. A flagstone walkway meandered all the way around the courtyard, with exotic ornamental trees carved into geometric shapes. On sunny mornings, he liked to breakfast on the terrace, where potted geraniums were set at precise intervals atop the balustrade.

His own Shangri-la, insulated from the insanity consuming the civilized world . . . except for the smell that floated in sometimes from the camp at Sobibór, only six kilometers away, a smell that didn't belong among the fields, the farmers, the forests, and the plowed earth.

A dusty brown mule lurched into view, hauling a wagon up the long drive. A delivery of hides. He didn't recognize the driver, the tanner must have hired a new man. Wysocki was already out there, directing him around the back. The hides were for Soroka. They were keeping him busy with a flurry of new saddle commissions (the Nazi officers loved their horses), a set of wagon harnesses for Falkner's drainage project, and oh yes, one of the Volkdeutscher farmers wanted his carriage reupholstered.

Reinhart's gaze settled on the wagon, broad, deep, and wide, stacked high with cowhides. His brows contracted in thought. And then he smiled.

It wasn't bad, it wasn't bad at all, he thought, pacing meditatively through the muddy lane to the stable. Having all his workers together in one place offered a distinct advantage. He didn't have to worry about the Gestapo accidentally rounding them up while he was away on business, for instance, which happened once to Falkner.

Here in Adampol, he was isolated from the horrors of the world outside by a thick forest . . . but it was a forest bristling with partizan activity. There were Polish partizans, Russian partizans, Jewish partizans. There was even a German deserter or two.

As for him, he didn't wear the uniform, and he had a reputation for being a good German, but he wouldn't count on it to save his life if he were confronted by a band of resistance fighters. His duties had him constantly traveling, on the road or in the fields, through the woods, in and out of villages. Everyone knew who he was. He'd taken to carrying a gun wherever he went.

He turned up the path that led to the stable. Linker, his stableman, had Fallada out in the middle of the aisle, brushing her down. She nickered inquisitively.

"Hold on a minute, princess," he said, and fished for the sugar cube he always kept for her in his pocket. She snatched it from his palm without a jot of gratitude. "How are you, my girl?" he murmured. "Did you enjoy your bath?"

She whinnied and tossed her head. Her forelock fell in her eyes like a little girl's bangs. The irises were a pale moonstone blue, practically human. Not for the first time, he thought he detected a sentient wisdom keeping watch in their opalescent depths. One of these days, he was certain, she would answer him.

Soroka's younger son was there, too, polishing the saddle his father had made. Though he was small for his age, the little redhead was agile and alert, an expert at making himself useful.

Reinhart lifted the saddle to inspect it, tilting his head one way, then the other. The leather shone with the translucent luster of an old oil painting.

"Good job, kid," he said. "You're going to be the best saddlemaker in Poland, just like your papa."

The boy wriggled and glowed under the praise. He was about the same age as his own Matthias, he realized, funny that he'd never noticed it before. With a surprising stab of regret, Reinhart wondered what his boys were doing at that moment. Getting dressed? Eating breakfast? Or were they already in school?

Soroka's boy wasn't alone, he had his little sister with him. She had made herself at home in the hay, where she was watching the barn cat nurse a litter of kittens. The cat, a mean yellow tabby, didn't seem to mind the little girl's presence, acknowledging her now and again with a switch of her tail or a slow blink of her yellow eyes.

Soroka and Wysocki lumbered through the stable doors, conferring in Polish. When they saw Reinhart, they switched to German.

"Novak is here with a dead sheep," reported Wysocki.

"Where?"

"Right outside. Should I tell him to leave it behind the stable?"

He scribbled his signature on the form Wysocki offered him. "Yes, same as the others." The carcass would be gone by morning. Officially, he had to account for his farmers' dead livestock. Unofficially, he left them where his hungry workers would be sure to find them.

He turned to Soroka. "All right, what is it, Haskel? You look like you're sitting on pins and needles."

The saddlemaker was carrying a package wrapped in a blanket. It smelled enticingly of neat's-foot oil. "First things first. What does Miss Ostrowski think of her new saddle? Does it need any adjustments?"

"Petra asked me to tell you that she has never owned anything that fits her behind as perfectly as your saddle. She made Linker carry it to her room so she could look at it while she's in the bath. She says you're an *artiste*. She also wanted me to tell you that your beautiful daughter raises the tastiest rabbits in the county."

Soroka chuckled, but tension hummed in the air between them like a live wire. "I have something for you," he said.

"I've been out all day visiting farms around Natalin," Reinhart said. "I have a metric ton of paperwork I need to fill out. Come to my office. We can talk there."

Soroka followed him past the grand staircase, past the stone fireplace with the earl's coat of arms carved in relief, past the alabaster bust of Mars, the god of war, that sat on the mantel. In his office, Reinhart pushed a stack of ledgers from a needlework chair and motioned for Soroka to sit.

The saddlemaker pulled off his cap and scratched his head. "That kid you hired to deliver messages for you. He's an informer."

Reinhart went wobbly in the knees. He had to sit down. "How do you know?"

"His bicycle. No Pole has a new bicycle unless he's working for the Germans. It's a dead giveaway."

His insides were turning to water. Where had he sent him? To Bobak, who seemed to have an endless supply of hard-to-find redcurrant jelly; to Ulinski, who organized French champagne . . . Zygoda, who could always be depended on for a Leica camera. "Christ. I've already sent him to three different places Rohlfe shouldn't know about. And those are just the ones I remember. What am I going to do?"

Soroka fitted his cap back onto his head. "From what I understand, it's, ah, not a problem anymore."

Reinhart sagged with relief. "Thank you, Haskel. How do you hear these things?"

"Oh, you know. A little bird told me." Soroka never talked about it, but he had a son living in one of the illegal Jewish camps in the forest. Was he also a partizan? Reinhart didn't want to know.

Soroka massaged a freckled hand over his sunburned neck. "Listen, Reinhart. There's no pretty way to ask you this. If it ever got to a point where you didn't think you could protect us anymore . . . you would tell us, wouldn't you?"

Reinhart's eyebrows steepled up. "I think you forget who you're talking to."

"I know, I know. Willy Reinhart, the man with the silver tongue. No one can say no to him! Do you know the story of the fireflower? No? Famous Polish folktale. In the heart of the forest, there grows a fern that blooms only once a year, on Kupala Night. The flowers of this plant are fiery flames. To collect this flower, you must enter the forest before midnight on the longest day of the year. Demons will test you, bombarding you with questions. If you allow yourself to be distracted, the fireflower burns to ash. But if you resist the demons, the fireflower gives you the power to read minds, find treasure, fight off evil!" The saddlemaker flashed a smile. "Sure you don't have a fireflower around here somewhere?"

Reinhart laughed. "You've discovered my secret. I keep it in a vase on top of the piano."

"You would tell us, though. If it was time to find a safe place to hide."

"You can count on me, Haskel."

Soroka puffed out his cheeks, relieved. "Thank you, Chief. It's not for me, you know. It's for Hanna, the kids . . . a man has to protect his family." Now he was embarrassed. He dropped his gaze to his shoes. "Better get back to work. Anshel will polish a hole right through the seat of your saddle." He bent over, retrieved the package at his feet. "Oh, this is for you. Last time you stopped by, I saw that you could use a new pair of boots." He unwrapped the blanket. Swaddled in the soft cloth was a set of high black riding boots.

With delight, Reinhart turned them one way, then the other, admiring the play of light across the lacquered leather. "Is there anything you can't do? You're like a wizard, Haskel."

The phone rang. Petra wanted to go dancing. Was there a way to make that happen tonight? Absently, Reinhart turned away to take the call, stroking his new boots. The saddlemaker folded up his blanket and withdrew, quietly shutting the door behind him.

Haas wanted to know if his saddle was ready yet.

In a tense meeting, Reinhart had requested a certain Yakub Freund, a pipe fitter, to be taken off the rolls for transport and instead channeled to Adampol. By reputation, the Chief of Employment was a true believer, a cold-hearted, steely-nerved National Socialist killer. Reinhart gazed into his dead-pool eyes, pushed a silver pocket watch across the desk, and Freund was his. But as he was leaving, Haas asked about his saddle.

Not long ago, Haas had executed the entire membership of the Jewish Council for acting too slowly for his liking. Reinhart wanted Haskel to put the saddle at the top of his to-do list.

"Tell Soroka to come see me," he told Wysocki. "It's important."

Soroka didn't come that morning, or even that afternoon. All that day, the drive was crowded with incoming deliveries of potatoes and onions, horse-drawn wagons jockeying for position with army trucks shuttling crates of live chickens to the train station. As if he didn't have enough to worry about, there was a troubling letter from home, Matthias had been expelled from school for keeping a flare gun under his bed. Then there were the phone calls,

unreasonable demands from the Fatherland: More potatoes.
More rye. More wheat. More everything, or else. And that
wasn't the worst of it.

As the sun set and the saddlemaker still did not appear,
Reinhart began to grow angry. He didn't treat his workers
like slaves, like the commandants of other camps did with
their Jews, nor did he close them in with barbed wire and
guard towers. But he was still Willy Reinhart, Regional
Commissioner of Agricultural Products and Services, he
held life and death in the palm of his hand, and he assumed
a corresponding measure of respect.

In the evening there was a social event in Włodawa for
the local Reich leadership, dinner at the SS club, followed
by a gala movie premiere. It was nearly midnight by the time
he returned from the theater. Meeting him in the domed
portico, a manservant took his coat and quietly informed
him that Soroka was waiting in the manager's office.

"I won't be long," he told Petra. She wore a sable stole
against the chill, furnished by his crack furrier, Silverberg.
As she flowed up the grand staircase, her new diamond
earrings glittered in the chandelier's golden light.

In contrast, the office of the manager was practically
spartan. Four white walls, a wooden desk, shelves lined
with ledgers, a bare bulb that hung from the middle of the
ceiling. Soroka was standing directly under the light, his
face shadowed beneath the brim of his hat. Reinhart noted
that his shirt was torn, which only inflamed him further;
was this any way to appear before the Kommandant of the
Adampol Labor Camp?

Feeling strangled by his dinner jacket, he stalked behind
the desk, slinging open his tie. A month ago, he might have
made a joke. But not today. Today he'd seen his excellent

miller, a girl of twenty, performing push-ups over a steaming pile of horseshit in the town square while policemen laughed and pointed guns at her head. Today he'd heard about a regiment of German soldiers slaughtered by God knows what in the Parczew Forest. Today the crew digging potatoes was shorthanded because they'd already taken so many Jews away. Today there had been that telephone call from the General Government offices in Kraków.

So, instead of joking, he told Soroka that men had been shot for less. That his so-called superiors were breathing down his neck. That by protecting the saddlemaker's family, Reinhart was risking his own life. That all the Jews in Poland, except for the necessaries, were going to be gone within the next three weeks. Did he not realize, Reinhart bellowed, how lucky he was, that there were tens of thousands of Jews transported every day, Jews who would break their backs for him, Jews eager to take his place?

Soroka stood perfectly still, nodding, nodding, nodding. The saddlemaker absorbed his anger the way the color black absorbs light. "Where've you been, anyway?" Reinhart searched in his pockets for a cigarette, his customary good humor restored. "I've just come from a movie in town. Scientists, sabotage, sexy blondes. I highly recommend it."

Soroka sounded tired. "The baby was sick."

Reinhart rolled his eyes, jamming the cigarette between his lips as he hunted for his lighter. "When *isn't* the baby sick. You should take him to a doctor."

The saddlemaker lifted his head. The pale blue eyes were red and watery, the honest square face swollen with grief.

"A doctor can't help him anymore," he said.

* * *

The last Jews were transported from Włodawa to Sobibór in the middle of November 1942. In three days, ten thousand lives vanished into smoke, like a colossal magic trick.

In the end, there weren't enough train cars to ship ten thousand people quickly enough, so on the third day of the Great *Aktzia*, anyone left on the platform was ushered to a scar of wasteland behind the tracks and gunned down. When the men tasked with the execution ran out of ammunition, they improvised with clubs.

As the guns chugged and spat, Rohlfe and Streibel stood well back. With their jackbooted legs spread wide, they discussed a particularly wild drinking party at the SS club, where a secretary named Else had climbed on top of a table and taken off her clothes. Apparently, she was not a true blonde.

An officer yelled, another one snapped a picture. To the shouted approval of his friends, a soldier hauled a pretty girl across the dirt, holding on to her long black hair. Babies were thrown into the air and caught on the tips of bayonets or shattered against the frozen ground. According to testimony later delivered to the tribunal investigating war crimes in the Lublinskie province, a burst of laughter erupted when a skinny local kid, not yet fifteen, was conscripted as a shooter. In this festive atmosphere, the last Jews of Włodawa waited patiently for their turn before the guns and, when they were called, ran forth with such alacrity that you'd think they were running to freedom.

Guns popped, Streibel's dog yapped ceaselessly, men warmed their hands before a fire boiling in a barrel. Between the smoke and the barking, Reinhart's eyes were burning, and there was a terrible pounding in his head. But then he spotted him, Goldfeder the jeweler, sprinting out of the throng to take his turn in front of the pit. Reinhart leaned forward on his horse. "There he is," he said.

Streibel screamed at the top of his lungs, and the line halted. With a few well-placed blows to the shoulders, the jeweler was cut from his neighbors and escorted away. "Choose me, Reinhart!" someone else shouted before being clubbed to the ground.

Streibel had a girlfriend, the girlfriend had a birthday. Reinhart would provide the gift, a diamond brooch, created by his new jeweler. He was glad to be finished here. He pulled on Fallada's reins.

But Streibel was feeling chatty. He laid a gloved hand on the horse's arched neck. She laid her ears back and snorted at him. "Your Fallada is the most beautiful animal in the district," he said enviously. "She makes my Tristan look like a mule, and he's got a pedigree as long as your arm."

He bantered back. "Well, it's a good thing I saw her first, then."

Streibel chuckled, then lowered his voice. "You know what's going on with Falkner, of course."

Reinhart felt a prickle of unease; a cold sheen of sweat branded the back of his neck. "No, I don't hear anything. We're in our own world over at Adampol."

"He's been taken in for questioning. Turns out he's a traitor. Signed work papers for anyone who asked, warned his Jews when *Aktzias* were scheduled, even hid them in his home." Heavily, Streibel shook his head, implying a slew of crimes too loathsome to detail. "We think he was aiding partizans. Can you believe it?"

No, he couldn't. He was genuinely astonished. The pounding in his head accelerated. "How did you find out?"

"Oh, we have our ways. People talk." A small shrug. "He

denies it, of course. You're chummy with your Jews, did you know anything about this?"

This question was tantamount to an accusation. Falkner's arrest might even be a lie, this casual interview designed to shake something loose. Reinhart knew he should say something to exonerate himself, but just now his mouth had gone dry, his tongue was glued to his palate. "No," he bleated.

Streibel turned his head, watching the operation with renewed interest. A row of four girls was up before the gunmen, with pale oval faces and big dark eyes, they must have been sisters. They were holding hands. The youngest was no more than eight.

Streibel turned his attention back to Reinhart. "He was never really one of us, you know. He didn't join the Party until 1938, when his job was threatened. He was even arrested once, in 1933, for distributing Communist leaflets. It's all there, in his file."

Poor Falkner, his nervous bobbing Adam's apple, the hank of hair that gave his head the shape of an upended lemon. In addition to the pretty wife with the disapproving gray eyes, there were two boys and a little girl. Reinhart wondered what would become of them. The chief engineer of the Berlin Drainage Project had more courage than he would have accorded him.

"You look nervous, Willy. Why? Don't worry, you're not in any kind of trouble. Everyone likes Willy Reinhart." An assistant handed Streibel a mug of coffee. He frowned at some information on a clipboard, scribbled his signature. "And why is that? Because they know you're a decent man. All kinds of people tell you all kinds of things." He took an unhurried sip of his coffee. "Say, Willy. How many Jews do you have over there, anyway? What is it, five hundred? Six?"

The smell of gunpowder and hot metal addled his senses. "No, no, nothing like that," he protested with forced conviviality. Streibel had called him by his first name to demean him; only inferiors went by their first names. It was freezing, but sweat was running down his ribs. "I have three hundred and fifty. Every one of them tops in his field, absolutely necessary to the war effort."

"None of them is necessary," Streibel said. "The goal was always to exterminate the Jews."

There was a dull buzzing in Reinhart's brain. He rallied with desperate gaiety. "Where's my head?" he cried, slapping his forehead. "I rode all the way out here to invite you, and then I nearly forgot! How long has it been since you've spent a weekend at the palace? Too long! Well, I want to make up for it. How about Friday? Good food, lots of liquor, pretty girls. Bring your men. Can you make it? What do you say?"

The Gestapo police chief's mirthless eyes studied him. By now, Reinhart had sweated through his shirt, he could feel it clinging to his skin. But then, miracle of miracles, Streibel's face lit up in a boyish grin, and he was patting him fondly on the arm.

"All right, Willy, all right." He was laughing, though no one had said anything funny. "You're a good man, the best! I'll see you on Friday." He was dismissed.

Reinhart wheeled Fallada around, urging her forward with a touch of his heels. He was wobbly with relief. Luckily, he was on horseback, walking would have been completely out of the question. He was almost out of earshot when he heard Streibel calling after him.

"Oh, and about Falkner. I'm going to send some papers over to the palace. The messenger will wait. It would be best for everyone if you signed them right away."

Without looking back, Reinhart raised his arm in fare-well. Fallada's hooves clipped across the frozen scree, carrying him away, far far away. A child screamed, pop, the screaming stopped. Feeling dizzy, he shut his eyes, then quickly forced them open again. You never knew who was watching. He slowed to light up a cigarette, protecting the tiny flickering flame with a cupped hand.

Stumbling along beside him, the jeweler was quaking uncontrollably. Reinhart snapped his lighter shut, inhaled deeply. In a few minutes, a healing sense of unreality would take over, he could depend on it, and then he'd be fine.

"Come on, Goldfeder, let's go home," he said, flashing his famous smile. "Trust me. Everything's going to be all right."

Later that night, for the first time in memory, he had trouble in bed. Petra tried her best, she'd been under him, over him, beside him, upside down, bottoms up, and on her knees, but there was nothing she could do, the events of the day had unnerved him.

They'd wanted him to denounce Falkner. *I, Willy Reinhart, do solemnly swear that. Abel Falkner did commit acts of treason with. Witnessed by. In the presence of. Sign here and here and here.*

He'd inscribed his signature with a flourish, knowing that it didn't really make a difference what he did. The powers that be had already decided that Falkner was a goner. If he didn't do as they said, he'd be a goner, too, Adampol liquidated, Streibel had made that perfectly clear. The statement he signed would almost certainly be used to condemn a man to death, and the vision of lanky, do-gooding Abel Falkner standing bound and blindfolded before a firing squad wouldn't leave him alone, inserting itself repeatedly between his dick and Petra's exquisite thighs. Just now she was seated on top, pert pear-shaped breasts jiggling fetchingly above his head. He lay back in the soft pillows and tried to enjoy it.

Falkner was the past, he told himself firmly. What mattered now was Adampol. His people trusted him, they depended on him to protect them, it was his duty to keep them safe. He was prepared to do whatever it took. There might be more *Selektzions*, more *Aktzias*, but they'd blustered through them before. One day, maybe soon, the war would be over. To rebuild, the winning side would need craftsmen, and then they would come to him. "Thank you for saving Stein, he's the best carpenter in Poland," they would marvel. "Thank you for saving Weinschneider, the best tinsmith. Freund, the best pipe fitter. Ottensusser, the best electrician. Flaumanhauft, Mannheim, and Kaminetzky, the best road-construction crew ever. Those were crazy times, weren't they? Let's put them behind us." And he'd be redeemed, every wrong, rotten deal he'd ever made, forgotten. It would be worth it.

Finally, Petra conceded defeat, slipping off into the covers. Wordlessly, she lay beside him, comforting him with her soft presence.

He rested a hand on the curve of her hip. "Falkner's been arrested. They've transported his workers and burned his camp to the ground."

Except for a slight widening of the eyes, her face didn't register any surprise. "What was he doing?"

"Hiding Jews. Helping partizans."

"What will happen to him?"

"Shot, if he's lucky."

She turned away from him on the bed. At first he felt the

mattress vibrate, just slightly, and then he saw her shoulders shaking. He reached out to touch her. To his surprise, she pulled away from him.

"What is it?" he asked, bewildered. "Is this about Falkner?"

"I was thinking about his wife. His children."

"But his wife hates you."

She pressed the heels of her hands into her eyes. "He has a son, a little fatty, maybe ten or eleven . . . I think his name is Michael. The other boys at school make fun of him, they call him mean names, I overheard him once in town, crying. It was at that place, you know, where all the SS wives go in the afternoon to have coffee. He was sitting at a table with his mother. She bought him an ice cream, and he was eating it and crying. She looked so sad. I heard her tell him that it didn't matter what people said as long as you knew inside of yourself that it wasn't true." Mascara was running in jagged black stripes down her cheeks. "What's going to happen to them?"

"I don't know. Maybe they'll send them to a prison camp."

She made an awful sound and covered her face with her hands. As she sobbed, her rib cage fluttered like a baby bird's wings.

He was baffled. This was completely out of character. Until now, his mistress had been calm, submissive, serene. Almost deliberately docile, now that he thought of it, content to receive his presents and entertain his guests.

Suddenly, he saw himself as she must see him, Kommandant Willy Reinhart, Regional Commissioner for Agricultural Products and Services for the German Reich, an official of the greedy merciless foreign forces that had come without provocation to steal her land and murder its children. The appointed representative of an evil and corrupt system that, when it tired of persecuting its enemies, consumed itself. For the first time in his life, he despised himself.

There was a throbbing in the region of his heart. Did he love her? She opened her arms and legs to him, yes. But she also conjured in him a sense of home that was more real than anything he'd left back in Germany. Since he'd known her, he'd had no desire to sleep with anyone else. For Reinhart, if it wasn't love, it was certainly something very close to it.

And what about her? Did she love him? he wondered. After all, he was a German officer, she was the village beauty. Maybe *love* was too strong a word for what they had together. He offered safety and protection in an unstable world.

Whatever it was, he hoped it was enough, because he was about to trust her with his life. Kneeling over her, he put his lips close to her ear. "Petra, Petra," he whispered, pushing strands of damp hair from her face. "Don't cry. There's nothing I can do for Falkner, it's true. But maybe we can still do something. Tell me, Petra. Do you happen to know anyone who might have a way to get in touch with the partizans?"

Her eyes blinked open, the lashes wet and clumped together. She scrutinized his face with a probing intensity, like she was searching for something she might have previously missed. With her long white fingers pressing the sides of his face, she kissed him. As he stared into her eyes, clear and pallid and changeable like the river, he felt himself grow hard again. She felt it, too, and pulled him down on top of her.

As he entered her, a thought fired once across his consciousness like a shooting star. Had their roles been reversed, Falkner never would have signed those papers.

They showed up just after lunch, Streibel, his mistress, and fifteen gunmen. Feasts were prepared, rooms aired, linens pressed, black-market brandy trucked in, the gamekeeper put on alert. A bevy of girls from the typing pool were rounded up, and if they weren't the prettiest ones, at least they were the most willing. He thought it wise to pack Petra off to stay with her mother.

His marvelous cook outdid himself, and so did the serving staff. There were roast pigs on gold plates, boar and venison and rabbit and pheasant, sauces and gelleés and hard-to-find condiments, wines, and liqueurs from every corner of Europe. The bosomy blond secretary he'd met in the Gestapo HQ showed up; she took his hand with a demure smile, but once she had some champagne in her, she leaned over and kissed a dark-haired girlfriend right on the lips.

After the meal, there were chocolates, brandy, cigars. A band of musicians played "Lili Marlene." People coupled off, swaying slowly on the dance floor, the girls leaning their coiffed heads into the soldiers' uniforms. Reinhart congratulated himself. Streibel had made no further inquiries into his Jewish workers. The hastily arranged hunt weekend was already paying off.

One man was still seated at his table, tapping his foot along with the music. He looked to be around Reinhart's age, with a wide, honest face, a friendly grin, brown hair parted neatly on the side. When he saw they were alone, he leaned forward. "Thank you, Herr Reinhart," he said shyly. "We really needed this break."

"It's always my pleasure to host our hardworking soldiers. Where are you from?"

"We're a police unit from Hamburg. My name's Engler." They shook hands. "Our work is difficult," he confided. "Very difficult."

Reinhart thought of the four sisters throwing their arms into the air and sliding into the mass grave. "Yes, anyone could see that."

"I have a wife, two little girls. So, personally, I find it very hard to shoot women and children. That's not why I became a policeman, you know?" The liquor was loosening his tongue. "Before the first operation, back in Józefów, our commanding officer told us that if any man wanted to be excused, he should just go. One of my friends, a fellow I've known for ten years, stepped forward. His sergeant tore him a new one, really lashed into him, but he just walked away. I thought about it, too. But, you know, I'm a career man, I have to think about my future. So I stayed."

Reinhart nodded, puffing on his cigar. It was all a dream, a strange and troubling dream. Soon he would wake up.

"Some of us have invented little tricks to help us get through it. Like my friend Diederich, for instance. He only shoots mothers. You can understand that—it would be worse for them to see their children killed before their eyes. And me, I just do children. They wouldn't be able to live without their mothers, so the way I see it, it's an act of mercy."

Reinhart drank a lot that night, more than ever before. The blond girl from the Gestapo typing pool had a generous bottom, a warm, soft weight snuggled in his lap. The room twirled around in an agreeable way. He was laughing, he didn't remember why. When had she taken off her clothes? Suddenly, he was in his room, sitting at the edge of his regal king-size bed. He had no memory of how he'd gotten there. Blondie was unbuttoning his trousers, working her way down his belly with her lips. The last thing he remembered before passing out was the sensation of drowning in a vat of Chanel No. 5.

The next morning he awoke to a sky that was a brilliant and unrelenting blue. He lurched to his feet, lumbered naked to the window. Drawing back the drapes, he cursed; the hunting party was already assembling in front of the palace. He pulled on his hunting clothes and hurried to join them.

Wincing against the cruel sunlight, he put his boot in the stirrup and swung himself onto Fallada's back. For this, he was rewarded with a walloping headache.

The hunt master tootled his horn, leading them at a fast clip down the road. Near the front gate, they turned in to the forest. Reinhart slowed Fallada to a walk, letting the others pass him by. Usually, riding was his greatest pleasure. Today bouncing up and down in the saddle was torture. "Go on without me," he instructed the hunt master. "Give them a good run. I'll catch up with you later."

It was unseasonably warm, the forest floor was thawing. Layers of mist hung in the air, lingering at shoulder height. A meandering creek tinkled against the rocks at Fallada's feet. Yesterday it had been iced over. She dipped her head and nosed around for something tasty.

A family of deer materialized from nowhere, promenading slowly out of the mist and onto the path. He caught his breath. Four does, each one a milky white. One dropped her lovely head to nibble at some moss, another pawed the leaves with her little pointed hoof, while a third kept guard over a luminous fawn.

Fallada snorted, alerting them to their presence. Four graceful heads bobbed up as one. Together, they switched their ears forward, studying Reinhart critically with their big dark eyes. Little gusts of steam rose from their leathery black noses.

Albino deer were extraordinarily rare. The gamekeeper hadn't mentioned them, perhaps he was trying to protect them. Just then the nearest doe turned her flank to him, presenting him with a perfect target. His heart beat faster. Quickly, he shouldered his rifle, curled his finger around the trigger, drew a bead.

Reinhart wasn't a religious man, but to see four of them at once was practically a sign from God. He lowered the gun to his side.

The does heard it first, the pounding of many hooves. As if they'd received a signal, they took off, bounding away into the forest.

Thirteen horses and thirteen riders sailed over the creek, spraying him with gouts of mud. The riding jacket was ridiculously expensive, made by a London tailor, he should have been furious, but all he felt at this moment was an abiding regret. He would have liked the does to get away, to continue with their secret and mysterious existence deep in his woods. He touched his heels to Fallada's sides and followed reluctantly after them.

If he'd been less hung over, he would have been paying more attention. A pine bough slapped across his face, knocking him out of the saddle and onto the ground.

His head was spinning, had he blacked out? Reinhart sat up. Dead leaves were pasted to his ruined jacket and fell from his hair.

Using Fallada's saddle straps for support, he hauled himself to his feet. Ruefully, he rubbed the back of his head; he'd lost his hat when he fell. In the distance, he could hear the sound of excited voices. The hunting party was on the banks of the Bug River, he could just make out their figures. Having waded a few feet into the powerful current, the does found themselves trapped. Water eddied around them, gray and leaden, lapping sullenly at the raw and muddy bank.

The hunters dismounted. Holding their guns, they advanced slowly on the cornered deer, coaxing them in gentle, soothing tones. As he watched, the does turned to face their pursuers, their slender legs braced for battle, their tapered heads lowered in defense.

It would all be over in a few minutes. He turned away, hiding his face against Fallada's neck. It was childlike, superstitious, almost, but he didn't want to see them destroyed.

A snowflake landed on his cheek. Surprised, he looked up to find the sky scudding over with iron gray clouds. Fallada whinnied nervously, stamping skittishly in the ashen leaves. "You just want to get back to your nice, cozy stall, don't you," he murmured, stroking her thick coat, the color of bittersweet chocolate. Oh, she was a girl, all right, she was flirting with him to get her way. Involuntarily, he shivered. The temperature was dropping, one snowflake became a flurry. The wind was picking up, too. Strange, the sky had been a cloudless baby blue not half an hour ago. Fallada swung her pretty face toward him, nibbled his hair. He smiled at the touch of her velvety lips on his cheek. "All right, all right. You know I can't say no to you." He reached into his pockets, feeling for the sugar cube he always kept there. As she took it from his fingers, he sighed. Those men were important guests, and he was their host. Like it or not, he should be there for the kill.

"Come on, girl," he muttered. "We'd better get over there." He took hold of her reins.

But the horse had other ideas. She planted her hooves in the spongy earth and wouldn't budge. "Sorry, Willy," she said. "I can't let you go down there."

Reinhart glanced cautiously around to confirm what he already knew, he was entirely alone. He must have hit his head harder than he thought. He seized the horse's bridle, staring into her liquid, lake-colored eyes.

Impatiently, she butted his chest with her big head. "We really must go. We're running out of time."

"You can talk?"

"Of course I can talk. I'm talking right now, aren't I?" Her voice was sweet and soft and silvery, as it should be, given her fine temperament and her aristocratic lineage, with a light Polish accent.

He shook his head. "No. I'm sorry to disappoint you, Fallada, but none of this is happening. I hit my head when I fell off your back, and now I'm dreaming."

She stretched out her long neck, burrowing her pretty little muzzle against his throat, tickling the hairs behind his ear. A real temptress. "Now, you listen to me, Willy Reinhart. I know a few things about you. I know when you're happy or sad and what you had for breakfast. You want to do the right thing, but sometimes you can't. You're scared of Streibel. You feel bad about Falkner. You're worried your workers don't get enough to eat, and sometimes, when you think no one is looking, you leave a sack of potatoes out where they will find it.

"So you see, Herr Kommandant Reinhart, I know all

about you. And I promise you that after this is over, we can chat until the cows come home. But right now, my dear Willy, *we have to get out of here.*"

A curtain of snow descended from the sky, thick, heavy flakes. With that, the temperature plummeted. Frigid air constricted the delicate passageways inside his throat and lungs. He couldn't feel his fingertips. *Plink,* the sweat collecting in his eyebrows and along his hairline burst into icy crystals.

Around him, the wind began to cycle in huge gusts, gathering itself into a spinning vortex of snow and ice, sucking away light and visibility. "Too late!" she hollered over the howl of the wind. "Hold on to me, Willy!"

There was a metallic thunder, like a million artillery shells firing from a million cannons. In the next moment, landmarks were erased. He didn't know which way was land and which was sky. With his arms around Fallada's neck, he hung on for dear life as she protected him with her body.

He twisted around, trying to catch a glimpse of the hunting party. Veiled behind a screen of falling snow, he could barely make out their silhouettes.

The deer were gone, but the men of the Einsatzgruppen still stood there, transfixed. What were they staring at? He blinked back the icy shards of snow burning his eyes and settling on his lashes.

The Bug River was overflowing its banks. Gentle ripples became little waves, the little waves grew bigger. When the wind hitched around in the other direction, they surged another five feet. Now they were the height of a man and edged with seething white foam that looked like teeth. The breakers organized themselves, purposefully piling wave upon wave. The water shot upward in a gunmetal-gray fountain, and before his very eyes, *the river stood up.*

The hunters fled, scattering in all directions. He could hear their cries. But the river stayed where it was, growing higher, higher, as high as the trees, higher.

For another moment the river flowed peacefully upward into the sky. And then, with a brittle crack, it froze solid, in the shape of a monstrous, curling fist.

Only then did it begin to move. With colossal legs like a truckload of tree trunks, the river left its bed to stalk the hunters across the flat, snowy terrain. Reinhart could feel the earth shake with each step.

As it closed in on them, the top began to crumble, like the crest of a wave before it hurls itself against the shore. There was a long, hollow creak, like the sound a glacier might make when it moves, and then the whole mass came crashing down, the frozen river detonating in an icy explosion, smashing everything below it into a fine white powder.

The concussive force of the blast carried him backward. He lost his grip on Fallada's neck, catapulting into the vast white void.

He opened his eyes when he felt Fallada's velveteen muzzle brush against his cheek. Once again he lay beside the meandering creek tinkling through the rocks. Everything was exactly the way it was in the moments before the storm: The sun was up, the temperature mild, the sky a tranquil, blameless blue, and Fallada was nosing hopefully around the creek for something tasty to eat. When he turned his gaze to the river, that was the same, too. Nothing had changed at all, the wide gray waters that marked the border with Russia rolled patiently toward eternity. Other than a set of bootprints stamped into the mud, of men and deer, there was no trace.

*  *  *

Escape from Sobibór! It was all the German colonists could talk about. A week ago, three hundred Jewish prisoners had murdered their guards and melted into the forest. The mine-fields got some of them, and the SS shot eighty more, but many remained at large in the six kilometers of woodland between Adampol and Sobibór, armed and desperate.

Blue shadows lay in the grassy lanes between the trees in his orchard. There were still plenty of leaves in the branches and more on the ground. As Fallada danced along, she shuf-fled them with her hooves, sending them skating through the air. She shook her head and nickered, telling him, he was certain, that she was grateful for the exercise. Affectionately, he patted her neck. For the past week, he'd kept her a pris-oner in her stall, unwilling to brave the woods. For now he thought it wise to stick close to the palace.

He gave a slight tug on the reins. Fallada came to a smooth stop, and together, man and horse surveyed their patch of the world, a panorama of stubbly fields shaved close for winter.

Nearly a year had passed since the attack on the hunt-ing party, and only today was the matter finally laid to rest, with an official stamped letter absolving him of blame. Obergruppenführer Odilo Globocnik, the SS general for the southeastern region, was eminently approachable; on all levels, his administration was satisfyingly riddled with corruption. For the price of a phonograph, a box of ba-nanas, a bag of salt, and a crate of gooseberry jam, someone in Globocnik's office was more than happy to dismiss the allegations that Reinhart, as the sole survivor, was in bed with the partizans.

A flock of gray geese flapped overhead, noisily honking. His stomach grumbled in reply, reminding him that he'd had no lunch. "All right, Fallada. Guess we should be getting back. Nearly dinnertime, isn't it?"

Only Reinhart knew what had really happened that day in the Parczew Forest; he'd witnessed the land of Poland rise up and defend herself. It saddened him that Fallada refused to speak again, but he still conversed with her, hoping to catch her off guard.

"I wish you could see how beautiful your mane looks today, rippling in the breeze! Like tongues of fire." She laid her ears back and snorted, and he was confident she understood.

The revolt at Sobibór had shaken him with its savagery. Synchronizing their movements with military precision, the craftsmen in the concentration camp's workshops rose up against their overseers in a coordinated attack. The shoemakers told a supervisor to come to their workshop and pick up his new boots. When he arrived, they were waiting for him with their hammers. At the same time, the tailors invited a Ukrainian guard to try on his new suit, then stabbed him to death with their scissors. As for the construction workers . . . well, he'd heard something about an ax. Not that he had any sympathy for those butchers over at Sobibór— on the contrary, they deserved whatever they got—but the ferocity the prisoners had exhibited gave him the chills.

He jigged up and down in the saddle as Fallada trotted through the apple trees. At the end of the orchard was a fieldstone fence, and beyond that, the woods. On most days, they sailed over the fence and went for a gallop. Fallada quickened her pace, gathering speed for the jump. He tugged back on the reins. "No forest today, my love. Not until things settle down." He guided her to the left, breaking through a lane of trees, and that was where he came upon them, three men and a girl, standing in his orchard.

Reinhart's nerves jangled an alarm. With one smooth motion, he lifted his hunting rifle, braced it against his shoulder. "*Halt!*" he roared.

Three of them froze. But the fourth, a scruffy young man, stared at him, his face cowled in shadow. And then he bolted for the stone fence.

Reinhart sighted down the barrel, aimed at a place between the shoulders of the ragged coat. "Stop! Put your hands up!" he cried. But the scruffy young man ignored him. Reaching the fence, he dived over it, scrabbling for something on the ground. *Good Christ!* What did he have back there? A gun? A knife? A grenade? As he swiveled around again, Reinhart pulled the trigger. A gunshot boomed across the barren fields, startling a flock of starlings into the air. Twenty feet away, the young man let out a gasp—"Ah," he said—and slumped against the stones.

For a long moment, nobody moved. Eventually, Reinhart touched his heels to Fallada's sides, and she jogged reluctantly forward. At the wall, he dismounted. "You," he instructed the others. "Turn him over."

They took his arms and rocked him onto his back. With dawning horror, Reinhart saw that he was just a kid, perhaps sixteen or seventeen. A burlap bag slipped from his fingers. Reinhart bent over and picked it up. A few rutted and discolored apples rolled out onto the leaves.

"Is he . . . is he breathing?"

"Dead," said a man in a dove-gray homburg.

There was a cart stationed under a tree to collect the last windfall fruits of the season. "Put him in the wagon and take him to Gestapo headquarters," Reinhart mumbled.

One fellow took his arms, another took his legs, and between them, they gentled him into the cart. The shabby little parade of Jews began rolling the wagon with its human burden back to Włodawa. He caught a glimpse of the girl's face as she followed behind, transfigured with anguish.

With the rifle balanced in the crook of his arm, Reinhart reached inside his riding jacket for his cigarettes. His fingers were shaking so badly, he couldn't work the lighter.

In the lengthening shadows under the trees, he discerned a figure. Reinhart had already swung the gun to his shoulder before he recognized the general shape and silhouette of Soroka's boy Anshel, the telltale fringe of red hair. Quickly, he lowered the rifle.

"Little saddlemaker, is that you?" he called. "Come out where I can see you. What are you doing out here?"

In his winter clothes, he was as round as a barrel. "You sent me to the woodsman's hut. I'm supposed to deliver a message."

Was that today? This morning seemed so long ago. Reinhart jerked his head in the direction of the departed wagon. "Do you know them?"

Anshel's face was the color of candle wax. "They used to live on my street," he said. "Before we came to live with you. Yitz . . . the one you . . . he's a couple of years older than me. I used to play buttons with him."

"Buttons?"

"You flip your buttons against a wall. If your button lands on someone else's, you get to keep his button, too."

"Oh . . . we used to play something like that . . . with cards . . ." He felt curiously detached, like he was observing the conversation from a very great distance away.

"Since the last *Aktzia*, they've been living in the woods. They were looking for apples." Then, almost inaudibly, "They were going to ask you for work."

Mechanically, he nodded. By now, Reinhart was thoroughly numb, but this much registered. He'd killed a boy, his name was Yitz. Before the Germans came, he lived with his family on Wyrkowska Street. On the last day of his life, he was starved enough to risk being shot for a few rotten, wormy apples he'd found on the ground.

Anshel was gazing worriedly at him, shifting uncomfortably from one foot to the other.

*You'll have plenty of time after the war to have a nice, long nervous breakdown,* he told himself sternly. *But right now you have to pull it together. Come on. Grow a pair.*

At that moment, Anshel Soroka would later tell his father, Willy Reinhart was as white as a ghost. Then he raked off his hat. Plowed his fingers through his hair. Smoothed his hand over his jaw. Smiled his crafty magician's smile.

"Go on, little saddlemaker," he said, swatting the boy with his fedora before plopping it back on his head. "Get moving. Your date is waiting for you."

Anshel set off running down the path toward the woodsman's hut.

God, he needed a smoke. He was still holding his lighter. With nerveless fingers, he clicked it once, twice, and then it broke apart in his hands.

Seized with fury, he heaved it into the trees. For a moment it hung there, a small black exclamation mark against the sky, before dropping out of sight.

"So, Reinhart, you killed a Jew." Partizans had cut the telephone lines so many times by now, the connection was tinny. Rohlfe was calling from Gestapo Headquarters in Włodawa, only a few kilometers away, but it sounded like he was calling from the moon. "What happened?"

There was an edge of incredulity to his voice. What he really meant was *You, Reinhart, shot a Jew? Reinhart the Jew lover? You're just like the rest of us after all.*

"I was out riding when I came upon some people, strangers, in my apple orchard. I commanded them to stop. One of them made a break for it, reached over the fence for something hidden. I thought it was a gun."

"But the Jews love you, everyone knows that. Why would he shoot you?"

There was a soft knock at his door. It was Friedman, the bookkeeper, a neat, boyish man with thinning sandy hair and a carefully sculpted goatee. In a previous life, he'd owned a bank in Berlin. Behind him, a porter wrestled with a gigantic rolled-up Oriental rug. "Where do you want this?" he half mouthed, half mimed.

If Reinhart were honest with himself, there was nowhere to put it, the palace was at capacity, but he had a weakness for pretty things. Highboys, dressing mirrors, and china cabinets cluttered the second-floor gallery like wraiths. In corners and hallways, all kinds of chests and tables and bureaus and cabinets accumulated, a pastiche of styles and periods, with marquetry and gold leaf and brass fittings. Not to mention the four grand pianos crammed into the conservatory. He covered the mouthpiece. "Put it with the others," he hissed, and waved them out of the room.

At the other end of the line, Reinhart could hear the scratch of a pen point on paper. "It's a very serious violation to kill a worker. All Jews are property of the Reich. There will have to be an inquiry, possibly a trial."

A trial? It hurt to breathe, like his lungs were lined with broken glass. What did Rohlfe know? Did he have enemies? Someone who wanted his job? Was he being set up? Did that hissing mean that someone was secretly listening in on an extension? What should he do?

The lie tumbled out of him. "They were partizans," he blurted. "The boy had a gun in his bag. You know the forest around my castle is riddled with partizan activity."

"Oh," said Rohlfe. "Well, that's completely different, you shot him in self-defense. You don't even have any guards out there, am I right? No wonder you're on edge." His voice dropped, became confidential, fearful, almost. "I'm sure you heard what happened at Sobibór."

"Yes. Brutal."

"Fucking animals. Those men had wives, families. You know my dog, Luther? Kolko gave him to me. He'd had a litter of puppies." He was morose. "They killed Kolko with an ax."

"Animals." He would have agreed to anything Rohlfe said, just to get him off the phone.

"And you don't even have a fence around your camp! You're the one with all the workers, have them build one. You know, I'm going to send you some guards. All these boys are just sitting around town getting drunk. It will give them something to do."

"That won't be necessary," said Reinhart hastily. "I'll put up a fence. Fantastic idea, Rohlfe. Thank you."

"About the shooting. I'm sending a man with my report. Just sign it, and we'll mark this incident closed."

A mighty sense of elation powered through him, leaving him dizzy with relief. It was drafty in his office, but sweat pasted his shirt to his back. "Thank you. And if this man happened to return to your office with a bottle of Hennessy?"

"I wouldn't say no. Heil Hitler," said Rohlfe.

"Heil Hitler," he replied.

With a click, he returned the phone to the cradle. Reinhart leaned back in his chair, covered his eyes, and began to laugh weakly. What a vast cosmic joke. Yesterday he'd shot an innocent kid dead. Now he'd lied to an officer of the law to get himself off the hook. Should he feel bad about it? The police force committed more heinous crimes than this one every day. What good would it do anyone if he ended up in jail or, worse, the eastern front? Adampol would be finished, his workers sent up the chimneys at Sobibór. In this war, his first responsibility was to his people. He was one of the good guys, a hero. So he'd killed somebody. In the heavenly balance sheet, he was still winning by a landslide. If the kid had stayed put instead of risking his life for a bag of wormy apples, he'd be alive. His death was a casualty of the times.

He was Willy Reinhart, Reich Commissioner for the Collection and Distribution of Agricultural Products, Savior of the Jews, with the power of life and death in the palm of his hand. He'd just passed a test of life and death himself; he thought he deserved a treat. He took a cigar from the box on his desk and ran it under his nose, savoring the sweet perfume of tobacco before clipping off the end of it with a tiny gold scissor and putting it in his mouth.

There was a squadron of mounted policemen, forty of them, cantering four abreast down the road toward Adampol. It was morning, just after breakfast. Outside, the sky was a brilliant heavenly blue, but it was brisk. He could smell winter in the air.

With a flutter of apprehension, he watched their approach from his office window, where he was cooped up with Friedman, going over the final numbers for the harvest. Then he sighed. "Better go warn Ostrowski that there will be forty more to feed today. And the horses are going to need water, tell Linker." More out of habit than hope, he asked, "Any word on Soroka?"

Regretfully, Friedman shook his head, then left the office. The saddlemaker had vanished two weeks ago, and Reinhart's anger was still fresh. A tangle of emotions roiled his heart, sometimes fury taking the lead, other times betrayal, or a deep, aching sense of loss.

He didn't deny it, that last episode had been a close one. On a perfectly random, ordinary Friday night, a squadron of Wehrmacht had rolled up to the palace. Without so much as a how-do-you-do, they went right to work collecting his Jews and leading them into the forest. Reinhart had been fast asleep. By the time Wysocki roused him, they were already half a mile away. He had to drive like a maniac to reach them before anything drastic happened.

Striding down the long line of terrified laborers, he'd found the commanding officer and gone right to work. Bullied, flattered, wheedled, persuaded. Blackmailed, coerced, cajoled, and threatened. Insisted, and wouldn't take no for an answer, that the officer accompany him to the castle and have something to eat. He had to make some phone calls, Reinhart explained, and the officer could help himself to brandy and anything else from the pantry while he waited.

Fortunately, he'd recently hosted Lischka, the Gestapo chief of Lublin. One, two, three, he phoned him up, explained the spot he was in (*My best workers! Middle of the harvest!*), then spent a few pleasant moments reminiscing. Lischka asked if he could speak with the officer in charge, and Reinhart handed him the receiver. A few choice words in the right ear, and the excitement was all over.

So yes, he could see how it might make Soroka a little jumpy. But he'd pulled it off, hadn't he? How could Haskel leave him? After all the times he'd saved them, didn't that mean anything? He was Willy Reinhart, the man with the silver tongue, no one could refuse him!

Since then, he'd tried to strike up a friendship with the bookkeeper, but it wasn't the same. Friedman was too refined, too courteous, too apologetic, too eager to please.

Soroka felt like family. He missed the saddlemaker's square, careworn face, his determined, plainspoken honesty. For the hundredth time that morning, he wondered where they were. Haskel knew all the roads, every path through the forest, every partizan, every horse, every wagon, every farmer in the province. Obviously, they'd gone into hiding, in someone's barn or root cellar. He was evenly divided between hoping they were safe and hoping they would come crawling back.

Outside, a rook stalked pensively through the grass. Reinhart turned away from the window, shrugged on his suit jacket, straightened his tie. He practiced a couple of cheery smiles in front of a small mirror he kept stashed inside his desk before drawing himself up to his full height and striding down the hallway.

An unfamiliar police captain waited for him under the portico. He clicked his boot heels together and smiled thinly through his toothbrush mustache. His breath came out in puffs of white vapor.

"Welcome, Captain. What can I do for you?" Reinhart greeted him with a friendly smile. But not too friendly; after all, he was a very important man, and he needed this officer to know it.

On the driveway, the police had divided into two columns and were making their way around the flanks of the house. Their horses' hooves struck sparks against the paving stones. Reinhart said sharply, "The palace and everything on the grounds are property of the Reich Agricultural Commission. Your men are not permitted to wander around by themselves."

"They're going to search the buildings," said the captain pleasantly. "We're here for your Jews."

He'd heard this line before. "I'm sure this is a mistake," said Reinhart genially, staring down into the strange officer's eyes. "These people are my best workers, every one of them a master craftsman, tops in his field. Absolutely necessary to winning the war."

This gimmick had always worked. But now, unperturbed, the captain returned his gaze. "Those are my orders." His voice was not angry, and it was not unfriendly. It was the voice of a man who had no doubts, no qualms, and no questions.

Reinhart felt a twinge of dread, the clammy sheen of perspiration collecting between his shoulder blades. "Of course, of course, we all have orders. Captain, why don't you come in and have something to eat? Your men, too, all of you, sausage and eggs for everyone, right from the farm, a real feast. I won't take no for an answer. I can promise you, you haven't eaten like this in years!"

"Sausage and eggs, that sounds wonderful," said the captain, allowing himself a rueful smile. "We left Różanka early this morning. But we're on a tight schedule. We have two other operations after we're done here."

"Różanka! Hmmm. Pretty girls in Różanka. Is Braumueller still the chief of police there?"

"No," said the captain. "It's me now."

"I see. Let's talk in my office. Can I offer you coffee? Tea? I know it's early, but something stronger, perhaps?"

The captain followed him into the foyer. Reinhart saw him glance appreciatively at the glossy woodwork, the polished floors, the paintings, the furniture; at Petra, who stood at the top of the grand staircase, remote and pale.

Wysocki edged out of the kitchen, his broad forehead a typographical map of worry. "Kommandant Reinhart, I was just going to send a wagon to Farmer Swaboda for some more bacon. I'm sure our guests are hungry. Also, with your permission, I'd like to speak to the gamekeeper. I haven't seen such a perfect day for hunting in ten years."

Conversationally, the captain said, "Tell your Polacks to go home and lock themselves inside."

Wysocki hesitated, his eyes darting to his master.

"*Schnell schnell!*" the captain yapped.

Another man might have been pissing his pants by now. But he was Kommandant Willy Reinhart, he'd snatched people from the jaws of death a hundred times. Why should today be any different? He just needed to get to his telephone. He ran through a mental list of contacts. Who loved brandy, women, hunting? Who craved custom leather riding boots, fur coats, diamond jewelry? He wasn't going to waste precious minutes with Haas or Rohlfe, not while these *schweineren* were out there rounding up his people. He would call Kastner, the Business Director of Agriculture, based in Chełm, or perhaps Lischka again. And if they failed to help, he still had an ace up his sleeve. He would reach out to Obergruppenführer Globocnik, who'd spent two sunny weekends at the palace last year and had recently been promoted to a new post in Italy.

Reinhart was too nervous to sit. Sliding behind his desk,

he stood hunched over the telephone, a handsome Bakelite objet d'art trimmed with gold. Who to call first, Kastner or Lischka, Lischka or Kastner? Lischka, he decided. Goldfeder had just finishing repairing the clasp on a five-strand pearl necklace. Lischka's ugly wife had a penchant for pretty things.

He lifted the receiver and cradled it to his ear. When the operator came on, he said, "Hello, Else, when are you going to leave your husband and run away with me? I need to speak to—"

A hand slapped down on the cradle, severing the connection. "No calls," the captain said.

Reinhart calculated. In his experience, some men didn't respond to pleasantries and gifts, they only respected authority. He revised his tactics.

"Do you have any idea who you're talking to, you cockroach?" he snapped. "I'm on a first-name basis with half the Reichsleitung in eastern Poland. I won't be told what I can and can't do in my own camp by a fucking *captain*." He stalked to the door. "Who's your commanding officer? He's going to hear about this. You can just bend over right now and kiss your ass goodbye." Forget Lischka, he would approach Kastner in person. How long did it take to drive to Chełm?

The captain had lashless, close-set eyes that trod the line between gray and brown without the warmth of either one, the color of a shadow sliding along the side of a building, or the barrel of a gun, like the one he was holding now. "Stop right there. You're under arrest, Kommandant Reinhart."

His legs loosened under him, and he gripped the back of the Louis XIV chair for support. "I'm— What? What for? What are the charges?"

"You're too close to your Jews," said the captain. The sun

gleamed on the death's-head badge on his cap, outlining it in gold.

Reinhart's throat closed up, it was hard to breathe. His mouth gapped open and shut, searching for the right words, but for once, he had nothing to say. "I'm going to be sick," he said unsteadily. The captain made a face of disgust, but he didn't stop him when Reinhart flung aside the velvet curtain, wrenched open the window, and leaned out as far as he could.

In the courtyard, an untidy procession of his workers was forming, the men gathered from their workshops, women and children from the huts, storehouses, and barns. A tall needle-nosed policeman bellowed that they were moving out, hiking through the forest to another work camp where their services were needed, and he wanted them to organize themselves into a line that was four across. Reinhart saw Friedman at the head of the line, arranging his family to the officer's specifications, always so helpful. Friedman had two sons, Reinhart knew; the youngest was only three. It was this little boy whom Friedman kept beside him now, taking his hand. Reinhart counted six soldiers. There had been dozens more. Where were they?

"Jews, march!" the needle-nosed policemen yelped. A few men turned around, darted inquiring looks in the direction of his office. The horror of the situation swelled up and overwhelmed him. *Dear God. They're waiting for me to show up and save them.* Then the line seethed forward, filing out of the courtyard and toward the woods. Reinhart leaned out as far as he could without falling. Once they passed the stable, they'd be out of his range of view.

But at the stable, the parade lurched to a stop. "First row," the policeman bawled, "follow me!"

Obediently, Friedman and his family scurried off, following the sergeant behind the stable and out of Reinhart's sight. Friedman wasn't a big man, but the little boy's legs still pumped to keep up with his father's pace.

For a long moment, there was a curious silence. Then *crack crack crack crack*. The gunshots echoed, reverberating off the windows and walls, loitering for a while on the thin, cool air.

The line shuddered like a living thing. The mass of waiting Jews writhed and churned, husbands and wives calling to each other in alarm. Another police officer trotted to the front. "All right, all right," he groused. "Let's have order!"

For the past three years, in a thousand other villages throughout Poland and the Ukraine, this approach had undoubtedly worked. But this was Adampol Palace, just six kilometers from Sobibór concentration camp, and each of Reinhart's handpicked Jews was a wary veteran of previous *Aktzias*. All hell broke loose. The line spun apart and dissolved, three hundred and fifty men, women, and children punting off in all directions. In a matter of seconds, there was no one left in the courtyard, nothing to see but the yellow lawn, some stripped trees, and a fountain wrapped in burlap for protection against winter winds.

Reinhart closed his eyes and concentrated. *Go, go, go,* he urged his workers silently. *There are only a few guards, and the woods are fifty feet away. You can make it. Come on, Linker! Come on, Goldfeder! Come on, Trachtman and Stein and Cohen and Amsel and Baumgarten! Faster, faster, faster!*

He didn't know which God had awarded him his magical abilities, Jesus Christ, the God of the Jews, Buddha, or the Holy Trinity, but he prayed to Him now with all his might. *This is it, Lord. Anything you say. I'll stop screwing around, I'll eat fish on Fridays, I'll go to church on Sundays, I'll leave Petra and cleave to my wife, I'll divorce my wife and marry Petra, I'll become a priest if that's what you want, only please, Holy Father, just one more miracle.*

It startled him away from the window, the unmistakable spitting of machine guns, so out of character with the bright blue morning. *Tat tat tat tat tat tat tat . . .* it came from all directions, and he realized that the missing policemen must have fanned out and made a perimeter around the camp. *Tat tat tat tat tat tat tat . . .* the barrage of bullets went on and on and on.

Groping for his chair, he lowered himself down into the cushions. Surrounded by items of peerless beauty, helpless in his handsome home, Willy Reinhart sat and listened to the gunfire.

It is finally quiet. The captain holsters his gun and departs; he has a special operation just like this one designated for Natalin, one town over. "You're free to go," he says before he rides off. "It was only house arrest."

He can tell his Poles to come out now, the captain adds with an ironic glint in his eye, he's going to need their help.

Has there ever been a silence as thick as this one? Every child can imitate the sounds of a farm. Cocks crow, pigs grunt, horses neigh, sheep bleat, the cow goes moo. But not here, not now. Crossing the courtyard, he sees no one. *Maybe it worked, maybe they all got away,* he thinks hopefully. He walks through the empty stable and steps into the paddock.

They are spread out before him, his Jews, his marvelous, gifted Jews, each one a master craftsman, tops in his field, crumpled and rigid on the hard-packed earth, their blood blackening the dust. Their eyes are open, as if they are still looking to him for help. He doesn't recognize anyone. Death has already begun its chemistry, altering appearances. He knows that if he turns, he'll see what's left of Friedman slumped beside the stable wall, but he doesn't have the courage.

The sun is beginning to sink over the trees. The day ends early in November, but today the golden light lingers, slanting a vibrant pink glow on the softness of a cheek, an outstretched arm, a shapely thigh, the arc of a throat, the inside of an open palm. When the first chilly breath of nighttime riffles through a young girl's hair, even the sun shivers, withdraws its warmth, and slinks away.

"Can you fix it? My wagon driver says he can't use the harness the way it is," said Rohlfe. "The breast collar needs to be replaced."

The Russians were coming. Today, tomorrow, no one knew for sure, but the German colony was packing up and leaving Włodawa. Truck after truck gusted down the road, their tires churning up clouds of dust that lingered long after they were gone, coating everything in a fine ashen powder.

Yesterday porters had begun carting Reinhart's furniture to the train station. A particularly fine bird's-eye maple tallboy was now going on the boxcar. The porters, a titanic tattooed Pole and a tiny bowlegged Ukrainian, shoved it into a niche between a forest of grandfather clocks and a dining room table carved from burled walnut. Stacked sideways and upside down and inside and on top of one another, the pieces he'd collected over five years filled three boxcars.

Reinhart's gaze roved restlessly over his furniture. "I don't have any more workers, Rohlfe. They're all gone. Anyway, that last saddlemaker had two left hands."

It was a sticky afternoon in late August. A well-fed fly hummed lazily around their heads. Rohlfe sighed. "I can't argue with that. Since last winter, the level of craftsmanship has really deteriorated."

That Reinhart had been able to find any workers at all was a miracle. After the massacre, no one wanted to work for Willy Reinhart anymore. "What can I say. My best people are buried in the ground."

"It's a shame to leave anything behind for those savages. But the Führer is a genius, he knows what he's doing. The army is stretched too thin. We'll regroup, and then you can be sure we'll be back."

Reinhart nodded to the soldier guarding the train. With a grinding screech, the boxcar door was closed and latched.

"I admire your dedication," said Rohlfe. "And I'm sure there are those in the Fatherland who will welcome your shipment of antique furniture. But what we'll really need is fighters. Better get going before the Ivans arrive."

"I'm leaving in a few hours," he said. Screw the Fatherland, he was routing the furniture to Breslau.

"Then I guess this is auf Wiedersehn. Good luck to you, Reinhart. What times we've had. I'm going to miss your parties." He crunched over the cinders back toward his car.

What the hell. He was never going to see Rohlfe again. He had to know one way or the other. "So who did it, Rohlfe?" he called to him. "Who gave the order to execute my Jews? Was it you?"

The Gestapo chief turned around, genuinely surprised. "No," he said. "I always assumed you did it yourself."

This was so ludicrous that Reinhart was momentarily

speechless. "Why would I do that? They were my best workers, every one a master craftsman, tops in their field."

A fly emerged from Rohlfe's ear. Its body was a metallic
gold, like the foil that came wrapped around chocolates. "I
figured you were covering something up. Maybe you got a
girl pregnant . . . maybe you liked little boys . . . maybe you
thought they were going to kill you while you slept." Adjust-
ing its lacy wings, the fly hopped down to his pink earlobe.
"If you didn't do it . . . who did?"

Rohlfe shot him a scornful look. "What's the difference?
Whatever else comes of this war, at least we accomplished
one thing: ridding Europe of the plague of Jews. The world
will thank us for what we did here. No one else had the guts."

An enormous green fly streaked out of Rohlfe's sleeve.
It circled his head a couple of times and came to a rest on
his cratered nose. "And what about you, Kommandant Jew
Lover? Tell me, how is it you survived that partizan attack
on the hunting party when everyone else was killed? Is it
just possible that you knew about it beforehand? I still don't
know how you talked yourself out of that one."

To Reinhart's amazement, a third fly, this one a flashy
electric blue, launched itself from Rohlfe's nostril and settled into droning orbit around his fleshy head.

Rohlfe sagged, haplessly pawing at his ear. "Ach, these
flies," he sighed gloomily. "I don't know where they come
from. They won't leave me alone." Distracted, he turned back
to his car. By the time he reached the door, his head was
enveloped by an angry black cloud of flies.

Once more, Reinhart navigated the rutted roads back
to Adampol, swerving around tanks, overburdened trucks,
refugees pulling carts, teams of horses towing artillery, officers on horseback, infantrymen on foot. Behind the wheel

of the Mercedes, he gratefully breathed in the stench of gasoline fumes; it was a nice change from the stench of death.

He turned down the avenue of cool green firs that signaled the entrance to the estate. Trucks had been coming and going at all hours, stripping the barnyard, the henhouses, and the pens of their inhabitants, emptying the silos and storehouses. They even took the beehives. After the commotion of packing up—the squawks and moos and grunts, the incessant sawing and hammering, the revving engines, the thudding of crates and sacks, the calls and commands of men—the silence was overwhelming.

Reinhart switched off the ignition and stumped slowly up the steps. Already, the castle exuded an air of abandonment. In the past few days, a gauzy film of dust had settled on the windows and the facade. Some departing infantryman had written his name in chalk on one of the sandstone columns. Reinhart used his handkerchief to wipe it clean.

He straightened up to admire his handiwork, then took a startled step backward. A soldier hung from a rope in the willow tree next to the automobile. While Reinhart stared, the hairs rising on the back of his neck, the branches creaked, and the soldier's corpse danced gently in a semicircle. There was a cardboard sign around his neck, with words printed in thick black strokes: *I'm a deserter.*

Suppressing a shudder, Reinhart wrestled open the heavy oak door and ducked inside. The click of his heels on the parquet floor echoed through the imperial, empty chambers. He let his eyes wander over the width and breadth and span of the Great Hall, the timbered walls, the murals painted by some 1920s artist whose name he'd never learned. On the stairs leading up to the second floor, looking like she owned the place, sat the yellow-striped barn cat. "Who let you in here?" he said, frowning. True, there were no couches or carpets left for her to ruin with her claws, but she could still wreak havoc on the drapes. "Scat! Shoo!"

The cat gave him a look of undisguised contempt. With a flick of her tail, she leaped to the mantel over the fireplace, where she wound in and out between the bust of Mars and a vase of shriveled flowers.

He went straight to his office. Sitting behind his desk for his final minutes as Reich Regional Commissioner of Agricultural Products and Services, he ran loving fingers over the cool marble surface, the whorls and swirls of the wood grain, the polished brass drawer pulls.

Petra's voice lilted through the galleries like a spill of musical notes. "Willy? Is that you?"

"In here."

She had exchanged her chic dress for a bulky brown skirt, a flowered apron, and a white babushka, but she hadn't managed to surrender her lipstick. She rested her suitcase on the floor. "The last truck left hours ago."

"I know. I needed something from my desk." A sense of irremediable loss tore at his heart. "You should leave, darling," he said quietly. "God knows what the Russians will do to women who shared German beds."

Not for the first time, Petra wondered if it was possible that her lover had shrunk in the last year. There were wrinkles she hadn't seen before, and flecks of gray in his hair. His legendary smile was rare and fleeting. The murder of those poor martyred souls behind the stable had broken something in him. He flew into unexpected rages, and complained of odors no one else could smell, things no one else could see.

Reinhart went to the window and cranked it open. Outside, a warm breeze rippled like a river through the tall grass. The onion domes of St. Adalbert's basilica were just visible over the treetops, shimmering like a mirage in the heat.

He tried to imagine shoehorning himself into normal life. Moving back to the cramped city apartment tenanted by his rigid, disapproving wife and children he barely knew. Workdays spent mediating between bickering siblings and their parents' money. Making small talk with neighbors and shopkeepers who had pushed an old woman out a window, or shot only mothers, because it would be too painful for them to watch their children killed.

"I'm not going back," he said. He hadn't known it himself until now.

"Not going—? Are you crazy? The Gestapo are hanging deserters."

He wheeled around, his sorcerer's green eyes hollow and haunted. "I don't belong in Germany, Petra. I belong here." She drew a sharp breath. He plunged on. "I've been thinking about it for a while, but now I'm sure. I want to stay. Can your partizan friends find me a place to hide until things settle down?"

Petra patted down her voluminous skirt. "I don't think it will be a problem," she said. "They were grateful for your help, especially with the supply train schedules. But Willy, we have to get out of the palace. The Russians will be here any time now."

"My bag is already packed. Let me get what I came for, and we'll go."

Critically, she surveyed the dashing cut of his suit, his crisp white shirt, the fresh shine on his onyx oxfords. "You're not going anywhere dressed like that. You look too prosperous. Let me find you a different shirt, maybe a pair of baggy pants with some honest proletarian dirt on them. Unless you prefer to be dressed like a woman. You'd look nice in a babushka."

Reinhart laughed. "Thank you, love. But don't just grab the first thing you see. If I'm going to be a woman, I want to look pretty."

"Wysocki may have something you can borrow. I'll see if he's still here."

Petra went off on her mission. Alone, Reinhart slid open the bottom desk drawer and removed his diary. Folded beneath the cover was his map of killing sites, dating back to 1939. Surely, after the war was over, there would be an agency to give it to, a commission appointed to investigate Hitler's crimes.

Under the diary was a black velvet bag with Hebrew words stitched in gold metallic thread. A few weeks ago, out for a ride on Fallada, he'd practically knocked over Soroka's youngest daughter, straggling down the road behind an assortment of farm animals and accompanied by a dog the size of a Volkswagen. She denied it, but she was definitely a Soroka, no one else in the county had hair like that. He was so pleased to see her that he'd swooped her up in his arms and hugged her. The Sorokas were alive! For a few days, he'd felt like the old Reinhart, with magic in his eye and a devil in his smile.

He pressed his cheek to the soft velvet nap. Inside the bag were Soroka's prayer book, a striped shawl, and leather phylacteries. It must have been a mistake, left behind in the rush to escape. When the war was over, the Nazis gone, the Jews returned to their homes, he would seek out Soroka in his shop and return it to him.

"You were right to leave me," he would say. "I couldn't

protect you. I couldn't protect anyone, only I was too vain to see it. I should have spent my days telling everyone I met to find a hole to hide in and stay there until the war was over."

He always insisted that the massacre wasn't his fault, the Jews of Adampol were destined for slaughter no matter what he tried. But now, with the German occupying forces fleeing to escape the punishing fury of the Red Army, he let the tendrils of his unconscious probe deeper. The morning of the final *Aktzia*, as he'd stood before his window and complacently observed forty Waffen SS troopers amble up his driveway, *why hadn't he warned his people to run and hide?*

That day in October, when the executioners had already driven his Jews into the forest before he managed to talk them around . . . that was also the day Soroka saw through his pretty promises and disappeared. The angels had been giving him one last chance, he saw that now. He had ignored it. After all, he was Willy Reinhart, the man with the silver tongue. He could talk anybody into anything.

He tucked the diary and the velvet bag into his valise, dropped his hat on his head, tilted it just so. He turned the key in the door to his office, then smiled to himself. Who was he locking out? The cat?

Footsteps crunched up the stairs leading to the palace. "I hope you brought me something green. It highlights my eyes," he said, holding open the front door.

A Soviet rifleman was silhouetted between the columns. Reinhart had taken him by surprise. He grunted what must have been the Russian equivalent of *Oh shit!* as he trained the barrel of his weapon at Reinhart's chest.

He dropped the valise and raised his hands in the air. Fear scoured him raw. Desperately, he dredged up his best smile, the one that greeted you like a long-lost friend, knew

your dirtiest secrets, and liked you anyway. The rifleman
yelled even louder. Reinhart didn't understand Russian. For
all he knew, he was wishing him happy birthday.

A muddy jeep with a red star on the hood wheezed to
a stop in front of the palace, and two Red Army soldiers
jumped out. One was an officer, with stars on his red epau-
lettes and a red band around his cap. The officer tugged off
his cap and wiped his forehead on his sleeve. He looked hot
and angry. When he saw Reinhart, he unleashed a torrent
of loud and furious Russian syllables.

Reinhart forced down the acid taste of panic. "Where
are my manners!" he cried. "Welcome to Adampol Palace!
Come in, come in! Let's get you something to drink, something to eat."

The officer let loose with more gobbledygook. In response, the rifleman prodded Reinhart with his bayonet.
They directed him down the steps, away from the house,
into the overgrown yard.

Impulsively, he turned around. "Who likes brandy, women,
hunting?" he sang. "You're in the right place. Are your men
hungry, Officer? I'll check the kitchen. I think there are some
sausages and eggs left over from breakfast. Let me send someone over to Farmer Swaboda. He always has the best—"

The officer gave a command. The rifle coughed. Reinhart
pitched forward into the grass.

The air was heavy with the scent of impending rain. At
the edge of the paving stones, a pandemonium of white
butterflies fluttered in ecstasy over a stand of wildflowers.
One came to rest on his upturned fedora, and it perched
there, opening and closing its papery wings.

When the officer saw that Reinhart was still moving, he
berated the rifleman. Then he took out his gun and walked

through the long grass. For a moment their eyes connected. Reinhart thought he saw something like pity. In all honesty, he understood their situation perfectly. They were hunting SS men, not farm administrators, but it was a bad day to be German. The officer raised his gun and fired.

# NEW YORK CITY, 1989

Julia was late. He was already there, wielding a tremendous black umbrella in front of the 92nd Street Y, where they'd arranged to meet. In her backpack were tickets to a concert. Leonard Slatkin was conducting the St. Louis Symphony Orchestra in a performance of Samuel Barber's *Adagio for Strings*. Seeing him, she slowed her pace. Was she really doing this? Not too late to run away, pretend she was sick.

Last summer Julia had participated in a Jewish heritage trip to Poland. A tiny, wizened old lady had chased her clean across a dusty town square for the sole purpose of returning her grandfather's long-lost tallis bag. The woman was wearing a shapeless housedress that looked like a hospital gown and a pair of cheap blue slippers. At first they thought she was an escapee from a mental hospital.

"She was beating a carpet on her balcony when she saw your group walk by," the guide translated slowly. "There was a saddlemaker named Soroka who used to live here. He had a daughter with hair like yours. She says she's never seen anything like it, not since the war. Soroka's daughter raised rabbits."

"Haskel Soroka was my grandfather," said Julia. "My mother raised rabbits during the war."

As the guide translated, the old woman's face broke into a blissful smile, conjuring up a ghost of the beauty she had once been. With a sigh of immense relief, she placed a bundle in Julia's hands. When Julia untied the knots, she found her grandfather's tallis bag under layers of burlap.

This was where things got weird. Beneath the velvet bag was the diary of a Nazi named Willy Reinhart. Apparently, the little old lady had been the lover of this Reinhart, who saved Julia's family not once but many times.

The Sorokas were elated. To think that their Julia had met someone they knew from the war years—incredible! A flurry of communications was fired off across the Atlantic Ocean to anyone who'd had anything to do with their survival. Upon Julia's return from Poland, her mother celebrated with a special Shabbos lunch. Over schnapps and poppy-seed cake, the *lantsmen* peppered her with questions. *Oh, Reinhart's lover was a beauty! Did you take pictures of the town? Is the shul still standing? Did you go into our house? Are they using our furniture? What about our shop, did you see it? Is Reinhart's castle still there?*

The handful of Włodawa Jews who had survived the Holocaust thought of one another as family. The table was crowded with short, stocky old men and bustling, round-faced women sharing their war experiences in a rapid-fire patter of Yiddish and English. Each of them had a Reinhart story. He'd rescued the bakery lady from a gang of SS men. He'd informed partizans of German troop movements and supply trains. He'd helped people he didn't even know about, her mother explained, for every time he'd warned her grandfather of an upcoming *Aktzia*, Zaydie had told ten more people that they should go and hide.

In the fall, Julia moved to Manhattan, scoring a grubby rent-controlled studio on a questionable block in Chelsea, with ambitions of making it as a furniture designer. By coincidence, the Nazi's grandson was in New York, too, studying international law at Columbia. The *lantsmen* had insisted they meet. At least she could give him the diary.

Now the grandson was peering hopefully into the face of each woman who passed, a tricky thing to do without looking like a creep. Julia took a deep breath and stepped forward.

He was facing away from her, gazing expectantly down Lexington Avenue. She walked up to the vast umbrella and said, "Hi. You must be Lukas."

He took a surprised step backward. This was unfortunate; he had positioned himself too close to the stairs leading down to the entry level, and now he stumbled, pinwheeling his arms to keep his balance, making a weapon of the umbrella. He would have tumbled down the steps if she hadn't reached out and grabbed his hand.

She had an extraordinary mouth, he was thinking as he righted himself, and swept the umbrella above them to protect her from the rain. The upper lip was longer than the lower, making her look unreasonably sad.

"Sorry," she said, giving him a wry smile. "I'm not making a very good first impression, am I." When she smiled, the effect was the same as when the sun came out from behind a cloud.

"No, no. It's me. I'm . . . " He grasped for the correct word, came up blank. How did you say *clumsy* in English?

"*Ungeschlickt.* Do you speak Jewish? Many of the words are similar to German."

He'd said the wrong thing, he saw it immediately. Her face chilled into a polite mask. "It's called Yiddish. Anyway, my parents speak it, not me."

"I'm sorry," he said carefully.

"Never mind," she said, but her tone was frosty. "Why don't we go in."

He collapsed the enormous umbrella and shook off the rain. It took them a comically long time to reach their seats; she'd purchased student tickets, situated at the very tippy-top of the nosebleed section.

The lights went down while they were struggling with their coats. The first somber notes broke over them, the strings quivering bleakly, gathering momentum and force. Julia felt the music thrum through her chest, overriding the regular beat of her heart. Violins strained upward in a haunting cry of waste and desolation. The instruments wept for the dead of every nation, in every war, for all time.

Slowly, gently, the piece drew to an end. If mourning could be translated into music, it would sound like this.

When the last chord faded to silence, the room exploded into deafening applause. Julia turned to her companion. To her astonishment, his eyes were wet. He smiled, embarrassed. "It vas . . . very beautiful, yes?" he said.

She cringed. It didn't matter that he was disconcertingly handsome, with green eyes fringed just now with long damp black lashes, or that he was pleasingly proportioned and dressed entirely in bohemian black. Every time he opened his mouth, he sounded like a Nazi.

"What is it?" he asked, seeing her expression.

She didn't answer.

Lukas felt a wash of disappointment. This wasn't going the way he had hoped. He'd come to this meeting with the saddlemaker's granddaughter expecting to hear stories of his grandfather's war heroics, but she was treating him like he was some kind of criminal.

The fact was, he knew very little about Opa Willy. All thin-lipped, bony-framed Oma would ever say about him was that he was a demon, with the power to weave spells with his words. His own papa barely remembered him, though he harbored vague memories of living in a castle. Uncle Matthias had known him best, and as a priest, he was supposed to have compassion for all sinners, but even he didn't speak of him. There was an understanding that he had done something terrible out east, and those things were best swept under the carpet and forgotten. Which wasn't unusual. Among his friends, no one talked about what their grandparents did during the war.

He helped her with her coat. She raised her arms to free the thick tumble of her hair from where it lay trapped under her collar. He'd never seen anything like it, long and wavy, with strokes of mahogany, ochre, copper, and caramel. Like a painting by a Renaissance master.

"I enjoyed very much," he said. "Thank you for the tickets." This time he saw her wince. "What's the matter?" he asked, puzzled. "Something I say?" He cupped his hand over his mouth, breathed into it. "Maybe my breath?"

This made her laugh. She hesitated before selecting the next words. "It's your accent. If you're Jewish, there's just something about a German accent that makes you shiver."

"But my grandfather protected your family."

"Yes. My mother's family. But on my father's side, the

Einsatzgruppen wiped out his whole village. He was the only survivor."

"Oh," he said.

Outside, the rain had turned to sleet. He hoisted his enormous umbrella over them both. But she was already inching away, eager to escape. "That's all right. I, ah, have to go."

Under the umbrella, his shoulders sagged. *What can I say?* he wondered. *What can I do to make her stay? Nothing,* he concluded. Given her family history, he might react the same way. Regretfully, he smiled.

The smile twinkled encouragement: *Come on, it's not so bad!* The smile promised that it knew your secrets and would keep them safe. The smile wanted to tell you a dirty joke, to buy you a drink, it wanted you to stop worrying. The smile threw its arm around your shoulders and called you friend.

She faced him in the rain, stray crystals of snow and ice catching in the parabolas of her hair. "You must look like him."

"That's what my grandmother tells me. Though she doesn't seem happy about it. What makes you say that?"

"My mom . . . I think she may have had a little crush on him. Whenever his name comes up, she mentions that he looked like a movie star. Though these days, I think she does it just to make my dad jealous." The corners of her lips tugged up in a sly grin. "Everyone with a Reinhart story says something about his smile. Even the men."

"Nobody in my family ever talked about him. I'm pretty sure my grandmother thought he killed all those people himself."

"Oh, no, no. My family agrees, the *lantsmen* agree, whoever killed those poor people in Adampol, they took him by surprise. He didn't know they were coming."

"How can you be so sure?" He desperately wanted to believe it. Too few Germans had offered resistance during World War II. Even if his grandfather had tried and failed, it was a thousand times better than the millions who turned their heads and pretended not to see.

She looked surprised. "Everyone knew. The Jews, the Poles, even the Germans. Willy Reinhart was a decent man. Oh, I almost forgot! I'm supposed to give you this." She began to rummage through her bag.

"What is it?"

"His diary."

"Oh yes, the diary! Tell me, how did you get it?"

"His lover—um—Petra Ostrowski—gave it to me. She found it in the grass after he was killed. She was going to destroy it—it was dangerous for her to keep it around after the Communists took over—but she could never bring herself to do it. It was all she had left to remember him by. We wanted to mail it to your grandmother, but she said she wasn't interested."

"That sounds like my grandmother."

Julia rewarded him with a quick smile. "But your dad thought that you might like to have it."

The sleet was pelting harder now, coating the sidewalk with a mix of snow and slush. She glanced up at the sky, frowned. "If I take it out here, it's going to get ruined."

"Perhaps we could go for a cup of coffee," he suggested cautiously.

She pushed the diary deeper into her bag for protection, slipped it back onto her shoulder. "I know a place, but it's a bit of a walk."

"I don't mind," he said. "But you must come under my umbrella. You are getting wet."

Together, the grandson of Willy Reinhart and the granddaughter of Haskel Soroka set off down Lexington Avenue. Behind them, the snow grew steadier, filling in the traces of their footsteps with a light dusting of white.

# ACKNOWLEDGMENTS

This book wouldn't exist without the devoted efforts of many extraordinary people.

I am indebted to my wonderful agent, Jennifer Weltz, for her insight, wisdom, and guidance. Thanks to the rest of my team at JVNLA, Ariana Philips and Tara Hart, for so many reasons. A special heartfelt thanks goes to Jean Naggar; without her faith and dedication, I wouldn't be a writer.

Great armloads of thanks to my eagle-eyed editor, Liese Mayer, for her vision, passion, and inspiration. Thanks also to Beth Thomas, my indefatigable copy editor. Many thanks to Katie Monaghan and Rosie Mahorter, my fabulous PR team, and to all the talented, marvelous people at Scribner for bringing this book to life.

My unending gratitude to *The Kenyon Review*, *Gargoyle*, *2 Bridges Review*, *Danse Macabre*, and *JewishFiction.net*, where these stories first appeared. Without their support and encouragement, the entire collection would still be sitting in a file on my desktop.

Many of the events in these pages were handed down to me by my mother, Brenda Soroka Maryles, who reported her war experiences with pitiless accuracy. My dad, Barry

Maryles, told me narratives of blinding courage and incomprehensible horror. I pass them on the only way I am able, through the filter of fiction.

I am deeply grateful to my uncle Philip Soroka, who tolerated my phone calls and answered my myriad questions, no matter how trivial. His sense of humor, his memories, and his knowledge of local history have contributed immeasurably to these pages.

My very warm thanks to Chaim Melczer, Paul Edelsberg, and Jack Pomeranc for sharing their Włodawa recollections with me. Joe Tenenbaum ignited my interest in partizans with a single sentence overheard at a Sukkot dinner: "So I jumped out of a tree, and I killed him with my knife." I am grateful beyond words to Dieter Schlüter, stepson of Righteous Gentile Bernhard Falkenberg, for sharing his family's war experiences and his photographs with me. Thanks also to historian Peter Kamber, and to the research staff at the Bundesarchiv in Ludwigsburg, Germany.

For some of my Jewish folklore, I turned for inspiration to three wonderful books: *A Treasury of Jewish Folklore*, edited by Nathan Ausubel; *The Diamond Tree: Jewish Tales from Around the World*, selected and retold by Howard Schwartz and Barbara Rush; and *Chosen Tales: Stories Told By Jewish Storytellers*, edited by Peninnah Schram. For the story "In the Land of Armadillos," I was inspired by the magical *The Street of Crocodiles*, by Bruno Schulz, and *"The Good Old Days": the Holocaust as Seen by Its Perpetrators and Bystanders*, edited by Ernst Klee, Willi Dressen, and Volker Riess.

Myriam Auslander, Ruchama King Feuerman, Leora Fineberg, Olivia Fischer Fox, Zalmie Jacobs, Deborah Landesman, Shelley Mendelow, David Naggar, Karen Benchitrit Naggar, Dan and Eileen Raab, Rena Bunder

Rossner, Steve Kendall, Elana Maryles Sztokman, Deborah Tannenbaum, Bluma Katz Uzan, Michale Wacks, Avi Weiss, Deena Yellin, Larry Yudelson, and Eve Yudelson, thank you for taking time from your busy lives to read the stuff I send you, and for being brave enough to tell me when it still needs work.

To all Maryleses, Sorokas, and Shankmans, my circle of uncles, aunts, cousins, nieces, nephews, and in-laws: Life is a journey, and it is a much better journey because I share it with you.

To my sister, Bernice, and my brothers, Chaim and Sam, thank you for your unwavering support, in a thousand different ways.

To my children, Gabriella, Raphael, Ayden, and Jude, you are the brightest lights in my sky. Thank you for putting up with me.

And finally, to my sweet Jon: You are the greatest miracle that has ever happened to me.

# ONCE UPON A TIME
# IN POLAND

"So I jumped out of a tree, and I killed him with my knife."

The truth is, anyone saying those words would have captured my attention. But the fact that they emerged from my mother's childhood friend, tiny, rotund, elderly Mr. Tenenbaum, was what made them so extraordinary.

In the kitchen, I corralled Mom and asked her what he'd been saying.

"Oh, just one of his stories," she said. "He was a partizan during the war."

This was the exact moment that I fell under the spell of my mother's war stories.

In my early years, I heard the stories traded back and forth across the dining room table at my grandmother's house. Since I spoke only English, and my grandparents only Yiddish, I had no idea what they were yelling about over the chicken soup and poppy-seed cake. And I didn't care. My bubbie's stories didn't interest me; they were something to be endured before we could leave for the playground. Certain words came up again and again, though I didn't know if they were names or places: *Selinger. Włodawa. Falkenberg. Sobibór. Adampol.*

I grew up, moved from Chicago to New York. Became an artist. Left all that depressing Holocaust stuff behind. Got married, had children. Now and then we would fly back with the kids to celebrate various high holy days. I was just returning to the Passover Seder table after putting Child #3 to bed when I overheard Mr. Tenenbaum's words.

The next night, as the babies slept, my mother and I sat at the kitchen table, rolling up tiny pairs of socks. She was a much better homemaker than I will ever be, a real *balebusta*. Before she went to sleep each night, the house was spotless, laundry put away, floors sparkling.

Hesitantly, I told her that I was thinking about writing a book and that I wanted to use some of our family stories. Could she repeat them for me in English?

I braced myself, waiting for her to scold me, tell me to stop wasting time. After all, I had three small children and a house to care for. But all she said was: "You should have learned Yiddish." And then she began to talk.

Back in New Jersey, I typed *Włodawa* into a Google search window and waited to see what would happen. One by one, photographs materialized on my monitor. The most adorable town square you ever saw, the houses painted in pretty pastel colors. Rolling fields. The lyrical, winding Bug River. The spectacular baroque synagogue that you could see from Mom's house, when Mom's house still existed.

Remembering the name Selinger, I typed it into another search box. There were Salingers, Zelingers with a Z, Zellingers with two LLs. When I saw an entry in the *Yizkor Memorial Book for the Town of Włodawa, Poland,* I knew I had found him. According to the Yizkor book, Selinger was an SS officer, commandant of the work camp in Adampol, eight kilometers from the town of Włodowa.

I sat back in my chair, thunderstruck. My family had been protected by an SS man? As I read on, the details matched the ones I already knew. Always wore civilian clothes, never a uniform. Had a reputation as a good German. Collected the craftsmen around him.

I wrote to the United States Holocaust Memorial Museum. A historian wrote me back that they tracked only lost Jews, not lost SS men. But they were kind enough to send me two pages of information. The first was from *The Encyclopedia of the Righteous Among the Nations*. Someone named Selinger had betrayed one of the Righteous, Bernhard Falkenberg, informing the Gestapo that Falkenberg was hiding Jews and aiding partizans. For his crimes, Falkenberg was arrested and sent to Mauthausen for the duration of the war. The second page was worse: Selinger was accused of making a phone call that resulted in the massacre of all his Jewish workers.

None of this made any sense. This couldn't be my Selinger, the Selinger who'd alerted my grandfather when *Aktzias* were imminent and told him to warn his friends; the Selinger who'd called the Nazis *Schweineren* and sent a wagon to bring my family to the safety of his castle. This couldn't be the Selinger who'd swooped my Aunt Esther into his arms, or the Selinger who'd sweet-talked the SS goons into leaving his Jewish workers alone . . . could it? Who was this guy?

The historian at the Holocaust Museum directed me to the war crimes archives in Ludwigsberg, Germany. I wrote, I emailed, I pestered. And while I performed my amateur detective work, the cancer that we thought my mother had vanquished in 1977 returned for a second try.

As I began to compose the stories that would become *They Were Like Family to Me*, the disease grew stronger, stealing her power of speech. While I learned more and more about her home town in World War II, she withdrew further and further away from us. When she fell into unwaking, unending sleep, I realized, with a kind of terrified astonishment, that I would never hear her stories again.

A few weeks after *shiva* ended, a manila envelope containing fifty-eight xeroxed pages of German testimony arrived in my mailbox. Typing the long foreign syllables into Google Translate, I read Willy Selinger's own words describing his years in Włodawa.

Did he snitch on Falkenberg? Selinger says he didn't. Did he summon the SS to his castle to massacre his workers? No, he says, he was under house arrest during this operation because it was common knowledge that he liked Jews. And what was the name of the officer who kept him under arrest? "I can't remember," Selinger says. And what of Sobibór? Did he know what was really going on in concentration camps? "I was six kilometers away," he answers. "Smoke and firelight, I have not seen."

To my chagrin, there was no photo. When I traced my fingers over the loops and whorls of his signature, goose bumps rose along my spine. As I wrote, I kept Günter Grass's controversial autobiography, *Peeling the Onion*, on my desk for inspiration. Controversial because, in its pages, the Nobel Peace Prize–winning author revealed that he'd been a soldier in the Waffen SS. From the cover, a young Günter Grass smiled craftily at me through a haze of smoke.

I had expected a tidy list of answers. Instead, I received a random set of court documents—typewritten testimony from many different people, offering different versions of the same events. Reading through them was like decoding a detective story.

This intersection, where truth, lies, and speculation meet, is the basis for the stories in *They Were Like Family to Me*. In my writing, I am drawn to human frailty, the persistence of humanity under the most inhuman conditions, the gray and uncertain no-man's-land that lies between good and evil, and the shifting nature of right and wrong in times of war.

Art removes us to a safe distance from actual horrors, allowing us to see in a new way what we already know. Fairy tales entertain children, but they also warn of danger. In a fable that my fictional author, Toby Rey, composes for his Nazi protector in "In the Land of Armadillos," he ends his allegory of a village complicit in a secret crime with this line:

"From that day forward, wherever the townspeople went, they were accompanied by the songs of birds. It filled their lives with beautiful music, but it also reminded them what they were capable of. *Remember*, the songs warned them, *and do not forget*."